Gold Coast Blues

by

Marc Krulewitch

Prologue

Stones crunching and popping off tires registered innocuously in the back of Tanya's mind as she sat in an armless swayback lounge chair swiping her finger across an iPad. She felt wonderfully cozy with her legs folded tightly underneath herself in jersey knit stretch pants and an oversized sweatshirt. At no time in her young life had she ever imagined *seeing* a house like the ones on the *Home & Design* website, never mind relaxing in a modern living room of concrete and glass looking into a leafy paradise. When she heard knocking and doorbell chimes, Tanya felt more annoyed at having to leave her comfy lounge chair than alarmed by the urgency of whoever was visiting.

She opened the front door to see her friend's familiar smile. He treated her like gold but his arrival deflated her mood a bit, reminded her that her days living in a suburban wonderland were coming to a close. Good things lay ahead, she knew, but a bittersweet mixture of hope and anxiety was also never far away.

"What's in the suitcase?" Tanya asked, as if she didn't know.

"Your train has finally arrived, my love," her friend said, locking the door then following Tanya back to the living room pulling a small metallic suitcase on rollers. Tanya returned to the lounge chair. Her friend dragged a chair over from a card table and sat in front of her. They made small talk for several minutes before he smiled broadly, put both hands on the suitcase handle, then struggled to lift it chest high, where he held it a few seconds before dropping it back down.

"Oh, my god!" Tanya said.

They both laughed. Tanya told her friend she couldn't wait to buy more *comfy* clothes like what she was wearing. Then tires skidded on gravel. Soon after, someone fiddled with the door. Tanya's friend jumped to his feet, then backed away from the living room entrance, dragging the suitcase with him.

That's when the guys with the guns walked in.

1

Ten days earlier.

The first day of Spring. Cold, rainy. Ten a.m.

Coltrane, a giant saxophone-playing rodent wearing a red beret, hung from the ceiling of Mocha Mouse, a kind of coffee shop–deli that had become my hangout. I had just finished reading an article in *The Partisan* about the most recent collection of rubber stamps given to the new mayor—the one who promised a city free of bookkeeping ploys or sleight-of-hand political maneuvers—when I looked up to see a kid standing in front of the door shaking the water off his leather jacket, scanning the room. Slim, about five-nine, his T-shirt clung to a severely chiseled physique. His shaved head and baby face reminded me of the screaming man in that famous painting. When his gaze reached the far corner of the room, he looked at me squint-eyed for several seconds, then advanced. His swagger meant business. As he approached, I recalled eyeing my holstered gun as I left my apartment. Alas, I'd left it behind.

"Are you Mr. Landau?" he said in blue-collar New Jersey.

"I might be," I said, unable to keep a straight face. My humor escaped him.

"Oh. I thought maybe—"

"Sorry. I'm Landau. What can I do for you?"

The kid took a seat and folded the jacket on his lap. "Mr. Kalijero told me to see you."

"First, tell me who you are."

"Uh, I'm Eddie Byrne." Eddie offered his hand. I took it. A spider-web tattoo stretched between thumb and forefinger.

"How do you know Detective Kalijero?"

"I don't know Detective Kalijero. But he's friends with a cop I know back East. Kalijero said you're good at findin' people."

"Tell me what Kalijero looks like."

"I just talked to him on the phone."

I folded the newspaper shut and pushed it aside. "Are you searching for birth parents?"

The kid screwed up his face. "No, no. My girlfriend, Tanya Maggio."

He handed me a photo taken in a booth where you sat on a stool while the camera flashed rapid-fire then spit out a strip of pictures. She bordered between cute and pretty with straight dark hair and a perky nose.

"How old is this picture?"

"It was a while ago," he said. "But that's what she looks like."

"When did you last see her?"

"Over a year ago." He started scratching the back of his neck. A bear claw of black ink graced his left forearm.

"Okay, if you want me to help you, then you need to tell me a story about Eddie and the gal he hasn't seen in a year. Let's start with where *you've* been the last year."

"Yeah, yeah. Sorry, I ain't never talked with a guy like you before. I've been away. So me and Tanya haven't been seein' each other so much but now I'm back and I heard she came to Chicago."

He was starting to annoy me. "You were away, like away in the Peace Corps?" I was pretty sure that wasn't it.

Eddie looked confused. "No, no. I don't know no Peace Corps. I just had some business out of town for a while."

I stared at him then took a calculated risk. "Just say it. *I was in prison the last year.*"

Eddie scratched his neck again then looked at me with a sheepish, *mea culpa* face. "Yeah, okay, I was, but more like three years. She stopped visitin' me over a year ago. I got my last letter six months ago. And then nothin'. She knew I was gettin' out. And we was all excited because I was gonna make a new start with her, you know? And then she takes off."

"Hang on. She came to Chicago a year ago, after her last visit to you in the can? Or six months ago, after her last letter?"

"I dunno. Her last letter had no return address or nothin'."

"You didn't even get an email?"

"Ain't no email in East Jersey State Prison."

"What about the postmark on the letter?"

More confusion. "I don't remember."

"What did the letter say?"

Eddie shrugged. "Nothin' special. Nothin' about leavin'."

"What about her friends?"

"Nobody knows nothin' except she took off for Chicago. And she was workin' at some fancy wine bar."

"And nobody knows why she left without telling you *nothin'*?"

Eddie turned his head away just enough to indicate he was about to lie—then he looked back at me and nodded.

"Well, I don't think I'm your guy. But it was nice meeting you." I picked up *The Partisan*.

"What? Why? I got money." From under the leather jacket he took a folded wad of cash in a rubber band, then reached across the table and dropped it in front of me. General Grant and the troops looked pretty well-worn, like they'd just retreated from Cold Harbor. I looked around the room. "That's five large," Eddie said quietly.

"You got balls, Eddie. I mean, this isn't a tough neighborhood, but if you go tossing 5K bankrolls around, it's only a matter of time."

Suddenly, his eyes narrowed, turning the nice kid into a serial killer. Just as quickly, he softened. "Yeah, well, I guess this is how I know to do business. It's just a down payment to show you I ain't full a shit. And I got plenty more. I really gotta find Tanya. She's been at my side my whole crappy life. She's never let me down. I don't care what it costs, Mr. Landau. I'll pay it."

He slouched in his chair, staring at the table. His lower lip quivered a few times. I picked up the cash and fingered the beat-up bills. Then I took two cards out of my jacket pocket and tossed them to Eddie. "Write your number on one of them. And tell me about this wine bar."

Eddie wrote down a number. "I don't got the name of the bar, except it's on the North Side and they serve the fancy stuff to yuppies."

"Maybe they don't drink wine in Jersey, but the North Side's a big neighborhood with a lot of fancy wine bars."

Eddie rubbed his temples. "It's near the river."

Actually, that narrowed my search significantly and I took this as a good sign.

2

The late morning rush at the Kutaisi Georgian Bakery was winding down as I parked in front of the place on Devon Avenue. Six months had passed since the owner had been arrested, along with Chicago's deputy director of the department of revenue, and two Russian gangsters, for their roles in murder, human trafficking, prostitution, and money laundering. The cousin of one of the murder victims now owned and operated the thriving bakery. In the course of my investigation, we had become intimate. Gradually, the bakery wedged us apart. Yesterday, she left a message asking me to stop by.

Tamar, a petite woman with jet black hair framing a beautiful, slightly Asiatic face, flitted through the kitchen and prep room, absorbed in her endless duties. I watched from the counter, curious how long it would take for my presence to break the spell. The apron and silly hat did nothing to diminish Tamar's loveliness. She approached me, obviously distracted, offering nothing in the way of intimate recognition.

"I should've told you to call first," Tamar said.

Before I could respond, she grabbed an employee's arm, spoke in her ear while taking off her apron and hat, then motioned for me to follow her to a table.

"I'm sorry I didn't offer you anything," she said after we sat. She looked about to cry.

"You look sad."

She sort of nodded her head. "I don't think I have the time or energy right now."

"For me."

"For us. Until I find people I can trust to help me run this place. It's not fair to you."

It's not you, it's me.

Disheartening scenes should be brief. "Call me when you feel more settled," I said.

"Thank you," Tamar said, then looked over to the kitchen where several employees were peering into the huge brick-domed oven. "I better get back; we'll talk soon."

Halt and catch fire, said the female computer to her boyfriend. We wouldn't talk soon, but that was beside the point. I watched Tamar put the apron and hat back on, quickly give directions to subordinates, then disappear into the prep room. Just in case my visit hadn't depressed me enough, I still had one more stop before beginning the fancy wine bar search.

Men called "associates" took care of Dad. They shopped, cooked, cleaned, and generally made sure Dad's life was agreeable. These perks were not from regularly paid insurance premiums, but from favors accumulated over decades of loyal service to individuals and organizations operating as a *de facto* syndicate. Sixteen years spent keeping his mouth shut in a medium security prison was worth a quality, long-term disability plan.

Dad rarely left his apartment in the 3700 block of Pine Grove, which is why I didn't bother calling. Through the door's oval glass, Arthur, a big bear of a man with a heart of gold, trudged toward me. I could tell by the look on his face, it had been a rough morning.

"What happened?" I said when he opened the door, then heard Dad shout, "Goddamn it!"

The two of us hurried back to his bedroom where Dad sat in a recliner watching an old *Bonanza* rerun. "What's wrong, Bernie?" Arthur said.

"The goddamn snakes are back! Look at 'em in the corner, slithering all over each other. I told you to get rid of them goddamn snakes!"

I pulled Arthur out of the room. "When did this start?"

"About two weeks ago he began seeing snakes. And then there was a hole in the back door, and a guy on the porch, in a black coat and black hat, was dumping the snakes through the hole."

"Has he seen a doctor?"

Arthur nodded as Dad shouted, "What the hell are you two talking about?"

"It's a type of dementia," Arthur said. "Lewy-something."

"Can they give him anything for the hallucinations?"

"They're trying different drugs but it takes time to work."

I returned to Dad's room and sat on the corner of the bed, next to the recliner. Dad sat slack-jawed, staring at Little Joe on the television. "Hi, Dad. It's Jules."

Dad turned to me. "Hey! Did you see the snakes? A whole pile of 'em."

"No, I didn't see them."

Dad eyeballed me. "Goddamn Arthur. Telling me there're no snakes."

"He's a nice guy and he works hard for you."

Dad looked back at the television. "I don't even know who all those people are. Do you know those people?"

"What people?"

"They're all over the place. I don't know who the hell they are. Are you hungry?"

"No—"

"Arthur!" Dad shouted. "Make Julie a salami sandwich."

"No thanks, Arthur. I'm not hungry."

Dad eyeballed me again. "What's the matter with you? Why're you so down in the dumps?"

His sudden shift to sanity surprised me. "I'm fine. Just got another case. Missing person."

"That's nice. You need any money?"

"I'm fine."

Dad turned back to *Bonanza*. I peered out the door. Arthur sat at the kitchen table reading the newspaper. When I looked back at Dad, his eyes were closed.

Around West Wacker Drive and Orleans Street, the Chicago River forked north-northwest, roughly parallel to busy Clybourn Avenue, which served as an excellent boundary to neighborhoods I thought might accommodate a nice wine bar. Webster Avenue ran through one of those neighborhoods and when I saw the *Auvergnat Vin Bar* I slowed down before parking across the street, in front of *Pâtisserie Grenouille*. A violin-playing frog dressed as a *maître d'*, and standing on a hunk of camembert, graced its window.

A black Porsche SUV with the license plate VINMSTR was parked in front of the Vin Bar. Although a wine tasting wasn't scheduled until four, the door was unlocked, which I took as an invitation to enter. The venue reeked of country cottage schmaltz. Large paintings of sweeping Rhone sunsets and Loire Valley vineyards covered the walls. Antique wooden cabinets and wine racks hung from exposed brick. A few tiny shelves of distressed wood blended in perfectly despite holding pamphlets advertising something called a "wine equity trust."

Behind the bar, a man carefully arranged a row of sidecar cocktail carafes. Near him, a gangly redheaded kid, who looked too young to be legally standing behind a bar, held a small spiral-bound notebook while studying a row of glass stemware, each holding a different shade of red wine. Standing in front of the bar, a man wearing a full-length black apron garnished with a stickpin of gold grapes looked thoughtfully over tables covered with bottles, glasses, and menus. He was tall with thick, black wavy hair, and his nose was slender and shiny. Around his neck hung a small silver saucer attached to a chain. I was practically in his face before he glanced at me and said, "Can I help you?"

"I'm sorry, I guess you're not open yet. But your door was unlocked."

"Yes, we don't mind if people curious about wine wander in. Unfortunately, the Provence tasting doesn't start for another hour."

"What's a wine equity trust?" I said.

Grape Man looked me over. Then he kind of shook his head a few times with a look of utter confusion. "Sorry. Who are you exactly?"

"I'm looking for a girl named Tanya Maggio. I was told she works here." I showed him my investigator's license.

"My god, you're serious."

"What's that supposed to mean?"

Grape Man let out a laugh-snort. "I've just never met a private eye before. I thought you guys only existed in the movies."

"Next time, I'll wear an overcoat and fedora. Do you know Tanya?"

"I've never known anyone named Tanya, and she certainly doesn't work here."

"What about the other staff members? Maybe they knew her before you arrived?"

Grape Man snorted again. "Ahhhh—no. None of them arrived before me. I hired them all—stole them all, some say. Only people with a proven background and education in serving and tasting wine can work here."

"Any other fancy wine bars on the North Side, near the river?"

Grape Man's face lit up. "Any wine north of here along the river is poured from a cardboard box into a plastic cup." A hearty laugh. I was the perfect straight man. "I put this place out of its misery six months ago."

"You're the *new* owner?"

"Six months ago. That's what I just said."

I wondered how long this guy would last in Eddie's world before someone shoved that pin down his throat. "And the poor huddled masses that made up the staff of the previous miserable establishment? All fled from the black-caped wine taster with the silver spoon around his neck?"

Grape Man gave me a savage look. "I hold diplomas from the Court of Master Sommeliers, the Wine and Spirit Education Trust, and the Institute of Masters of Wine. And I'll be damned if I'm going to let you walk into my wine bar and insult me." As he continued describing my disrespectful behavior, I put a card on the bar, then bowed deeply as I backed away.

3

She worked at a fancy wine bar, I thought while driving. Maybe in Eddie's Jersey neighborhood wine equaled fancy. After turning back on to Clybourn, I pulled over to answer my cellphone.

"You're the guy who was just in the wine bar?" a male voice said.

"Yeah. Who is this?"

"I heard you talking about Tanya and I saw your card sitting on the bar. What's up with her? She in trouble or something?"

"Were you the redheaded kid studying the wine?"

"Yeah. I'm Ted Goldberg. I'm training."

"How do you know Tanya?"

Ted paused. "Uh, how do *you* know her?"

"Uh, did you *read* my card? Under my name it says *private investigator*."

"Wow. So she is in trouble, huh?"

Here again, another kid getting on my nerves. "I didn't say that, Ted. Some folks are worried. I've been hired to find her. Now, be a good lad and tell me everything you know about Tanya."

"We all worked for the previous owner when it was the *Webster Avenue Saloon*. I was in the kitchen but I hung out with the waitstaff a lot. Tanya and I were sort of friends but this other guy, James, probably knew her best out of everyone who worked there. Although Spike knew her pretty well too."

"Spike? The guy's *name* is Spike?"

"Tanya told me his real name. Landon 'Spike' McFadden. He tells everyone to just call him Spike."

"Where can I find James and Spike?"

"James works at Arbitrage on Armitage. Spike, uh, I'm not sure."

"Were James and Tanya dating?"

"Well, I guess they were dating—maybe. She was real pretty and we kidded him that she was out of his league."

"What would James say about her?"

"He didn't talk about Tanya much. Although he did tell me once, she never talked about herself. Everyone knew they came from different worlds, you know? She was kind of rough around the edges. Not stupid, just not educated. I think James liked that. He got kind of whipped on her, actually. None of the girls liked Tanya, that was obvious."

"And what happened between James and Tanya?"

"She kind of blew him off. And then she just disappeared not long before the place shut down."

I made Ted promise to leave my business card on the bar, but save my phone number in his contact list. Then I promised to do the same.

Arbitrage on Armitage, a coffee shop or an exhibit of oxford-cloth performance art. Both depictions worked. I did not approve, however, of the incongruous decor. Antique financial charts should not hang from walls painted earthy tans and warm grays. The choice of chrome, granite, and stainless steel made the place as cozy as an operating room. Rising steam from a coffee-cup silhouette on the staffs' aprons formed a mallet-wielding polo horseman. This long-established symbol of class privilege contrasted sharply with the uneven angular black hair of the kid behind the counter. He looked like the anti-barista.

"Can I help you?" he said, doing his best to smile.

"Are you James, the guy who dated Tanya?"

His smile disappeared. "Why? Who are you?"

"I'm a private investigator. Ted Goldberg told me you worked here." I handed him a card. He held it like he wasn't sure it wouldn't bite him.

"Is she okay?" James asked with a dramatic hair flip.

"I'm trying to find out. A guy at that new wine bar referred me to you. He said you all worked together."

He nodded while examining my card. "Yeah, a while ago."

A couple of V-neck wool cardigans with suede elbow patches walked in, took their place behind me, stared at the menu on the wall. "You got a break coming?"

"What do you want? I haven't seen her since that place shut down."

I took out my wallet and dropped one of Eddie's fifties on the counter. "That's for nothing. I'll be over there. If you can get away and sit with me for a few minutes, you get another."

James looked over his shoulder, grabbed the fifty, then greeted the next in line.

My only choice was to sit practically elbow to elbow in the row of two-tops along the wall. I must have looked odd without a laptop or coffee, just *The Partisan* and a laminated card of barista terminology to keep me company. Arbitrage guaranteed a perfect cup of coffee, regular, skim, or soy, and explained the trials required to become a certified Arbitrage barista. Meanwhile, a row of customers had formed along the counter and looped back around the pole of the rope line. A man closer to my age joined James to help with the rush. The speed and dexterity the two displayed mesmerized me. I watched them *dose, tamp, pull,* and *steam* as deftly as most of us tie our shoes.

When the crowd thinned out, James said something to the other guy, who then glanced at me, nodded, and patted James's shoulder before the kid walked over.

"Holy shit, you guys are good," I said as James took a seat. "How long does it take to learn all that?"

James shrugged. "So what do you want to talk about?"

"Was that your boss? He seems like a nice guy."

"Yeah, he's all right. But it could get busy again so—"

"Tanya. You met her working at the bar. What kind of bar was it?"

"Is she okay?"

"Don't know. She's missing. I've been hired to find her. That's all I know. Tell me about the bar where you worked together."

James nodded. He looked worried. "It started out as a place to get local microbrews. I thought we were doing pretty good. We had a lot of regulars. On a Saturday night I could go home with a couple hundred bucks in my pocket."

"So the clientele were young like you or more professional types?"

"All kinds. Too pricey for the guys who order Bud on tap. But anyone else could come in and hang out."

"I heard the place described as a fancy wine bar."

James chuckled. "I wouldn't go that far. Like I said, we were doing good. I know Tanya was psyched with the kind of money she was making. But then the owner decided to experiment with wines. He thought he could get more of the highbrow crowd. We all thought it was a stupid idea."

"The cultivated Chicagoan didn't come forth."

"What a moron. Doug Daley just started buying cases of wine. Tens of thousands of dollars of inventory that just sat there. It's like he thought if he just bought the right stuff, the right people would show up. He pushed out half the beer choices to make room for wine."

"And during this time, you and Tanya were dating?"

James hesitated. "We were seeing each other."

I waited. "That's not the same as dating?"

"I *wanted* to be dating. Just us, you know? But she kind of wouldn't go there."

A lightbulb lit up. "You were sleeping together, but you weren't exclusively boyfriend-girlfriend." James nodded. "Okay, tell me about Tanya."

"She showed up several months before the wine transition began. At first she didn't really fit in. But she was trying so hard, it was obvious. She was sweet to everyone. Even though we were all waiters and bartenders, most of us had been to college and were just trying to make some money while figuring out what to do with our lives. Tanya was seriously working class. The other girls used to laugh at her accent. She didn't understand why it was funny, but it didn't bother her. Sometimes we couldn't understand what she said and we'd all laugh."

"What did you like about her, besides that she was hot?"

"Once we started talking, I saw that she was very curious. We talked about all kinds of stuff. She asked me a lot of questions."

"What kind of questions?"

"Oh, about politics or world events. Then she started asking questions about me and my life. But it took a while for her to talk about herself. It was like she didn't understand why anyone would be interested in her. Gradually, she opened up to me."

"What did you learn about her?"

"Well, she grew up in a kind of scary place, near Newark, New Jersey. She said it wasn't terrible but I don't know. It sounded pretty bad to me. Her dad was in prison for selling drugs and her mom was a hopeless drunk. She tried to take care of her, but she wouldn't stop drinking—or couldn't stop. Finally, it killed her. Tanya won't touch alcohol. Some of the waitstaff teased her for that. It's stupid."

"What happened to your relationship?"

James readjusted himself in his chair. "I don't know. After a couple of months, she just started cooling things down. She wasn't mean or anything, but she wouldn't tell me what was going on. And it got really hard to work with her. Before I knew it, it was like I didn't exist anymore."

"What about Spike?"

"Assistant manager. Douchebag. Acted like a guido/wiseguy around Tanya."

"What did Tanya think of him?"

"She would imitate him and do a more convincing guido. It was hilarious. At first, he got angry, but after a while, he laughed too. Spike was actually nice to her and Tanya seemed to be the only one who didn't hate him."

"And the boss? How old was he?"

"Doug? I don't know. Maybe fifty-something."

"Besides being a moron, what kind of guy was Doug? What was he like to work for?"

James thought about it. "He was a stupid clown, actually. With me, he'd say 'Hi, how're you doing?' like we were good friends, even though he didn't know my name. And he was always hitting on the chicks or joking around to see how they would react. He liked to shock people with bloody magic tricks, like pretending to carve his leg up with a steak knife or sticking this huge needle through his arm. The guys thought he was a jerk."

My first murder case also involved a man in late middle age clinging to a fantasy of youthful vitality that was irresistible to younger women. "Was Doug married?"

"I don't think so. He didn't wear a ring."

"You think he could've been doing anything illegal, like using the bar as a front?"

"I don't know. And he didn't talk business with us before a shift like most bars or restaurants do with their staff. He just did what he wanted. No discussion. A lot of times he would be the bartender so he could try out his magic tricks. Tanya said he had a magic tricks supply business on the side— although I promised not to tell anybody. He was also very involved with some kind of wizard society. That's the stuff he really cared about. I think the bar was really just a hobby. I mean he was rich, so I don't think he gave a shit if the place lost money."

"He hit on Tanya, I assume?"

James didn't like my question. "Yeah? So? He hit on everybody."

"Take it easy. She was cute, right? Personable. Inquisitive. Doug was rich, I assume not hideous—"

"She wasn't fucking Doug!"

"Relax! I'm not saying she was. But I have to ask these kinds of questions."

Neither of us spoke. James stared at his lap while visions of Tanya having sex with Doug tore into his heart.

I said, "Don't let idiotic scenarios take over your mind. Trust me. I've been there. Some women are vulnerable to an older man with money—it's a security thing. A desire to be taken care of, they say. But everything I heard tells me Tanya wasn't like that. She took care of herself. She didn't want to be kept by some asshole just because he had money. She probably thought the guy was a joke."

James looked at me. "I saw her sitting in his BMW—once."

"That doesn't mean anything," I lied. "Do you know where Doug is now?"

"No idea." He looked around the café. "I'd better get back."

As he stood to leave I put another fifty in his hand and said, "I'm sure she's fine and she's nowhere near that dumbass boss. So don't waste your time on it."

James put the money in his pocket and pretended he didn't think I was full of shit.

4

Toxic chemical stink assaulted my nose as I opened the door of the converted Old Town walk-up where I rented an office. New paint, updated lighting, and durable industrial carpeting depressed me. I had grown attached to the original Art Deco time warp of a lobby. I found comfort in the murky light and moldy smell of neglect.

I leaned back in my ergonomically designed high-back chair and felt the pressure release from my lower spine and thighs. It seemed unfair that not everyone could afford a chair like this. I dialed Kalijero's number.

"Hey, Jimmy, I apologize for interrupting your retirement, but do I owe you a finder's fee?"

Silence, then, "What the hell are you talking about, Landau?"

"The Jersey kid looking for love."

"Oh, yeah, Cooper's guy. You take it?"

"I didn't think I would, then he showed me a pile of cash. You got anything you want to share?"

"I don't know anything, I'm retired."

"How are you spending your retirement?"

"Let's see. Today I'm watching some TV, then I'm going to cut my toenails."

"You sound depressed."

"Fuck you, I'm not depressed."

"Fine, you're *joyous.* Your cop buddy in Jersey—"

"Buddy? Cooper's a prick."

"Okay, your cop prick in Jersey. Tell me about him."

"Here's the short version. Detective Cooper is the son of a guy I met at the academy and served with until he got killed responding to a domestic. I tried to help his mom bring up the kid. Smart little shit. Got good grades. We convinced him to go to college. Graduated from Northwestern! And then I don't know what happened. He became a rebellious prick. He could've done anything he wanted with that brain of his. Suddenly he wants to be a cop. Go figure. Went to New York and wound up in Jersey."

"And that was the end of him, huh?"

"Before he left, he knocked up a nice Irish girl. I knew the family. We almost got him to do the right thing. He hung around long enough to name the kid after himself, then ditched her. But he wasn't shy about using his dead-cop father as a reference. It got him on the force."

"Where in Jersey?"

"A crap-hole called Irvington. Mostly poor blacks and Puerto Ricans. Gang and drug infested. I hear he drives a nice car. Years ago, rumors got back to me that he makes extra money working with the local businesses—if you know what I mean."

"You want to help me on this or are you too deliriously happy being retired to do anything else?"

"Tell me, Landau, why is it that every time you get a murder case you and I become old pals?"

"Who said anything about murder? Tanya Maggio's a missing person and I got a feeling she's missing on purpose. And apart from you putting my father in prison, we have nothing to talk about except when I'm investigating something."

"But that's what I don't get. You think I *want* to talk to you. I've got plenty of people to hang out with. They may drink a little too much, but I sure as hell don't *need* Jules Landau trying to pull me back into the murder—I mean missing *bodies* game."

"I worry about you, Jimmy. Guys like you can never really retire, so when an interesting case comes up—" The call dropped. It was our way of saying goodbye.

I called Tasty Harmony and ordered their Bigboy Burger—rice, bean, and soy patty on a toasted roll—which would be waiting in front of my apartment. The place was just down the block. I was such a good customer they billed me monthly and ran the food over. Then I called a little *carniceria* also in my neighborhood and told them *Señor Gato* needed a delivery. Eddie's number was next. A male voice mumbled, "Jackson Hotel." That dump rents rooms by the hour. I hung up and dialed again. Same result.

"You have a guest named Eddie?"

"I don't know."

I described him.

"I don't know."

"I'll tell you what. If you see a guy that looks like him, tell him to call Jules Landau. He's got my number. Okay?"

"Uh-huh."

While driving home I wondered why a guy with a load of cash would stay at a slum like the Jackson. A prison cell was five-star compared to the Jackson. After lucking out with a parking spot only three blocks away from my place, I walked past Tasty Harmony and waved at the guys who kept me properly nourished. As expected, two packages waited outside my apartment. Seconds after picking up the bags, I heard the thump of Punim's paws hitting the floor before she ran to the door.

From one of the bags I took out a plastic container of small animal organs and dropped a few into Punim's bowl. While she dug in, I fell into the recliner, tore into my sandwich, and replayed the day's events. On one hand, there wasn't much I liked about Eddie. His heartbroken aloofness annoyed me. Go back to Jersey and suffer in silence if you want to act like a tragic hero. However, I couldn't deny that the bankroll and his lousy first impression made me pretty damn curious. On the other hand, I liked what I'd learned about Tanya. She was cute in a blue collar kind of way. And she was smart. In my book, curious people are smart because they *want* to learn. Combined with her working-class sensibility, I found this incredibly sexy. I wondered what she saw in a jerk like Eddie.

Unlike many of Chicago's historic enclaves that have lost their ethnic flavor, the Near West Side neighborhood of Greektown had maintained its culture primarily through food and festivals, the popularity of which had helped foster gentrification. For prices starting in the mid $300,000s, one could buy a condo in the surrounding blocks and live only steps from a Hellenic gastronomic paradise.

And then there was the Jackson Hotel. The stench of urine and tobacco greeted me in the lobby. A skinny man with sunken eyes sat behind a glass counter holding a comic book in trembling hands. I stood at the counter several seconds before he blinked a few times and looked at me.

"Yeah?"

"I'm looking for someone. You got a guest register?"

"No."

The last surviving Quaalude addict was my guess. "Cool. Then I think I'll just walk around and see if I can find him."

Ten stories made up this horror hotel, but I chose the stairway over the ancient phone booth of an elevator. Shouting Eddie's name down the hallways of shabby carpeting, cigarette butts, and dead roaches, I felt not the least bit self-conscious. Besides the occasional grunt or television chatter behind closed doors, there was no sign of life. By the seventh floor I started wondering if Eddie gave me this number as a ploy to avoid unwanted attention—like a real control freak might do. As I opened the door to head up to number eight, I heard my name shouted from the lower part of the stairwell in that unmistakable Jersey accent. I shouted back, "Meet me downstairs," and began my descent.

Once in the lobby, Eddie Byrne showed not the slightest expression of surprise or contrition for putting me through this trial. "He told me you were lookin' for me," he said.

I put a twenty on the counter and thanked Quaalude Man. "You gave me the front desk phone number because you don't have a cellphone?"

"Nah. Don't need one."

"C'mon," I said and pulled Eddie by the arm outside. "Why the hell are you staying in that dump?"

Eddie looked hurt. "It ain't so bad! You shoulda seen where I been livin' the last three years. How would you like a roommate takin' a crap five feet from where you sleep?"

I guessed having a room to yourself was an incomparable luxury. "Okay, sorry. How the hell did you expect me to get ahold of you? You think that walking-dead phantom behind the counter was going to take messages for you?"

"I was gonna call you. Why you so mad?"

"You're getting a cellphone just so you can talk to me. When we're done working together, throw it away if you want." I dragged him down the street to the first discount appliance store I saw and bought a prepaid phone. A burner, the criminal element called it. He took it without complaint. Then I suggested we find a place to talk. We ended up in a Greek coffee shop. They served us dark brown sludge and a plate of white cheese, olives, and cucumbers. A small sampling of the bitter goo convinced me to forego any ambition of developing a taste for it. Eddie took several sips, each a little larger, as if defying the flavor, challenging it to defeat him.

I said, "You had no contact with Tanya during the final six months of your prison stretch. Right?"

He sipped. His mouth no longer puckered from the flavor. "Yeah."

"I spoke to a guy who worked with her."

He looked alarmed. "Just workin'? Was he datin' her?"

"They were friends. Nothing more."

Serial killer face returned. "How do you know? Where is this guy?"

"Listen to me, Eddie. You have to fucking grow up if you want my help. If I say they were just friends, then believe me. If you can't, we're done. And if I thought they were more than friends, I would've said so. Got it?"

Back to street kid. "Yeah. I'm sorry, Mr. Landau."

I let several moments pass, hoping Eddie would snap out of his pathetic posture. "I'm going to tell you what I believe are facts. And you're going to have to deal with it like a big boy. Tanya's friend said the owner used to flirt with the chicks—including Tanya. One time he saw Tanya sitting in the boss's BMW. That doesn't mean anything, but we have to look at this equation. You know what I mean?"

"No. What?"

I took a deep breath and let it out. "You grew up in Newark?"

"Irvington."

"A white boy in Irvington? Must've been rough," I guessed. "How'd you land there?"

"My dad was born there and never left. The neighborhood changed but we stayed. It was just the way things were."

"Tanya too?"

"A few towns over. Not great but nothin' like Irvington." He looked around, drummed his fingers on the table.

"You don't like to talk about yourself, do you?"

He thought about it a second then shrugged. "Nobody ever asks me nothin' about myself."

"What I mentioned earlier—the equation. Hear me out and then tell me if you think it's crap. For the first time, Tanya breaks away from the working-poor world she's always known. She gets a job in a bar with upper-middle-class young people. She sees they're really not too different from her other than their education, some money in the bank, and probably parents to fall back on if things go south. It feels good to go home with a pile of cash every night. The boss starts hitting on her. He's way too old for her and she doesn't take him seriously. Still, she notices the nice cars, his clothes, he probably has a great place in Lincoln Park. See where I'm going?"

He looked pained. "I don't see her goin' with some guy just 'cause he had money."

"Okay. But it's the only thing I got to go on until we find more people who knew her. Tell me again, who told you she worked at a wine bar in Chicago?"

Eddie pushed his chair back a couple of inches and then looked around again. "Her friends from home."

"Is she still in touch with these friends?"

"Nah. They don't know nothin'."

"You mind if I ask them—"

Angry Eddie appeared. "They don't know nothin'! And don't go pokin' around there neither."

I paused to let the words hover in the space between us. "Okay, here's the deal. I'm going to walk in one direction and you'll walk in the other. Then you're going to think about whether you really want me to find out what happened to Tanya. If you decide my services are in fact desired, you will call me and tell me so. Your admission will serve as an agreement that you will never again bark orders at me. If you break that agreement, our association will immediately end—and, yes, I will keep all the cash you gave me."

I walked out without looking back.

Home for the evening, leaning back in the recliner, I wondered if I needed more vices. Guys like Eddie had plenty of vices, including self-destructive qualities that required guys like me to pretend to be tough. Maybe stupidity was my vice. Acting tough when it didn't come naturally or even feel good. Sadly, SOBs like Eddie respected strength. The top motivations for stupidity: money, sex, obsession with younger women. What else did I have to go on? Would Tanya Maggio have been seen sitting in an older man's beat-up Oldsmobile?

Eddie's call came sooner than expected. "Hey, Mr. Landau, I'm really sorry—"

"What's up, Eddie?"

"I didn't mean to sound like a dope. I mean, you got a job to do and that's why I'm payin' you. And I need your help. You don't gotta worry about me no more. And I promise I'll keep payin' you. You don't have to worry about that neither."

"Why did you freak out at the thought of me talking to Tanya's New Jersey friends?"

"Well, it's just that you're a stranger and they're kinda tight over there. . . ."

Eddie spent the next ten minutes stammering about why I wouldn't be welcome in his native sandbox, suggesting it was for my own good that I should stay away. A juncture had been reached, one that shouted for me to drop the case. Every cell in my body waved a red flag while the shadowy, impetuous, stupid side of me delighted at the prospect of a plunge into the unknown.

"I appreciate your input on my well-being, but I'm going to do what I want to do whether you approve or not. You still want me on the case?"

"Yeah, yeah. Okay, that's fine. I'm not tellin' you what to do or nothin'. I'm done with that. Okay?"

"Hold on to that cell phone. I'll let you know when I'm ready to talk to someone from back East." I hung up before he could respond.

Doug had wanted to convert his yuppie pub into a snobby wine bar. Across the street, a café with a frog played violin on a chunk of camembert. I fell asleep thinking about French cheese.

5

By the time I got to *Pâtisserie Grenouille* the next morning, most of the tables were already occupied by someone reading the paper or eating a crepe. Classical music played softly as the patrons enjoyed their organic, French roast, fair-trade coffee.

The woman behind the counter appeared intensely preoccupied while she wiped down the machinery and put various components of the coffee-making trade away. Several times she held up a shiny metal object to study it before deciding where it should go. When she noticed me, she quickly wiped her hands on her apron and apologized. Her nametag said Brenda.

"We just had a rush," she said with a self-conscious giggle.

Brenda's crow's-feet betrayed an otherwise youthful face. She looked at me wide-eyed, waiting for me to say something. "How's the cheese business?" I asked.

She hesitated. "Oh, we have lots of cheese. I make cheese crepes every morning—"

"I was just kidding."

"Wait here," she said and dashed into the back, returning with a crepe on a plate. "First-time customers get a free sample."

The joyful anticipation of Brenda's expression left me no choice. "I never eat cheese crepes alone," I said. "But you're probably too busy—"

"No, actually, I just have one rush in the morning. Mostly the same people. The next busy time won't be until the light-lunch rush."

She showed me to a table and said she'd be
right back. I watched her chat with the other patrons
while collecting dirty plates on a tray. An old man
with a bushy white beard and a black beret watched
her from a table against the far wall. He pushed his
chair back then slowly stood and carried his plate to
her. She thanked him warmly. He doffed his cap to
reveal his bald head and walked out. When she
returned, her eyes moved back and forth between
the crepe and my face. I pushed the plate to the
middle of the table. "We have to share. If I eat,
everybody eats."

She took a fork and cut off a piece. I cut off the
end, managing to avoid any cheese. "I think I'll use
more lemon in tomorrow's batch," she said.

"Is it worth being open every morning just for a
handful of regulars?"

"Oh, yeah, well—I don't know. They're so
loyal. I mean I don't want to let people down. I love
so much to cook for others—*duh*! And you meet so
many people in this business. Are you new to the
neighborhood?"

I told her my name and put a card on the table.
When she read it her eyes widened again. "You're a
private investigator? Really? I'm Brenda Gallagher,
by the way. I own this place if you hadn't figured
that out."

"Did you know the guy who owned the pub
across the street before it became the fancy wine
bar?"

Her face returned to the distracted demeanor I'd noticed when I first walked in. She studied the tablecloth a moment and then gazed out the window toward the *Auvergnat Vin Bar*. "Yeah, I knew Doug Daley," she said, cutting off another piece of crepe. Saying his name seemed to elicit pain.

"What about the staff? Did you know any of them?"

She nodded. "A few of them. We used to have after-hours parties on Friday and Saturday nights."

"Did Doug attend the parties?"

"Yeah, at first. He kidded around with the girls. He liked gory magic tricks, like in the movies. I remember one time Doug pretended to push a knife into his stomach. *Ugh.* Then we would chat, just the two of us at a different table. He was very interested in learning about French wine. He thought if he could attract the pricey wine crowd it would be mutually beneficial to our businesses."

I took out the picture of Tanya. "Did you ever see her?"

"Oh, yeah, she was a sweetie. Is she in trouble?"

"What do you remember about her?"

"I remember her well because she didn't drink, so I would make her a cup of cocoa. Once in a while she would join me outside for a cigarette, but she was trying to quit so I discouraged her."

"You and Doug became friends—or more?"

Brenda sighed. "It's none of your business, but I thought he was interested. We spent a lot of time together—"

"I'm sorry. I'm just trying to figure out Tanya's whereabouts. An old boyfriend of hers seems to think she's gone missing."

"Doug hung around only during working hours or after he closed the bar—*duh*! I'm not good at reading people. You're probably really good at reading people, aren't you? Since that's your job."

"What changed your mind about Doug?"

"His wife."

"He's married?"

Brenda gave me a conciliatory smile and nod. "Right? See what I mean? I should've seen it. Not all married men wear rings."

The more I heard about Doug Daley, the sharper he came into focus. Brenda's vulnerability to a man who shared a common interest in French wine would have been hard to resist. He wanted to learn, she had the knowledge. Doug had no problem using people, even if he hadn't mentioned he was married. But she would've still needed to shave ten years off her age to have had a chance.

"How did you find out he was married?"

"Margot started coming into *Pâtisserie* for an occasional glass of wine. We got to be friends. She often referred to 'her husband' and I had no idea it was Doug until she showed up at one of the after-hours parties."

"How did Doug's employees react to her presence?"

"Hard to say. I was so shocked and upset, I wasn't paying attention."

"If you don't mind, Brenda, was Doug a real hunk or what?"

Loud laughter. "Oh, yeah. Well, he was nice looking, in good shape. Not very tall but still GQ handsome with a full head of grayish hair with streaks of white. He always looked me in the eye when he spoke, like he was really interested in what I had to say."

"I heard he was doing fine with the microbrews and that his desire to turn the *Webster Avenue Saloon* into a snobby wine joint tanked his business."

Brenda considered my statement. "Yeah, I don't know. You should probably be one or the other. Did the wine thing ruin his business? I can't say. He just kind of sold out and hit the road."

"Do you know where he went?"

"I never saw him again after he shut the *Saloon* down. And since the accident, Margot hardly ever comes in—but she's still around."

"What accident?"

Brenda looked surprised. "You didn't know? I'm sorry. Doug was killed in a car wreck early last month, in New Mexico. Margot showed me the article."

I sat back in my chair and tried to absorb the significance of Brenda's words to my case.

"What do you mean 'but she's still around'?"

"Margot lives down the street. She's been kind of reclusive since the accident. Her windows are always lit up at night."

"Can you show me the building?"

Brenda stood and motioned for me to follow her out the door to the sidewalk. "See that rounded room with the dome roof sticking out? That's her place."

6

It was one of those buildings that made you wonder what the hell people had been thinking. A classic Victorian transformed into a red-brick rectangle, sprouting bay-window lesions. Margot Daley's apartment included the lesion that faced Webster Avenue. Despite the intercom system, I was instantly buzzed through. At the top of the first flight, her door was halfway open.

"Mrs. Daley?" I called out.

"Call me Margot," I heard before she came into view.

Once upon a time she had been breathtakingly beautiful, a redhead that hushed a crowded room upon entering. Older now, she was still pretty, with

41

a smattering of gray streaks and a few vertical lines around the lips that did nothing to take away from her elegance. Sunlight streaming through the bay window revealed a spacious mustard yellow apartment and walls decorated with French impressionist prints. An expensive-looking lamp sat on what looked like a fancy grand piano. Oriental rugs covered the floor. I found myself drawn to the multicolored paper butterflies adorning the chain to the attic door.

"The butterflies help me forget there's a dank loft up there."

I said, "Persian on the floor, Tiffany on the baby grand?"

Margot laughed and nodded approvingly. "A cultured man, no less!"

Her voice had the slightest echo of a smoker's rumble, although I saw no ashtrays and detected no tobacco odor. She had quit just in time.

"I'm Jules Landau, a private investigator. Were you expecting someone?"

"No. I enjoy having visitors, so whoever rings comes in. I'm having a glass of pinot noir. Would you care to join me?"

"No thanks."

The furniture was luxurious in the traditional style, fully upholstered with wood trim. "Please sit," Margot said and lay on a chaise longue in front of the bay window. A small end table next to her held a half-full glass of red wine. In blue jeans, her figure could be that of a teenager. I took the love seat, along with its view of Margot's profile.

"I hope you weren't serious about letting anyone in who leans on the buzzer," I said.

"You don't know me but already you're worried about me?"

"I'd have to be in a coma not to be disturbed by images of what could come walking up those stairs."

Margot smiled. "You're sweet but perhaps too imaginative. I don't fear the city or what it has to offer. This couch is my favorite place to relax and feel the warmth. No matter how cold it is out in the streets, this chaise is a comfy haven. You can always create a little space of comfort for yourself, regardless of where you live. And I keep a .38 revolver in the desk drawer."

I wondered how comfortable she would feel when some crackhead stumbled into her bedroom.

"You seem remarkably indifferent that a private investigator has dropped by."

Margot shrugged. "If you show up here investigating, I assume you want to talk about my husband."

"I'm sorry for your loss."

"Duly noted."

"I've been hired to find a woman who used to work with your husband." I stepped over to her with the picture of Tanya Maggio. Margot didn't move, just glanced at the photo and then returned her attention out the window.

After I sat back down she said, "You're wasting your time. Doug killed her."

The matter-of-fact way she mentioned murder blindsided me. "You want to tell me how you know this?"

"I just know."

"And have you told the police you 'just know'?"

"They're both dead, what's the point?"

"Well, her family might appreciate knowing."

"I'm sure he did it, but I can't prove it." All of a sudden, she seemed less like a victim.

"Tell me your theory."

Margot sighed then turned to me. "It just makes sense. He killed her and then he killed himself."

"Officially, he died in a car accident, right?"

Margot swung her legs off the lounge, then walked to a writing desk against the wall, where she opened a drawer and took out a newspaper article. Without a word, she handed it to me and lay back down. A large photograph showed the charred, mangled remains of a car severed in half after crashing head-on into an oak tree.

"They identified him through dental records—though it took a couple of days to find his jaw."

44

"But you're saying the car crash wasn't an accident?"

"I'm saying there were only a handful of trees on that lonely stretch of highway in the New Mexico desert. There were no skid marks. He wasn't wearing his seatbelt, plus the airbags in his BMW convertible did not deploy. Also, the cops think the gas tank was almost full—"

"I get it. Why would your husband have killed Tanya Maggio?"

Margot hesitated. "Why do men kill women?"

Answering questions with questions was inherently suspicious behavior. "Why does anyone kill anyone?" I countered.

Margot laughed. "Doug fell in love with her. She went along with it for a while, a flattered young woman, understandably mesmerized by his wad of cash. I found out he took her to Cancun. How could a working-class kid like that resist? But after a while, she probably felt trapped with this older man. When she started pulling away, Doug's attraction became an obsession. You take it from there."

"Did Tanya go with him to New Mexico?"

"I assume so. Around Thanksgiving, he closed the place and they ran off together."

"When did you realize he was having an affair?"

Margot sat up and dropped her legs over the side of the chaise. "When he closed his bar and ran off with her last Thanksgiving."

"You had no idea before then that something was going on?"

Margot took a deep breath. "I thought he was spending more time with his friends who shared his passion of magic tricks. I know he and his buddies ran an internet supply business. Everything was very secretive with those guys. But I should've know better. Anyway, what difference does it make now?"

I let a few moments pass. I expected her to throw me out soon. "When Doug up and left, he must've angered some folks. Had he paid his creditors off? Did he abandon the lease?"

"I was his landlord. I bankrolled his business. I bought the BMW he wrapped around a tree."

This sudden shift in ballast upset the equilibrium of my working theory. Doug suddenly became a pathetic loser who took advantage of his loving wife's trust to squander her money and run off with a younger woman.

"What's the matter, Detective? You look dazed."

"Call me Jules. And I'm a private investigator. Did Brenda call and tell you I was coming over?"

Margot smiled. "Sweet girl. Needs more self-confidence."

"You didn't answer my question."

"She thought I might be angry because she showed you where I lived."

"Were you?"

"No. I told you I like visitors."

Margot turned her attention back out the window. She seemed remarkably comfortable splayed out in front of a perfect stranger. Too comfortable, as if anticipating something inevitable.

"If you don't mind—is this your *main* residence?"

"This is my home. I could afford much more, but this is all I need. Doug and I had that in common—I thought. Have a nice car, take nice trips, enjoy hobbies, start a bar—whatever. But we don't need an apartment on the Gold Coast or a country house or a place on Maui."

An extended silence, then I said, "But why? Had your marriage—"

"Men desire younger women, Jules. It's not complicated."

"He must've had a plan, though. Something more complicated than wooing away a naïve woman using your wealth. Was he stealing? Are you missing large sums of money?"

"Of course."

I thought it strange that she didn't elaborate. "Will you be able to recover any of it now that Doug is dead?"

"I'm working on it."

"So the police are involved?"

"No."

I stared at her profile. She had mentally left the building. "I know settling an estate can be complicated—"

"It's not complicated!" she shouted, scaring the hell out of me. "I'm sorry," she said. "I had no right to raise my voice. It's just that sometimes— It's just that money and younger women are not complicated concepts or motivations. I think you'd do your client a favor by just accepting the obvious. They're both dead and that's all that matters."

"But you won't tell me how you know for certain Tanya is dead."

Margot stood and walked to the door. "I really don't want to talk about this anymore. It was nice meeting you, Jules. Pick another subject to discuss next time you drop by."

I left, but forgot to leave a card. While walking back to my car I tried to re-create the tone of her voice in her last sentence—and what the hell she was talking about, for that matter. Despite her outburst, I didn't perceive anger, rather fear and disappointment, with a touch of expectation.

7

"How many goddamn times I gotta tell you I'm retired?" Kalijero said.

"I'll pay you as a consultant—just to have a conversation on the phone, to give me your opinion. You don't even have to get out of your easy chair."

"I charge five bucks a minute."

"That's three hundred an hour. You trying to save up so you can die in a Gold Coast condo?"

"No, I spent forty years as a cop. And I'm worth it."

It was true. "Deal. Fifty-something dude has business bankrolled by rich wife. He runs away to New Mexico with twenty-something after stealing even more of his wife's cash. Then he dies in car wreck. Wife says it's suicide after he murdered twenty-something who got sick of him."

"How the hell does she know this?"

"That I don't know."

"Well, it sounds like she knows a lot more than you do. The young broad. Is that the Jersey boy's girlfriend? You gonna tell him to get the New Mexico police to start digging up the desert?"

"I'm not sure if I should tell my client anything yet. But I'm wondering just how well your cop buddy in Jersey knew him."

"I don't know about that. He's ancient history to me. As far as I'm concerned, Cooper is still a prick. And I can't see him in Irvington and not being a crook. But what do I know?"

"Eddie freaked out on me when I suggested I might get in touch with Tanya's friends back East."

I could hear Kalijero thinking through the extended silence. "So he's hiding something. You said he's paying you in cash, right?"

"Yep."

"Keep that it mind. You know what I mean?"

He meant drugs.

Eddie answered, "Hello?" as if he wasn't sure which end of the phone to speak into.

"Hey, let me buy you lunch. Okay?"

I counted to five, then heard, "Yeah, sure, but you don't have to pay or nothin'."

My impression was that New Jersey people had a special fondness for pork, so I gave him the address of *The Pork Hut,* a greasy spoon within walking distance of his hotel. *The Pork Hut* did an enormous take-out business of pork sandwiches. Little money was wasted on trying to get people to eat in, and it showed. All the vinyl seats were slit open and the floor was almost as sticky as the tables. I arrived to see Eddie sitting at a table, looking at the menu.

"What do you think?" I said. "Garden State quality?"

For the first time Eddie smiled like he knew what I was talking about. "The number three works."

A hunk of pork with egg and cheese on a kaiser roll. "What is it with you Jersey boys and pig meat?"

Eddie shrugged. "We like eatin' our own."

His deadpan coolness evoked loud laughter followed by an embarrassingly loud roar from Eddie, who I'm sure had only tried to sound self-deprecating. Either way, the moment seemed to break through one of those walls that stood between almost-strangers and the first degree of trust. After we composed ourselves, I put our new relationship to the test.

"I'm a curious guy, Eddie. I hope you don't mind me asking why your dad didn't take the family and move out of Irvington?"

Eddie's stare suddenly had a menacing quality, like a sociopath about to blow someone's brains out. Then he blinked a few times and averted his gaze. "I guess he was afraid or didn't know where to go."

"But what about you—his kid? He wanted you to grow up in a shithole neighborhood?"

"You know about Irvington?"

"Two days ago you called it a ghetto. And Kalijero told me something about it."

Eddie nodded. "My aunt said Vietnam messed up my dad. He came back and started drinkin', druggin'. He didn't give a shit. Just worked in the steel mill and got blasted. Married his high school girlfriend and they partied together. Been that way my whole life."

The waitress arrived. When I ordered a salad, she gave me a dirty look.

"How did your dad keep a job if he was drinkin' and druggin'?"

"He did it after work, I guess."

"Bad habits like that cost money. The steel mill paid pretty good?"

Eddie shifted in his seat and looked around. "Well, I guess so, until they shut it down when I was a little kid. And, uh, he started workin' with my uncles and cousins. They started buildin' fences for people and other stuff."

Silence descended. I watched Eddie push a packet of sugar back and forth between his hands. "Was any of that 'other stuff' illegal?"

"I don't know."

"You get into a lot of trouble as a kid?"

"I got really mean, especially after drinkin'. Fightin' was the only way I was gonna get respect."

"That's how you got to know this cop, Cooper?"

Eddie chuckled. "He couldn't wait for me to turn eighteen. He kept sayin', 'When you turn eighteen, Eddie, it's the big house. Your ass is mine!'"

"He took an interest in you."

"He kept bustin' me for any goddamn thing and tried to get me to snitch. They wanted to know stuff. They thought I'd rat 'em out. A real dumbass."

"Okay. I'm an eight- or nine-year-old kid growing up in Eddie's Irvington neighborhood. What's my day like?"

Eddie didn't need time. "Steppin' over dope-sick junkies on the way to school. Hidin' any money I had in my socks. Gettin' held down while someone stole the shoes off my feet. Syringes layin' all over the playgrounds. Gettin' jumped in stairwells or locker rooms . . ."

When the food arrived, Eddie began devouring his pork, egg, and cheese sandwich while I picked at a plate of yellowish iceberg lettuce.

"This investigation could take a while," I said. "What're you going to do with your time?"

Eddie stopped chewing, looked at me, then resumed chewing. "I don't know."

"Gonna do some *other stuff* for your uncles?"

Eddie chewed a bit more. "What do you mean?"

"I don't care what you do. But make damn sure I don't see anything I can't ignore. If the cops have the slightest suspicion I know about *other stuff*, I lose my license—if not more. Got it?"

Eddie finished his sandwich, licked his fingers. "I don't want you feelin' sorry for me 'cause I'm ghetto. I tell you stuff because you *asked* me."

"You ever consider that Tanya might be dead?"

Eddie's eyebrows creased. "No."

"Was Tanya involved in *other stuff*?"

"I told you she wasn't from Irvington. She stayed away from—"

"She didn't stay away from you, right? Just tell me she wasn't doing anything she should not have been doing and I'll believe you. Okay?"

"Tanya never did nothin' bad. She's not that way."

As if on cue, we both leaned back in our chairs. "I met a woman who thinks Tanya was murdered by Doug Daley, her boss from the *Webster Avenue Saloon*. In New Mexico."

Eddie rested his forehead in his hand for a few moments. "Why would he do that?"

"Maybe he loved her to death. I don't know. Tanya could be alive and well."

"If you don't know, why you tellin' me this?"

"You should know I'm not going to get the New Mexico police involved. They might get in the way of finding the truth, especially if she's intentionally hiding."

"She's got no reason to hide, Mr. Landau. I swear."

"You've been in the joint three years. How do you know?"

"Because—I know."

"You just know she has no reason to hide and the wife just knows she's dead. Am I the only one who doesn't know something?"

Eddie sat and stared at his knees, like a discouraged little boy. Then he said, "Just do what you think is right, Mr. Landau. I just want to find Tanya."

8

Three bulk-mail envelopes lay on the floor inside the door to my office, waiting to be recycled. After propping the door open with a wooden shim, I leaned back in my chair, feet on desk, and thought about the seven bucks I'd dropped on a plate of wilted lettuce. Then I thought of Eddie's words, "She's got no reason to hide." Hell, Eddie's fish-eyed stare alone made me want to hide.

An unknown number appeared on my cellphone.

"Are you the private investigator guy?" a female voice asked.

"That's me."

"I'm calling for a friend of a friend. They want to hire you for an easy job."

"Why isn't the friend of a friend calling to hire me for an easy job?"

"I don't know. She asked me to call so I'm doing it. You'll get your normal fee just for picking up a package."

"Did she say what the package was?"

"I have no idea. I just need to know if you'll do it. It would take like a couple of minutes. You give

55

an envelope to someone, they give you the package, then someone will pick up the package from you."

"When?"

"Sooner is better. They're just waiting for my call and then you'll get more instructions."

"You sound like you're full of shit. Come to my office now. Then we'll talk about instructions."

The woman sighed. "Sir, I'm not involved other than making this phone call and bringing your fee and the envelope. If you agree, someone else will call with the details."

"I'm going to ask a question out loud, knowing you won't know the answer. Why doesn't the *someone else* who is going to give me the details also give me the money?"

"My friend thought it had to do with trusting the someone else."

What the hell. If they wanted to give me the money up front, I could always back out. "Okay. Bring the envelope and a separate envelope with ten one-hundred-dollar bills—my fee. It's three-thirty. I'll give you till four to get here. After I get the package, I bring it back to my office. Tell your boss, take it or leave it." I hung up.

If the woman or her *friends* knew my phone number, they probably had my address or knew where to find it. If not, then it was probably bullshit. In the meantime I called Johnny "Bail Bonds" Duggan.

"Johnny Bail Bonds."

"Jules for Johnny."

"Hold please." Irish flute music, then, "Holy shit, how you doin' Jules?"

"I like the flute."

"Tin whistle."

"Sorry to do this to you, but can you put someone on standby in my lobby ASAP? Until about six tonight?"

"How complicated is this?"

"I just need someone to tell me who's heading up the stairs for a visit. It should be one person. If it's more than one, I'll need backup. And if someone is waiting for me on the landing before I return, I want to know. Charge me extra for standby status. And if nobody shows, charge me double."

"Got my three best dogs sniffin' out jumpers right now, so me and Sheila will do this one for brother Jules!"

"You're awesome. It's much safer when Sheila is around. Call me when you get here."

Twenty minutes later I heard the lobby door slam shut and then tentative footsteps climbing the stairs. The caller must have gotten here before Johnny. I missed the stairway's cranky old character, how it groaned with age before the landlord gagged it with a carpet runner.

A cute, strawberry blond teenager appeared in the doorway. "You're in the right place," I said. She handed me two envelopes. "Thanks," I said. She sort of smiled and headed back down the stairs. I looked out the window to see Johnny and Sheila watching the girl jump into a waiting car. My phone rang.

"There's a redhead—"

"I know, forget her. Make yourselves comfortable." The lobby had a couple of love seats.

An envelope with my name contained a thousand bucks. I opened the other and saw a tight quarter-inch stack of C-notes covered in tissue. Maybe five grand. About ten minutes later, another phone call.

"In front of the Oriental Theatre," the male voice said.

"Who are you?"

"Errand boy. Who'd they send with the money?"

"Are you the one they don't trust?"

The voice snorted. "The dumb bitch thinks I need a bodyguard to deliver the money."

"Who is the dumb bitch?"

"Doesn't matter. You meet me at the Oriental. We give them the envelope, they give us the package. Then we bring it—"

"To my office."

"Yeah, fine."

"What's the package?"

"I don't know."

"I'll be there at five," I said. "What's your name, Errand Boy, and how will I know it's you?"

"Just be there at five. I'll figure out who you are."

The Oriental Theatre was a restored Art Deco remnant of the 1920s movie palace era when the word "oriental" was characterized in film by white guys portraying Chinese guys like Detective Charlie Chan. On this night, traditional Celtic step dancing awaited the crowd milling about in the lobby. A warm air mass had parked over cold Lake Michigan, bringing cloud cover and premature dusk to a March evening. Even the streetlight sensors thought it was too dark. Under the marquee, smokers puffed in the chilly spring air.

It was ten to five. I pictured Johnny and Sheila sitting in the lobby of my office building. The crowd now included families glowing with anticipation of the show. Stepping out of the multitude, I stood on the curb near some taxis, touched the envelope of cash in my breast pocket, then returned my hand to the gun in the pocket of my overcoat.

From behind me a voice shouted, "Mr. Landau." I turned to see a skinny man approaching. He didn't appear older than nineteen. His hair was cut high and tight and slicked back in a Prohibition-era gangster style. He stopped about two feet from me. A smattering of freckles across the bridge of his nose combined with his haircut to create a macabre impression of premature aging.

"I'm him," I said, "and who are you?"

"I'm the voice on the phone," he said staring at me with a quizzical expression and annoying smirk. I knew he was a punk.

"Why are you here? I mean, what's your role in this transaction, supervisor?"

"The dumb bitch thought maybe you'd be more at ease if I was here too, since we spoke on the phone."

"Yeah. I feel so much better now that you're here. Where's the person with the package?"

"Too many people. There's an alley—"

"Fuck you and your alley!" I reached into my coat to grab the envelope. The punk stepped up, poked me in the ribs with a snub-nosed revolver, then hid the gun behind his open jacket.

"It's a well-lit alley," he said.

The freckled face–oily hair combo created just enough creepiness for me to go along with the plot twist.

"Just so you know," I said. "I *legally* carry a Glock 9 and can *legally* shoot someone threatening my life—in a well-lit alley."

"Walk straight to the corner. Turn right, then right again into the alley behind the theater."

I led the way, turned on Dearborn, then turned into the alley supposedly haunted by victims of the 1903 fire that killed hundreds. It was indeed well lit but did not resemble a conduit with any commerce-related value other than providing a back door to various establishments. I had a clear view in both directions and checked behind every ten seconds or so to see the kid trailing me by a few feet. In front of me, the alley ended as a kind of *cul-de-sac* that probably used to be an active loading dock until it was bricked up. When I came within about five feet of a short, dark stairwell on my right, the punk told me to stop and turn around. I did as told. "Fuck you, Margot!" he shouted, his face joyfully deranged. Later, I recalled a scuffing sound, like the heel of a hard-soled dress shoe on concrete, and then my world began spiraling down.

9

No voices of lost loved ones telling me it was not my time, but the tunnel was there, long and dark with a light at the end. Not a particularly magnificent illumination of radiant bliss, but light nevertheless. At some point, I became aware that my eyes were open, the ground was cold, and the light was of the 250-watt variety the city had installed a few years earlier—to help reduce crime in alleys.

I dragged myself to the wall and looked around. All alone with a throbbing head in a deserted, well-lit alley. At least the pain from Tamar's breakup had been usurped. On the back of my head, a small lump, but no blood. Must've been hit with a flat surface. I slipped my hand into the breast pocket of my coat where the envelope with five grand no longer resided. Then to my coat pocket where my Glock remained. The punk had showed up about five. My watch said eight or nine after. A couple of minutes chatting, another five minutes to walk around the corner and down the alley. The blow had stunned me, but I didn't think it knocked me completely out. Either way, the trauma lasted less than a minute—in a well-lit alley.

Slowly, I maneuvered into a squat and lifted myself up, scraping against the wall. I get a phone call and two hours later I'm mugged in an alley. That's a lot of trouble just to steal five grand, assuming the package had really been worth a whole lot more. It made as much sense as someone paying me a grand to get whacked on the head.

From the alley entrance a figure entered my peripheral vision. A throbbing head and nausea overruled any impulse resembling curiosity or fear. I closed my eyes and rubbed my forehead. Having just been violently divested of five grand in a well-lit alley, what did I care if someone came back to finish me off? At least the throbbing would stop and I wouldn't have to worry about barfing in public.

"Mortal or spirit?" a female voice said.

I opened my eyes to a pretty brown face. She stood about three feet from me with her hands buried in the pockets of a khaki double-breasted raincoat. A headband held her long curly hair off her forehead, and a close-fitting belt outlined a figure as appealing as her face.

"Well?" she said, her eyes widening as if I tried her patience.

"You ask me that as if it wasn't a stupid question."

She cocked her head just a bit to the side and thought a moment. "If one knew one was hanging out in a haunted alley, one would know how logical the question was."

"And you expect that ghosts simply answer these types of questions?"

"Some do."

"And those who don't, what do they do?"

"Usually they vanish. It's how they run away."

Silence. Then I said, "Tell me something. How do I know if *you* are real?"

I felt her hand close around my wrist and release. "That's how you know."

I stopped rubbing my forehead and looked at her. "What's your name?"

"Amy."

"Amy, did it occur to you that I just had an unpleasant experience?"

"Judging by your posture and knowing you are mortal, that would make sense. Are you okay?"

"Besides the throbbing in my head and a bit of nausea, I'm okay. So you just happened to be walking by?"

"Sort of. I investigate paranormal hot spots. It's rare that I see someone hanging out in an alley during a damp night like this—especially this alley. What were you doing here—may I ask?"

This chance encounter in a well-lit alley had reached a crossroads. Would my answer effectively dismiss this nice lady from my life or would I pursue a conversation, if only to avoid a lonely evening aching over Tamar and trying to formulate possible consequences of the previous three hours?

"Walk with me," I said and Amy followed, keeping a three-foot space between us. I tried to subtly close the distance but she maintained the cushion. "I'm a private investigator. I'd been hired to accompany a kid exchanging cash for a package."

"You're really a private eye?"

She had a childlike excitement in her voice. I gave her one of my cards and showed her my license.

"Wow! What synchronicity! I was hoping I would meet a real private eye one day. Someone who would let me use my psychic abilities to help solve a case."

"Don't assume I'm that someone."

"I hope you don't mind me saying that I'm surprised an experienced investigator would walk into an alley with an envelope full of cash."

"Initially, we met in front of the theater. That's where I was told the transaction would take place. My contact decided to march me back here at the point of a gun. A lot of trouble for five grand."

"You counted the money?"

I hesitated. "It looked like five grand. How do ghosts feel about 250-watt bulbs?"

"It's mortals who are afraid of the dark. Maybe there was a lot more in that envelope than five thousand."

I didn't give her thought much credence, but it was possible. The cool night air had eased the pain. It occurred to me that whoever thumped my head took care to inflict only minimal damage. A plank of pine squarely hitting the top of my skull came to mind.

"What does it mean to investigate the paranormal?"

"It's a personal investigation. I experience the energy of spirits and see what information I can glean."

"They speak to you?"

"You could say that."

"So are all paranormal investigators as good looking as you?" Before I could gauge a response my phone rang. "Landau," I said.

"Jules? Me and Sheila are in the lobby. Nobody has showed up yet. But I just got an SOS and the jerk can afford to pay for SOS service. Do you still need us to hang around?"

It took a moment, but Johnny Bail Bond's voice transported me back to when I called him around three-thirty.

"Johnny! No, no, go ahead. Take off."

"You sure? You sound weird. Are you okay? You want us to call the cops?"

I assured him everything was fine and gave an abbreviated version of the events. It took a while for Johnny to relax and stop insisting I say a code word—like "peanuts"—if someone had a gun pointed at my head. Not until he finally believed the genuine irritation in my voice did he let me go. I put the phone back on my belt and noticed I had drifted from the middle of the sidewalk to the front of a shuttered jewelry store window. Amy was nowhere to be seen. Heartache, by way of Tamar, returned.

10

Punim landed with a thud somewhere among the shadows on the hardwood floor. Sitting on the couch, I stared at the streetlamp partially illuminating my apartment through the warped glass of the old wooden sash windows. Punim's toenails tapped lightly across the floor before she appeared as a black silhouette on the windowsill.

"I want to report a mugging," I said over the phone to Kalijero.

"Someone snatched your purse, Landau?"

I gave him a quick rundown of the evening's adventure but skipped the part with Amy.

"A girl calls up and asks you to deliver an envelope of cash? Then you get mugged by a punk who knows the rich broad?"

"He cursed her name as a signal for someone to crack me on the head."

"And you were supposed to deliver the cash for a package of who the hell knows?"

"Something worth at least five grand."

"Did you count the money?"

"It looked and felt like five grand."

"Never take a job unless you know every goddamn knowable fact. And if they don't want to tell you, walk away. That's investigator 101."

"There was a novice quality about the whole thing—"

"Novices get you killed. You want to be treated like a professional, Landau? Start acting like one and quit taking stupid risks. Amateurs panic, yeah? Be happy you're only out a grand with a bash on the head."

"I still got my money."

"Sometimes jobs are meant to look amateurish."

"If the job had something to do with the missing girl, I'm thinking it was Margot's money."

"So rich wife had something stolen and instead of calling the cops, she hatched her own plot, and at the last minute included you."

"The punk. He was like nineteen. He said the *dumb bitch* worried about him."

"Assuming that's Margot, she made you the punk's bodyguard."

"So instead of swapping the package, punk steals five grand?"

"A one-inch stack of hundreds, Landau. How much money is that? Take a guess."

"One inch is at least twenty grand. There was a quarter inch at most in that envelope."

"Well, then, maybe you're right. It was an amateur trying out his wings."

I flashed back to the punk's face just before I went down. There was a premeditation about the way he told me to stop and turn around.

"Trying out his wings by double-crossing Margot."

"Whatever they stole must've been worth a lot more than what you brought. Go visit the rich broad again and get some answers." Kalijero hung up.

It figured that Kalijero would leave me with *Go visit the rich broad*—as if sitting alone in my shadowed apartment didn't evoke enough *noir* corn. Had a bottle of scotch been at my side instead of a can of ginger ale, the cliché would have been complete.

It was already nine a.m. when I got out of bed and checked the towel on my pillow. No blood. In the shower, I wondered if Amy had been a ghost. Then I remembered my comment about how attractive she was and felt like a jackass. Two bagels and sixteen ounces of cold pomegranate yerba mate later, I drove to my office. Visiting my office at least once a day was important, an "intuitive career consultant" told me. Something to do with the universe responding to my intention. Having the newspaper delivered to my office helped with my intention to go there.

There was still a morning chill in the air, but the sun was out. Miraculously, I found a parking place in front of my building and walked up the three flights to see Amy sitting in one of the club chairs, reading my newspaper. At her feet lay a three-foot-long two-by-four. I didn't have a secretary and I thought having the chair on the landing created a de facto reception area—to help with my intention of attracting clients.

"You appear and disappear just like a ghost," I said.

Amy folded the paper and handed it to me. She wore a brown leather jacket with quilted shoulders and snug-fitting blue jeans. "I'm sorry I walked away but you seemed quite absorbed in your phone conversation—and then something came to mind."

I unlocked the door and held it open. She left the wood on the landing, then passed me, trailing a faint smell of lavender. "How long have you been waiting?"

"I don't know. Forty minutes or so. I was going to leave when I finished the paper."

"I assume you would've slipped a buck under the door. I charge the newsstand price, you know."

She smiled and sat in the matching club chair in front of my desk. Her smile didn't fade as smiles usually did. I no longer felt like a jackass and even entertained the thought that I had a chance. She said, "Have you figured out who sent the package and what it was worth?"

I looked at my watch. "You mean between five o'clock yesterday and right now? Well, I got a hunch on the first part. And I think you're dying to tell me about the second part."

"After I walked away yesterday, I got this feeling I should go back to the alley. So that's what I did. And when I got there, I saw this guy looking around like he'd lost something."

"Mortal or spirit?"

"I didn't want to startle him so I approached slowly. As I got closer, I could tell he was really angry. He kept calling someone under his breath a 'stupid motherfucker' and a whole lot of other nasty words. When I finally asked him what he was looking for, he just stared at me. Then he said, 'Screw it,' and walked away."

"A pissed-off ghost."

"So I started looking around. First I found that piece of wood, probably used to bonk you on the head, and then I found this."

From her pocket she pulled out a cork and put it on the desk. I picked it up, tried to make sense of a faded image and ornate lettering. "The package was a bottle of wine?" I said.

"I think so. But not just any wine. It had to be special."

"Do you know much about wine?"

"I know bottles can go for thousands of dollars."

"The cork was probably a memento. There's a hole in the bottom that might have held a key ring."

"I think that guy was part of the setup."

"And he realized he was missing his prized cork and came back to find it because it was potentially a clue that could point to him as the scumbag who mugged me."

Amy didn't appreciate my sarcasm. "For an investigator, you're pretty narrow minded."

I wasn't sure what her comment suggested, but I got the point. "You're right. Every potential clue could lead to a big break. I guess I'm annoyed I didn't think of it first."

"You didn't go back to the alley, did you?"

"I should have. So the person was prepared to pay five grand in an alley for a bottle of wine. That would mean the wine would really have been worth much more, like what? Ten grand? How many people drink bottles of crushed grapes worth that much?"

"Rich folks."

I leaned back in my chair. Amy stared at me. Her knowing smile seemed peculiar. I hadn't mentioned Margot to her. "I'm investigating a missing girl, not missing wine."

"Does the package being a bottle of wine makes sense to your case?"

"I don't know. Even if the cork belonged to a pricey bottle, what's the meaning of it? They already drank the bottle but still got paid five grand? I can't even speculate what it has to do with the missing girl."

"Tell me about her. Who hired you?"

Yesterday she sounded childlike in her enthusiasm. Today she resembled a captivated child. "Look, I appreciate your help but I'm not looking for a partner. And I couldn't pay you. How about I buy you dinner instead?"

"I don't want money. I like the challenge of figuring out puzzles. I'm an *investigator*, remember?"

"I don't deal with ghosts. These are real people who can be real dangerous."

The wondrous face became an angry adult. "I'm clairvoyant. Sensitive. I can communicate with energies most people have no idea exist. I want to help figure out who mugged you and why. And there's the missing girl. This desire brought me back to the alley where I found the cork. Is that curiosity so difficult for you to understand?"

It really wasn't that difficult, assuming one believed in her psychic ability. "Let me find out a few more facts, okay?" I turned over one of my business cards and asked for the best way to reach her. She took it, quickly scribbled her number, and walked to the door.

"And if you're thinking about calling me for any reason other than the investigation—forget about it."

I guessed dinner was out of the question.

11

What could be learned about a bottle of wine from its former cork? A quick Internet search found a family-owned wine shop only a few blocks from my office. For years, I had routinely passed *Der Weingott*, taking no notice of the place. I pulled open the heavy door. An atmosphere of reverence and veneration covered me. Once my eyes adjusted to the low lighting, I was struck by the beautiful walnut woodwork, finely detailed stained glass, oak wine casks, and a variety of arcane-looking wine paraphernalia.

"How can I help you?" asked a thin, gray-haired man in a fine charcoal suit.

"I'm trying to match a cork with its former bottle."

"Excellent!" the man said with a smile. "I love a good mystery."

The man introduced himself as Paul Price, then handed me one of his cards. I reciprocated, then handed him the cork. He took glasses from his jacket's breast pocket and began studying it. A few times he looked up, as if wanting to say something, then returned to the examination. Finally, he said, "Come here for a minute."

I followed Paul through a large room resembling a millionaire's private library with shelves of corked bottles lying on their sides. Paul's office was through a door masquerading as wall paneling. Once inside, he placed the cork under a large magnifying glass with a bright light. He studied it a few more minutes and said, "Where did you get this cork?"

"I found it."

"Really? Where?"

"In an alley. So what can you tell me?"

"I can tell you that this cork belonged to a very expensive bottle of wine. See this?"

Through the glass I saw the faint image of the letter "R" intersected by several arrows. "That's a logo, I assume?"

"Yes. Now above the 'R,' there's a word written across. It's very small and faded, but what does the first letter look like to you?"

I focused again on the tiny image. "I would say it looks like an 'L.' "

"Exactly. That's the five-arrow logo of Lafite Rothschild."

"So it was a pricey bottle of grape juice?"

Paul gave me a courtesy chuckle. "One of the most expensive. And here's something else to consider." He adjusted the cork so I could make out the imprint of the year 1947. "That year is one of the most sought-after vintages of Lafite Rothschild."

"What would a bottle cost?"

"Four to five thousand. You said you found this in an alley?"

I explained that I had been hired to exchange money for a package I think was a bottle of wine but was robbed of the cash instead. Paul nodded as if I had told him I ate French toast for breakfast. "You don't seem surprised by this."

"Was this a stolen bottle of wine?"

"I'm not sure, why?"

"Unfortunately, since the value of fine wine has soared in recent years, so have theft and counterfeiting. Restaurants, wine shops, wine collectors are all targets. So if your client had been robbed of a bottle of Lafite Rothschild, I'm not at all surprised."

"Counterfeiting wine? How is that done?"

"Pretty crudely—but with a lot of success. Printing techniques are increasingly sophisticated. Vintage labels are reproduced and put on different bottles. Old style fonts burned into wooden crates, creating the illusion of antiquity."

"But how can you get away with it? I mean once they taste the wine, isn't the game over?"

"An absurdly small number of people have any idea what an old wine tastes like. Even many Gold Coast collectors can't tell the difference between a rare wine and some cheap filler. And on the occasion someone realizes they've purchased a fake, many won't alert the authorities. Instead, they sell it to try to get their money back. Complicity is a huge problem."

I thought about the money involved in my caper. "But there are bottles of wine worth more than five grand, right?"

Paul laughed. "Oh, yes. Much more." He opened a desk drawer and took out a magazine. "To get an idea of the kind of money we're talking about, take a look at this when you have time." He handed me a magazine called *Wine Kibitzer*. "This edition is dedicated to the largest fraud cases of the last ten years or so."

"The price was five grand. If the wine had already been stolen and this was a ransom, why pay face value for a bottle you already paid for? You might as well buy another bottle from a reputable dealer rather than give your money to the crooks. And why would a crook expect his victim to pay twice for the same bottle? They'd be better off selling to someone else."

Paul took a moment. "You make an excellent point."

I said, "See that gouge in the bottom of the cork? I think it was attached to someone's key ring."

Paul played around with it under the magnifier. "The cork structure probably weakened from being taken out of someone's pocket over and over. They should have drilled a hole right in the center instead of in the bottom third. From your observations, you seem to be suggesting that the cork had nothing to do with the robbery."

"Well, even if the cork was just a keepsake, the guy probably knew something about wine. Maybe it was just a bunch of punks who already drank the bottle but wanted to get some easy cash. Maybe there never was a bottle of wine."

Paul frowned. "People wealthy enough to buy Lafite Rothschild will purchase it by the case."

"Which means they would have stolen the case. A hundred thousand dollars' worth of wine."

A woman dressed in a black skirt and matching jacket knocked on the door. "Dad, your investment appointment is here," she said and hurried away.

"Getting ready to retire?"

"Hardly. They're here for wine investment advice."

"Investing in something they're going to drink?"

"No. In uncertain economic times, people park their cash in commodities that traditionally have always appreciated or at least held their value. Some people buy art, some buy diamonds. I knew a guy who put all his money in vintage guitars. And then there are those who buy vintage wine." Paul opened a drawer and handed me an old paperback. "Here, take this. It's out of date but it will give you the basic information on the wine world."

Before I could thank him, Paul began walking quickly to the foyer. He greeted a well-groomed forty-something couple before leading them to a private tasting room. The taste of money would be rather dry, I thought.

12

"Come in, Jules," Margot said as I reached the top step. The door was ajar.

Once again, she had buzzed me in without using the intercom. Once again, Margot lay on the chaise longue looking out the window while I took the love seat. A glass on the end table held vestiges of pinot noir. She swung her legs off the chaise and looked at me. "Are you okay?" she said.

"You spoke to your errand boy, I assume. He told you he blew your cover?"

She searched my face. Tears brimmed forth. She started to say something but stopped short as the waterworks began. When she regained her composure she said, "I thought it would be simple. If I had any idea you could be hurt—"

"Why didn't you just ask me to do the job? What's with the cloak-and-dagger bullshit?"

She studied me again. "I'm trying to apologize."

"I'll accept your apology if you include the truth. Let's start with my business card. I don't remember leaving one here."

A blank look, then, "You left one with Brenda."

"Who was the girl who called and came over?"

"Jennie Adler. She works for Brenda. I asked Brenda if I could borrow her for a quick favor. Neither of them knew any details. I drove Jennie over, waited, then took her back."

"Who was your greaseball errand boy?"

Margot looked puzzled. "You mean Spike? He's just a college kid we met when we lived in Evanston. He used to run errands for us to make extra cash."

"Spike? The Spike who worked at Doug's bar?"

"Yes. He was Doug's assistant." She walked to the attic chain of paper butterflies and stroked one lovingly. "All handmade in India," she said then walked into the kitchen and returned with a box of tissues. She blew her nose a few times and dabbed her eyes.

"Then you called Spike to run another errand?"

Margot started crying again. "It was supposed to be easy and quick. Nothing to it. I swear I never would've knowingly sent Spike—or you—into a dangerous situation."

"So Spike was supposed to make the swap and at the last minute you decided I should be there."

"After you left yesterday I started thinking about what you said. That some crazy could just walk up those stairs—and like a fool I would let them. And then I started thinking about Spike and that he should have an older man with him. I still thought it would be easy, but why not have someone like you who legally carried a gun—just to make sure?"

My turn to study Margot. "Uh, you do know Spike pulled a gun on me, right?"

"What?" Margot whispered. Her expression of horror appeared genuine.

"Let me guess. The little bastard told you we got mugged in *front* of the theater surrounded by mobs of people, and you believed him. Sorry. Spike stuck a snub .38 into my gut then walked me back to the alley. I got jumped right after he said, 'Fuck you, Margot.'"

Margot staggered back to the chaise. "I can't believe it. I mean, I believe *you*. But I can't believe he would do that."

"Believe it. I noticed you buzzed me in without using the intercom."

Margot thought for a moment and then said quickly, "But I knew it was you. I saw you from the window walking down the sidewalk—you parked on Webster."

Good guess. "Where's Spike?"

"He called me in a panic. He said he ran away after you got hit on the head."

I thought of Spike's arrogant expression just before I got hit. "What exactly did Spike know about this easy job?"

"He knew nothing about the arrangement! Only that we asked him to exchange one package for another. I kept him in the dark on purpose—to protect him. He didn't even know the package was a bottle of wine."

"You're sure he didn't know?" I said.

Margot looked at me wild-eyed. "Yes. I just told you I kept him in the dark. I was afraid he wouldn't understand the value of wine."

Her last comment made no sense. "You're a wine connoisseur, eh?"

"Well, no. But you knew Doug had turned the pub into a wine bar—"

"How would I have known that?"

"You talked about it with Brenda. She told you she taught him about French wine."

Margot had done her homework. "So you think Spike couldn't resist stealing the five grand and that's all there is to it? Who stole your case of wine?"

Margot hesitated. "Ten cases."

"Holy shit! When?"

"Two months ago."

"And you don't think Spike had anything to do with it?"

"No, I don't believe it. He's been a great help to me until now. He succumbed to taking the cash, that's all. He grew up very poor."

"Where was the wine stolen from?"

"A wine storage facility."

"Okay. Here's what's bugging me. A wine expert told me a bottle of Lafite Rothschild costs four to five thousand. The ransom was five thousand. Why would you pay for the same bottle twice?"

"If the stolen wine was Lafite Rothschild, I would agree. But the stolen wine was *Mouton* Rothschild."

"How much per bottle?"

"Around twenty thousand."

I wanted my eyes to pop out like a cartoon character. "Twenty grand multiplied by two hundred and forty bottles?"

"Half of that. Wine cases have twelve bottles."

"And the thieves wanted to swap a 20K bottle for 5K?"

"I don't think they realized what they had and thought five thousand sounded like a good price."

"I found this Lafite Rothschild cork in the alley. It was used as a key fob. Do you think the same person would have kept a Boone's Farm screw cap?"

"How would I know how these people think? And I don't appreciate your sarcasm."

Margot wheeled herself around to stretch out on the chaise. I studied her profile as she gazed out the window. Any sign of anguish had vanished. Now she just looked pouty.

"The thieves broke in to a storage facility? Don't they have to compensate you?"

"They have to investigate first—like insurance fraud. It takes time. "

"Have you investigated Doug's staff? Didn't that place have security cameras?"

"If the police started asking questions, the thieves would've sold it at a deep discount and still pocketed a lot of cash. I didn't care if I had to pay for it."

"So they were going to sell it back to you one bottle at a time?"

"The one bottle was supposed to be a test to see if they really had my Mouton Rothschild."

"You think they'll call again?"

Margot sat up and faced me. "Can you help me get the wine back?"

"Unless the wine has something to do with the missing girl, Tanya, I'm not interested."

"But I'll pay you!" she shouted, once again startling me. "You can have a bottle as payment!" I didn't respond. She calmed down. "I did it again," she said. "I had no right to talk to you like that."

"I don't like wine."

"Keep it as an investment! I'll give you two bottles. That's forty thousand dollars in a commodity that has given double-digit returns the last ten years."

Forty thousand was a hell of a lot of money, about four times my net worth. The rich have been getting richer the last thirty years. I dared to predict their future looked bright and would include insanely expensive wines.

"If I can find your wine in the process of finding Tanya, I'll do what I can. But the girl will be my first priority for as long as it takes."

Margot jumped out of the chaise, ran behind the love seat, then wrapped her arms around my neck. "Thank you, Jules," she said and kissed my cheek.

Her weird behavior canceled out how nice her touch felt. "Margot, you need to chill out! I really don't know what I can do for you."

"Yes, yes, I understand," she said, although her voice remained ridiculously upbeat. For some reason she seemed to have a lot of faith in me.

<h1 style="text-align:center">13</h1>

The Audi sedan merged on to Webster Avenue as soon as I walked out of Margot's building. I didn't think much of it until I reached my 1983 Honda Civic and heard the tires squeal as it executed a sharp U-turn and pulled up to me. The window lowered and I saw Amy angling toward me over the passenger seat. "Let me give you a ride. Get in."

I leaned through the opened window. "You're following me?"

Amy frowned. "Oh, don't make a big deal out of nothing. Just get in and hear me out."

The sharpness in her voice put me off, but I did as told. Amy pulled another U-turn and we headed east. "So what the hell are you doing following me?"

"I know you think I'm a nut but I'm supposed to be involved in this investigation. It's just the way

I am. There's a puzzle that needs solving and I want to help."

"I told you, I work alone—"

"But it's not about you, it's about me. It's what I want to do—what I have to do. So many innocent young women are taken advantage of. Tanya Maggio's energy is calling me. I'm not sure she's alive anymore and the least I can do is offer my skills to make sure she's found and someone is brought to justice."

"You expect me to understand what you just said?"

Amy pulled over near DePaul University. "Haven't you ever felt a calling, something you *have* to do—even if you can't explain why and nobody understands you?"

"What? You think I get respect? Most people don't know private investigators exist outside of movies. They think I'm joking. But, yes, I'm drawn to it."

"Because you're reckless. You don't give a damn."

"About what?"

"About anything. You're like me. If something turns you on, you check it out to find what's behind it. Doesn't matter what others think. That's a reckless way to live."

She had that look of cocky anticipation, as if she knew she had me pegged. I wanted to tell her she had revealed a great reason for us to be more than friends.

"You want to play investigator with me?" I said. "Fine. You can share what you know or think you know. But you're on your own. You take your own risks. I'm not going to be responsible for something happening to you."

Amy's expression did not exactly exude gratitude. "Gee, thanks, Jules. How privileged I am to be allowed to help you."

"You say you picked up Tanya's energy. How do you do it?"

"I'm going to pretend you asked that question without overt cynicism. For people like me, the energy comes through *you*. The barrier between the concrete world and abstract consciousness is just a thin veil of perception. If you are focused on her, then at some level you are communicating with her simply through your desire to find her. Think of me as eavesdropping on *your* conversation."

Intelligent, pretty, she saw little difference between empirical and hypothetical reality. But only two letters separated the words "psychic" and "psychotic." "I don't like being followed."

"Last night I spent some time on the Internet. The wine collecting world isn't that big. Not at this level of value. When you start breaking out the niche groups, you find a small circle that collects antique wine. I don't even think they drink the stuff. It's just a place to park money, like an investment."

Amy took a piece of paper from her purse and handed it to me. It was a lengthy obituary of a philanthropic wine collector, Dr. Thomas van Bourgondien, who donated his bottles to various charities once they had attained a significant value.

"Interesting guy," I said. "What about him?"

"Read the last few lines."

"'Preceded in death by his wife, Sarah, survived by his daughter, Margot Daley.' How did you find out where she lived?"

Amy hesitated. "I did some more searching on the net."

"Is Margot Daley the only antique wine collector in the city? How did you settle on her house as where you'd find me?"

"I had a hunch—"

"Don't start with the 'energy' bullshit, Amy. Falling back on your psychic powers as an explanation isn't going to fly every time. In fact, the more you use it, the more I wonder who you really are."

Amy sighed. "Okay, you got me," she said. "A friend in law enforcement told me where she lived."

"That still doesn't explain why you were so sure I would go to Margot's house."

"I wasn't sure, but Margot's father was a North-Sider. I had a hunch she was a North Side kind of gal. I gambled and my hunch was correct. That's my explanation, take it or leave it."

"Your explanation stinks but I'll let it go for now."

"You want to tell me what Margot has to do with Tanya? You thought her disappearance was related to the stolen wine."

This time I hesitated. "Okay, you got me. I don't know and if I did I wouldn't tell you."

"You are really starting to annoy me. Do you want my help or not?"

"It's not about me, it's about you, remember?"

"Fuck you."

I supposed I deserved it. "Sure. You can help me. But like I said you're on your own. If you got info you want to share, fine. But it's going to be a one-way street. I'm not going to risk you getting hurt because you know too much. The state gave me a license, they can take it away."

Amy sighed. "I wonder how a guy like you—who probably doesn't have many friends—would be any good at this job."

"Maybe not having friends is an advantage. Or I make up for it by being *reckless*. And like you said, I don't give a damn."

Amy offered to drive me back to my car. I declined, choosing instead to see if the fresh air would inspire my mental energies to figure out why this beautiful stranger would willingly take crap from me. Despite my view of intuitive abilities, I thought the passion in her voice for investigating the spirit world was sincere. And true to my reckless nature, I was attracted to the mystery of her sudden appearance in the same alley where I had been jumped.

14

It always felt good to be home. Despite an absence of only four hours, coming home to a reclining chair and sleeping cat had taught me to appreciate simple comforts. I called Eddie.

"It's Jules Landau. How're you doing?"

"Huh? Yeah, I'm all right."

"Where are you?"

"Out."

"You mind coming north? See a little more of the city? I'd like to have a meeting."

"What about?"

I waited for the punch line. "What do you think? About why you're paying me, yeah?"

"Okay, yeah. You got new information?"

"Go ahead and make that assumption if it'll get you here."

I gave Eddie directions but couldn't shake the feeling he was pretending to listen. About an hour later I heard the outside door to my building open and then Eddie's footsteps on the stairs. I stuck my head out the door and watched the top of his bald head ascend toward me.

I said, "You always stare straight down when you climb stairs?" No answer. "How does our subway compare to New Jersey's?" Eddie had no opinion of the subway.

At the top of the landing Eddie said, "So you got info on Tanya?"

He followed me in and took a seat on the couch. I returned to the recliner and said, "How's business?"

He raised his eyebrows but ignored the question. "What have you found out about Tanya?"

"Don't get your hopes up. I want to tell you about yesterday evening's events. Maybe something will come to mind—something you'll want to tell me."

Eddie took a breath and let it out. Then he unclenched his jaw. "Okay, start talking." I pretended he didn't just give me an order.

"After our lunch yesterday, I got a call. Someone wanted to pay me a grand to pick up a package in exchange for a pile of cash. I've dropped a lot of business cards around town so it's no big surprise to get a call for a job, although this type of job was a first."

"What was in the package?"

"An expensive bottle of wine. So I showed up at the meeting spot, got hit on the head and relieved of the cash. I found out later the wine had been stolen from the wife of the guy who ran off with Tanya. The same woman who told me Tanya was dead."

"You don't know Tanya ran off with him. He might've kidnapped her or blackmailed her to go."

"We already discussed this. Tanya leaving willingly is the working theory."

Like the previous day, Eddie's cold, blue-eyed stare put me on guard. The image of him diving at me with a knife clenched between his teeth flashed through my brain.

Eddie said, "So what about Tanya?"

"This *other stuff* you're involved in. Would that include theft?"

Eddie's face reddened. "I know you think I'm a scumbag, but I do what I gotta do to survive. You don't understand how I grew up—"

"Lots of people grow up in crummy neighborhoods and don't become criminals."

"It—it's more than that. Trust me."

"I'm trying to keep the trust thing simple. Can I trust that what you're *not* telling me has nothing to do with Tanya disappearing?"

"I got nothin' to do with stealin' wine. I don't know what that's about." He pulled an envelope from the breast pocket of his leather jacket and laid it on the coffee table between us. "You been workin' hard. You gotta know I 'preciate it."

I could clearly see the well-defined rectangular outline of cash stuffed in the business-sized envelope. Eddie leaned back on the couch, looked around the room. I stared at him until he met my eyes then averted his gaze—just like he did at yesterday's lunch.

"I'm going to ask you this one time. And I'm going to *trust* that you'll tell me the truth. Is that cash drug money?"

"No way! I swear to Christ that money is clean."

He leaned forward, stared at the floor between his knees, began flexing his hands open and closed. I said, "We've got Doug, Tanya, and Doug's wife, Margot. Margot says they're both dead. Margot has an expensive bottle of wine stolen. We know Doug tried to convert his beer joint into a wine bar. How the hell is Tanya connected to this?"

Either Eddie knew the question was rhetorical or his fidgeting indicated he didn't know what to say. "I never even saw Tanya drinkin' wine," he said. "You order wine where I'm from and you might get your ass kicked."

"Let's go back in time. How often did Tanya visit you in prison?"

"I don't know. Couple times a month."

"What did you guys talk about?"

Eddie scratched the back of his neck. "Just how I was doin', how she was doin'; family and friends."

"You said nobody stayed in touch with her after she left?"

"Yeah."

"Bullshit. One of her friends told you Tanya was in Chicago—but you claim none of her friends know anything."

Eddie stood up. "Word got around and I heard somethin', so what?"

"So you *heard* she went to Chicago. That's all you heard?"

"Yeah."

"And then later, word got around that she was working at a wine bar—but none of her friends knew anything."

Eddie started pacing around the room. I sensed the danger.

"You don't even know what a pathetic liar you are, do you?" I said. He stopped walking and glared at me. "It's over, Eddie. I know you're full of shit. So why should I trust you? Tell me why I should even consider continuing this investigation?"

"I'm payin' you!" he shouted.

I picked up the envelope. It weighed like four months of income. "Take your fucking money," I said, then tossed the envelope his way.

Eddie watched it slide across the floor and hit the wall. I thought any second his head would explode. Then he rested his hands on his hips and stared out the window. I stretched out on the recliner. Eddie desired my help but knew he didn't deserve it. It was not in his nature to slink away like a frightened child, and he knew beating the crap out of me wouldn't remedy his pain either. We stayed in our respective positions for probably a few uncomfortable minutes before I attempted to put him out of his misery.

"If you leave and take the money, we're done. If you leave and don't take the money, I'm still working for you. But it also means you acknowledge and accept I will go anywhere I want and ask all the questions I want, if only to find out if you're lying to me. And, yes, in my rules of the game, withholding information is the same as lying. Take it or leave it."

Offering the only acceptable option had a cathartic effect. There was a difference between acting reckless and acting dumb. I didn't mind being reckless. If Eddie wouldn't tell me everything he knew, I could justify acting reckless to find the truth on my own. But if Eddie wouldn't pay me to snoop around his old neighborhood, I would be dumb to keep him as a client. Fatigue followed closely behind the catharsis. My transition into dreamland assimilated a closing door and Eddie's feet pounding down the steps. I could've lifted my head to see if he had taken the money, but the effort seemed pointless.

15

Knuckles banged against solid wood then stopped a few seconds before starting up again. I sat up and surveyed the empty room. Through the lingering haze of an afternoon nap, I reconstructed the scene that had taken place about a half hour earlier. Once out of the recliner, I saw the envelope still on the floor against the wall and then opened the door to stare into the face of retired police detective Jimmy Kalijero.

"Are you going to let me in or not?"

I stepped aside. "You could've called first."

Kalijero lumbered in and fell back into the recliner. He still looked rather dashing for a man past sixty, his silk shirt unbuttoned enough to reveal a gold Parthenon dangling above his sternum. His head of wavy silver hair also lent Kalijero a sense of mythical Greek nobility. I picked up the envelope then sat across from him on the couch.

"When are you going to put some pictures on the wall? This place depresses me."

"It seems having too much time on your hands brings out the useless critic. What's next, you don't like my haircut?"

Kalijero frowned. "That kid who left a little while ago. Jersey boy?" I walked to the kitchen, took two cans of ginger ale from the fridge, then handed one to my guest. "No Tanqueray?" Kalijero said.

"Funny. What were you doing out there?"

Kalijero held his gaze on me longer than I liked. He looked worried. "Where are you in the investigation?"

"Since we talked last night? The package was a bottle of wine stolen from Margot Daley and worth about twenty grand."

"How did you figure that out?"

"Margot told me."

"What else?"

"I have a cork one of the pirates dropped in the alley. It had once plugged a bottle of some other pricey vintage. Someone was using it as a key fob."

Kalijero laughed. "That was awfully convenient. No business card with it?"

"I can't think of any reason why they left it there intentionally."

"To lead you to the broad with money— Margot."

"Then they must've known I was investigating Tanya Maggio. Otherwise, how could they assume I would make the connection to Margot?"

I thought a little more and concluded the cork was irrelevant. "I would've made the connection to Margot regardless."

Kalijero's expression said he had moved beyond wayward corks. "How does the missing girl figure in?"

"No idea."

"What does Margot think?"

"She thinks both her husband and Tanya are dead. I told you that."

"Do you believe her?"

"Why shouldn't I? She showed me the newspaper article, crash photo and all. Jimmy, what are you doing here?"

Kalijero nodded, hesitated, then said, "I got curious about Cooper, the cop I knew years ago. The one in Newark who told the kid Eddie to find me. It appears the rumors were true—only more so. He's now King of the Shithole. The arrogant prick holds court out in the open, in a strip joint surrounded by suckling guidos. Here, a buddy of mine sent me this because I thought he was kidding."

Kalijero reached into his pocket, pulled out a folded piece of paper, then slid it across the coffee table. I unfolded a somewhat pixilated fax machine photo of a man sitting with a bunch of guys at a booth.

"Do you think your buddy could email me a jpeg of this photo?"

Kalijero looked horrified. "Do what?"

"Never mind. How dirty are we talking?"

"Start with a certain product that holds its value—especially in ghettos. Think of the cash it brings in. From there, who knows how dirty."

"Things that hold their value. I have a feeling you're not talking about Warhol paintings." I tossed the envelope on the table. It landed flat with a loud "thwack." "The sound of money crashing."

Even Kalijero seemed surprised at the potential sum suggested by the envelope's mass. "You may want to rethink this client."

"Thanks a lot. After you sent him to me. And he swore to Christ the money was clean."

"Oh, yeah? I swear to Christ I'm Archbishop Ieronymos."

"This picture will come in handy if I go out there and check things out."

"Go out where? Irvington? You're out of your goddamn mind if you go snooping around Cooper's territory!"

"You can't just *assume* Eddie is drug-connected with Cooper! If I have to go to Irvington to find out, I will."

Kalijero slowly ran both hands through his hair. "Just listen! You don't have to go to Irvington. Word is, Cooper is branching out. Wants to make inroads into other city shitholes."

"And you think that's Eddie's assignment, here in Chicago?"

"He's loaded with cash, Cooper's known him his whole life. Doesn't that make sense?"

"But what about Tanya? And since Cooper is from Chicago, you'd think he'd already have connections here."

"He might."

"A cop?"

Kalijero pretended not to hear me. "When I suggested rethinking this client, I wasn't joking."

"I've got almost ten years in this biz including two solved murder cases. Remember? When are you going to stop talking to me like I just got a junior G-man badge from a box of Corn Flakes?"

Kalijero pushed himself up from the chair. "You got anything to eat?"

He walked into the kitchen and started opening cabinets. After he found my sourdough pretzels he leaned back against the counter and started eating out of the box.

"You always were cocky. I don't know where it came from because your old man wasn't like that. Even after—"

"Stop with the guilt over putting my dad away. Forget it. You were just doing your job. I've said that a hundred times. I liked you better when you thought I was just a punk with a two-bit hoodlum father. This sentimental side of you is nauseating. Especially since Frownie died—"

"You're really determined to be a prick, aren't you, Landau? Your dad didn't want you in this business and neither did Frownie. But Frownie knew you'd do whatever you goddamn wanted no matter what others said. So he took the time to train you, to make sure maybe you wouldn't get killed—right away. And, yeah, since Frownie died I feel a little more responsible. So what? You got any friends, Landau? What I hear is you got nobody. I'm probably the closest thing you have to a friend and I don't even like you!"

Kalijero stood his ground, angrily crunching on pretzels. I saw a divorced, childless man figuring out where he belonged after a law enforcement career had justified his existence for forty years. He had a lot of experience to offer, but if access to knowledge required adopting a *de facto* father figure, I'd prefer taking my chances with fate.

I said, "You should know by now that I'm not going to drop a case for you or anyone else. So why bring it up? I mean, either you help me or you don't, Jimmy. And if you do want to help, there can't be any conditions attached."

Kalijero said nothing as he walked back to the chair, pretzel box in hand. I watched him get comfortable, then stare straight ahead in a chomping trance. About ten minutes later, he placed the empty box on the coffee table next to the envelope of cash and stood. Before walking out he said, "Enjoy the kid's money while you can. Eventually, the stink will rub off on you until you can't even stand yourself anymore."

Kalijero's exit left an ache in my gut. I thought of him making the effort to drive here, taking the time to watch my apartment, thinking about what he wanted to say. I should be flattered to get that kind of attention from a man with his experience. His career had spanned the last decades of my family's peripheral involvement with small-time crime syndicates, ending abruptly with my father's imprisonment when I was a teen. Maybe his retirement had allowed the connection he felt with the past to fill the void police work left behind. Maybe I should ask myself why I cared what Kalijero thought.

16

From across the street of *Pâtisserie Grenouille,* I stood in the languishing afternoon light, taking little comfort in the feeble warmth, but feeling unexpectedly lighthearted from the promise of March sunshine.

Brenda Gallagher stepped outside for a smoke. A few puffs later she flicked the cigarette into the street and returned to the café. I waited a while longer for business to pick up before slipping through the crowd and sitting at a table in the center of the room. Brenda pulsated joy as she ran her business, her smile never wavering as she fluttered about serving various desserts, chatting with devoted patrons, or offering advice on the best white wine with a puff pastry or lemon soufflé. Once again, I noticed the old, white-bearded man wearing the black beret, sitting by himself at a table against the far wall.

I recognized Jennie Adler, the woman who did a favor for Margot. When the rush settled down enough for Jennie to maintain things, Brenda stood in front of the swinging doors to the kitchen, surveying the crowd while wiping her hands on her apron. When her gaze came my way, I smiled and waved. She glanced over her shoulder, laughed, made a goofy expression, then walked over.

"Hey! Jules, right? The detective who came in the other morning?"

"Private investigator. I see you're busy, but can you spare a few minutes?"

"Sure, Jennie's got it under control."

"Jennie's what's called a strawberry blonde, right?"

Brenda laughed. "Yes, that's definitely strawberry blonde."

"Why are her lips pink?"

"Because that's the lipstick strawberry blondes wear—*duh*!"

"Of course! Anyway, you mentioned that Doug wanted to learn about wine. That you taught him about wine?"

"Well, yeah. French wine is my specialty. Why?"

"How about Margot? Did you talk about wine with Margot?"

Brenda thought about it. "I don't remember that. She would just come in and order a glass and we would chat."

Jennie appeared with a white bowl and two spoons. "Thank you, sweetheart," Brenda said. Jennie smiled at me and left. "You look worried," Brenda said and spooned out a heaping portion of custard.

"Did it strike you as odd that Doug Daley would come here to learn about wine considering his wife is a wine collector?"

Brenda looked as if she might spit the custard back at me. She swallowed hard. "Who's a collector—Margot?"

"Yeah, Margot. What exactly did you two talk about?"

"I don't know, small talk. The challenge of running a business. Men. Maybe a little about our backgrounds—where we grew up. That kind of stuff. As for wine, Margot would just order a glass from the list. She never mentioned being a collector."

"I wonder why she wouldn't mention it?"

Brenda shook her head. "Good question. Maybe she wasn't crazy about my wine selection and didn't want to sound like a snob. I mean, it wasn't like we were *great* friends or anything. We got along but in the very limited context of hanging out for a while after hours."

"Yet you warned her that I was on my way over to her house."

Brenda's eyes widened. "I never did that! Why did you say that?"

"That's what Margot told me."

"Well, she's lying! Why would I do that? Where she lives isn't privileged information. Everyone who worked at the pub knew where she and Doug lived."

Consecutive spoonfuls disappeared into Brenda's mouth. She ordered me to pick up my spoon and use it. The irritation in her voice gave her a confident demeanor, like she was a different person. I liked this person.

"That bitch!" Brenda said. "Why would she say that?"

"Sorry for this—but she also said you gave her the business card I left here."

Brenda fumed as she finished off the custard. "I'm going over there—"

"No! Don't do anything—as a favor to me. Pretend we didn't have this conversation. I'm not sure what she's up to, but it's better if she thinks her plan is working."

"You're looking for that girl Tanya, right? Can you at least tell me if Margot has something to do with that?"

Brenda's stare almost elicited a summary of events since our last meeting. I stopped myself in time to keep the focus on Margot. "She's convinced Doug killed Tanya and then himself. The car wreck was no accident."

Maybe too much information at once. Brenda looked wounded. "That can't be. I don't believe it. Doug a murderer? Was he having an affair with that—that kid?"

"That's one theory."

"Some kind of obsession-murder thing?"

"Why wouldn't Margot have taught her husband about wines? I doubt very much that Doug did not know Margot had a wine collection—his own wife?"

We silently considered my question until Jennie ran over to point out the line of customers reaching almost to the door. Brenda transformed back into the affable host, radiating the kind of happiness reserved for the long suffering artist finally finding their audience. I wondered how long she had toiled as just another nameless entity among the multitudes seeking recognition in the culinary arts. Could Brenda's current foodie devotees have known where she had been before she arrived? Timing was the key, I thought, then it hit me.

17

"Oh, that's right," Amy said over the phone. "I wrote my number on one of your business cards. How flattering that you should call me."

"That obituary you showed me on Margot Daley's father. What was the date?"

"Where are you? Is that Piaf singing in the background?"

"I'm at a café. Could you find the date for me, please?"

I heard her fumbling through papers. "The date was printed. A top-notch investigator would've noted the date."

"Yes, I have much to learn."

She mumbled something and then announced a date from the previous September. I hung up before she could ask any questions.

The condition of Margot and Doug Daley's relationship suddenly surfaced as a crucial detail. Margot said she had no knowledge of the alleged affair between Doug and Tanya until he shut down the pub and ran off with her. Initially, I took this comment to mean their marriage had been a going concern up until Doug's sudden departure. But what if that wasn't the case? What if, like many couples, they had drifted apart in every aspect, despite living together under the guise of marriage? Two months before Doug left, Margot's father had died. Included in her inheritance was his wine collection. What if Margot had recognized the value of the collection but knew deep down that her marriage was not thriving and was, instead, headed toward divorce? Would she have informed Doug of her newly acquired bottled wealth? In the meantime, Doug discovered on his own that his father-in-law's collection represented an investment valued much higher than a connoisseur's love of fine wine.

And then there was the matter of Margot implicating Brenda in two lies. If not Brenda, who warned Margot that I was on the way over? From whose business card had she gotten my number? She could have said she looked it up in the phone book. I retraced my steps from Eddie walking into Mocha Mouse and quickly found my answer across the street at the *Auvergnat Vin Bar* where I distinctly remembered placing my card on the bar before bowing to the master of grapes.

The black Porsche's VINMSTR license plate proclaimed the *sommelier* was in residence. Art Deco wall sconces and candlelit tables had transformed the rustic décor I remembered from my daytime visit into French country elegance. Bottles backlit with a luminous glow added a touch of chic. Most of the tables were occupied by couples talking quietly over wine and finger sandwiches.

Around the oblong bar, a mix of men and women sat waiting to meet someone or pretending to look that way. I observed two guests appearing to have no interest in each other, and sat between them. The bartender greeted me with a menu and introduced himself as Bruce. Standing in his shadow, I recognized Ted Goldberg, the skinny redheaded kid who worked with Tanya, dressed the same as Bruce in a white shirt and black bow tie. Ted avoided eye contact while Bruce claimed he'd be delighted to answer any questions, then walked away before I could respond. For several minutes I feigned interest in the wine list. The designated regions of France and Italy brought to mind their association with the Second World War instead of grape characteristics.

As I pondered the Allied breakout from Anzio, Bruce interrupted with, "Any questions?"

"Is the boss around?"

Bruce cocked his head slightly. "Is something wrong?"

Ted glanced my way. He was holding a list from which he chose bottles to be stood upright in a designated area under the bar.

"Not at all. I just want to chat."

"Well, there is more than one owner." He didn't elaborate.

"The guy who wears a silver saucer around his neck and a cluster of grapes on his black jacket."

Bruce nodded. "Yes. That would be Jeremy Godello, the *sommelier*. Uh, can I tell him who you are?"

I handed him one of my cards. He read it, gave me the evil eye, then spoke quietly to a young woman server who took the card and disappeared into the kitchen.

"This must be a lot better than working in the kitchen," I said to Ted. He smiled, nodded quickly, then returned to his list. A minute later, the woman server tapped me on the shoulder.

"I'm sorry, Mr. Godello is too busy to talk right now."

"Well, thank you very much for trying," I said, and after getting Bruce's attention, tossed a ten-dollar bill on the bar.

"Oh, that's not necessary," Bruce said, but I insisted and continued toward the entrance, stopping behind a tall cabinet used to store antique wine paraphernalia. I waited long enough for my presence to have been all but forgotten, then walked directly into the kitchen. The crew glanced at me with no particular interest. A second set of swinging doors on the opposite side of the kitchen enticed me. I pushed through to find myself in a short hallway leading to an open door where Jeremy, the *sommelier*, sat in a steno chair hunched over a desk, crunching numbers on a calculator. Close to Jeremy's right arm, a corked bottle stood next to an almost empty wineglass.

"Are you the som-elly-er?"

"Oh, my god!"

"What's a wine equity trust?"

"You're not supposed to be back here!"

"I just want to talk—"

"I don't have time to talk."

"I heard you lost my card—gave it away—and I wanted to make sure you got the new one."

"I don't know what the hell you're talking about—"

"The business card I gave you a few days ago. Margot Daley said you gave it to her and that's where she got my phone number."

Jeremy's face exuded fear. I thought he would burst into tears. "You want me to call the police?"

"Why did you warn Margot I was on the way over from Brenda's café?"

"She—she's a friend of mine. I saw a strange man walk into her building so I called her."

Holy cow, this guy was easy. I walked into the office and sat on the small vinyl couch opposite his desk.

"I don't know anything about that missing girl," he said. "I told you that."

"Yeah, I remember. And I'm flattered you remembered why I had originally stopped by. But you've got to be wondering how I came to know Margot. Right?"

Jeremy rotated his chair around to face me. "Obviously, Brenda told you about her."

"And why do you think I needed to know about Margot?"

"What do you want from me? I'm just trying to run my business. And—and you just walk in here acting as if I'm some kind of criminal. . . ."

His attempt at victimhood contained both pathetic and comical elements. Judging by his stilted hand gestures, he may have had acting lessons. I let him ramble on about how hard he'd worked to attain his station in life.

When he finished I said, "Why did you feel it was necessary to warn Margot I was coming over?"

Jeremy jumped up from the chair. "What is it with you? I don't know anything about the goddamn missing woman!"

"Are you really that arrogant or just that stupid? What are you hiding?"

Jeremy held up his cellphone as if threatening me. "I'm calling the cops."

I held up my hands. "Don't shoot! Just hear the big picture—so maybe you'll understand where I'm coming from. And then you can call the cops."

Jeremy surprised me by obediently sitting back down. "All I did was tell Margot you were on the way over."

"Tanya Maggio worked for Margot's husband. They left town together. Now Doug Daly's dead, she's missing. Little things like warning people are interesting to investigators. The babe-in-the-woods monologue was you shouting that you knew more than you wanted to tell me. And now there's all this valuable wine missing. You are a wine expert who owns a wine bar. You are friends with Margot, the woman you warned I was coming to visit."

"That's all circumstantial—"

"You're doing it again!" This guy was a gift. "You open your mouth, you tell me you know something."

"Bullshit. You're trying to get me to incriminate myself."

I laughed. "You're doing a brilliant job of it without my help."

"Fuck you." Jeremy started dialing.

I watched him tell the dispatcher he owned the *Auvergnat Vin Bar* and that a man was refusing to leave his establishment.

"Make sure you tell them how hard you worked to get where you are today," I said and walked out.

18

Pressure points poked my torso before morphing into a ten-pound weight distributed across my chest. My eyes opened to puffy white whisker pads bordering a black nose. Punim leaped down from my bed and ran to her food bowl—as was her custom.

I sat up, noted the blue sky outside my window, pondered my investigation's latest spin—some kind of bond between Margot Daley and Jeremy Godello—then re-examined the vagaries pulling me along the unknown route of my investigation: a missing girl, stolen wine, a cagey client named Eddie Byrne, and Spike's face before I got KO'd. Subtle mannerisms imprinted on your brain for a reason. Spike's smug expression gave something away, but what? Flagrant amateurism, I thought. A sweet boy robbing his way through college. What of Margot's anger at the suggestion Spike was in on the scam? Phony outrage? Maybe the kid was playing her. Maybe they were both playing me.

Punim ate a turkey heart. I called Margot. "It's Jules Landau."

"Yes?"

Dead air. "Yes? Yesterday, you hugged and kissed me. Today it's 'Yes?'"

"I didn't mean it that way. You took me by surprise. How are you?"

"Tell me again about your relationship with the sweet college boy, Spike."

"A college kid we met in Evanston. He ran errands for us, helped with small projects around the house. Eventually, he worked at the bar as Doug's assistant."

"He became a pal to Doug and Margot?"

Even over electromagnetic energy waves her approaching irritation was practically tangible. I braced myself. "It's really condescending to speak to someone in the third person," Margot said, scarcely able to control her anger. "Yes, we enjoyed having him around. Doug and I never had children, after all, and we got to know him very well. Raised by a single mother, he barely knew his father—"

"Would Spike have had access to your wine storage facility?"

"He knew about it. But nobody would've had access but me. Spike didn't steal the wine, Jules."

"Oh, yeah, he just steals *your* cash when trying to buy the wine back. I forgot."

Margot sighed loudly. "Doug ran off with Tanya before the wine went missing."

"But Doug could've told him the access code. Could Spike have been in touch with Doug *after* he left town and before he died?"

"Really, Jules. You're starting to sound unhinged." She hung up.

Calling Margot an arrogant, manipulative bitch would've been unprofessional, but proclaiming my feelings to an audience of one cat seemed appropriate. And Punim was a good listener. Just as Spike's pompous, shit-eating grin gave him away, so did Margot's passive-aggressiveness. One could only act a part for so long before offering a tell. Yesterday, Margot was the guilt-ridden victim radiating gratitude. Today, instead, a distracted, impatient, innocent bystander.

To understand what a thief would be up against trying to burglarize a modern wine storage facility, Paul from *Der Weingott* recommended visiting The Vintner's Treasure, a ground floor business of exposed brick, marble, steel, and glass, indistinguishable from the ten stories of luxury lofts overhead. Wearing a lavender polo shirt, close-fitting jeans, and a little hair gel, I entered The Vintner's Treasure to find myself in a combination tasting lounge and kitchen that would be agreeable to the most discerning of urban professionals. I sat only a moment before a smiling, fiftyish man in a gray linen sport coat walked over, introduced himself as Peter, then led me to an open office in the corner of the room where we sat opposite each other on matching black leather and chrome chairs.

"So, Mr. Landau, how may I help you?"

"Well, I'm really just on a fact-finding tour. The wine—it's stored *underground*, I assume? That's why it's so safe?"

Peter looked a bit crestfallen. "Yes, everything is belowground, of course." He pointed to a wide staircase. "One could use the stairs or elevator, depending on how much product one was moving in or out." He cleared his throat. "Did you have something particular in mind—with regard to a storage facility?"

"Security is my main concern. What if someone acquired my magnetic key and password?"

Peter either laughed or cleared his throat again. "That would just be the first stage. Before getting to the vault the thief would have to contend with five layers of security doors providing the type of redundancy no criminal would want to contend with. Any fluctuation in condition will at once notify our private guards as well as the police. And if you were still apprehensive, we provide an extra measure of protection—something extraordinary for those with the resources.”

“Currently, I have a small collection, mostly for consumption. I’m looking to expand my portfolio.”

He eyed me suspiciously. “What *segmentation* are you thinking about? *Premium* wines?”

Nice try, Peter. “That word ‘*premium*’ has such a subjective quality. I have an opportunity of possibly obtaining many of cases of Lafite—as an investment.”

His face lit up. “We offer services for those desiring to diversify. Our professionals long ago recognized wine as an asset class, just like gold, silver, or art.”

“Excellent. If I’m going to invest, it would be specific vintages that have significant second market potential. A vintage with no more than, say, half a million cases produced.”

“Perhaps I could give you the name of a broker who could help you get started?” Peter handed me a card. “Using one of our brokers will make the transition quite seamless, practically from the supplier to your vault. He’s quite well connected—you should know.”

Peter held his gaze on me. “Okay,” I said. “*What* should I know?”

“Investments in fine wine are only a minuscule part of the market. Over the years it has become common for many producers to hold back a limited number of cases—to age them. When these reserve wines come to market, the demand is quite high. The key is knowing when a reserved vintage will be offered.”

I raised my eyebrows. “And your boy gets the early bird specials.”

“As do a select group of others.”

I pretended to ponder Peter’s words before changing the subject back to security. “What about video surveillance or detection devices?”

“We have devices along the perimeter of the building, as well as motion sensors, and smoke and humidity measuring instruments—all standard for a facility of our caliber.”

“I apologize for belaboring this point, it’s just that a friend of mine has many wealthy clients, some of whom are deeply immersed in the wine culture. And when I mentioned my desire to start investing in fine wines, he cautioned me to *never* assume a storage facility is foolproof, and that an appropriate insurance policy would also be required.”

“Your friend is correct, which is why we include insurance as part of the storage contract. I think you’ll find the cost almost negligible. Of course, one can always *over*insure.”

“Negligible because the odds of a successful robbery are small?”

“Exactly.”

“But it does happen, right?”

Peter thought about it. "I'm sure somewhere it has happened."

"According to my friend, it happened here in Chicago. Ten cases of Mouton Rothschild worth over two million dollars."

Peter shifted in his seat. "I hadn't heard."

"Really? I can understand the moneyed interests keeping such news quiet, but I figured within a niche industry like this, there were no secrets."

This time I held my gaze on Peter and watched his eyeballs bounce around the room. He squirmed a little more in his seat. Too much time passed for him to get away with lying. He was a salesman, after all, who had sitting before him a potential client worth a fat commission on top of a potential broker kickback.

Peter took a deep breath and then crossed one leg over the other. "Well, certainly, we do hear things. But what's true and what's rumor isn't always clear. And superstitions are always in the back of one's mind in a small competitive market like ours."

"Airlines don't brag about their crash records."

"Precisely."

"Although one could argue the consumer has the right to know how safe his investment is. I assume this market is free from government regulations. And a business has the right to assure a client that mistakes made elsewhere are learning opportunities."

Peter was starting to like me. "Absolutely! Which is why I can—with confidence—tell you that the rumored breach would have been avoided here."

"I guess you're not superstitious."

"Science trumps superstition. Are you familiar with biometrics?"

"Like digital fingerprinting? Is this the 'extraordinary' measure you mentioned earlier?"

"We offer up to a four layer biometric security package. Signature recognition is the first layer. Then the digital fingerprint. Third is the iris scan. The fourth layer takes the iris scan to the next level. It's complicated, but think of being able to use the contractions of the pupil to determine the authenticity of an individual's identity."

I said, "The cost is determined by how many layers one desires, which would then be partially offset by a less expensive insurance payment."

"You have a mind for business, Mr. Landau. Come, let's have a look at the vault."

I followed Peter to the wide staircase spiraling down into a subterranean arched hallway. From there, we journeyed through four separate steel-reinforced security doors designed to look like they came off the hinges of a medieval castle. Once Peter got us through the final door, we entered a temperature-controlled catacomb of floor-to-ceiling shelves packed with bottles. It reminded me of library stacks, except these racks were connected to mechanized levers that opened up walkways between the walls of wine, giving access to private collectors.

"And depending on the total value of the commodity being stored," Peter continued, "we envision some instances where the purchase of insurance would be deemed superfluous."

Canister spotlights added to a feeling of recently discovered antiquity, as if visiting an archaeological display. I said, "Layers upon layers of security available for the right price."

"For some, peace of mind is beyond cost."

Peter led me back to the stairway. He began the ascent then stopped and said, "Would you rather take the elevator?"

I declined. At the next turn I said, "The facility from where the wine is rumored to be missing, they did not have this technology?"

"If there was a breach in security, this technology could not have been in use. I have no doubt."

"Unless it was an inside job."

Peter waited until we reached the top step to say, "An inside job trumps all other scenarios. That is why you must trust your employees."

"How would *they* get away with it?"

"They wouldn't get away with it. Any action to disarm our security layers would be recorded electronically. Everything that is taken out is recorded, everything that is put in is recorded, every keystroke is recorded, somebody has to give the command. . . ."

Peter went on to describe their surveillance technology as a devoted, intelligent employee that would never waver from its duty. Then he wrapped up our visit with a final, joyous allusion to a security system being an "omniscient, omnipotent oenophile," and I joined him in a hearty laugh.

19

Margot probably knew the people who stole her wine, I thought, while washing the gel out of my hair in the kitchen sink. But why would she pretend not to know anything and still beg me to get involved? The repetition of six notes on an electronic keyboard reminded me I had changed my ringtone to "Timeless."

"You owe me an apology," Amy said. "You hung up on me."

It took a moment, but I remembered calling her from Brenda's café. "Why would you even care if I hung up on you?"

"You don't think that hurt my feelings?"

"Not in the least. Besides, I could claim *your* cellphone dropped the call, and that *you* hung up on me."

"But you'd be lying."

122

"True. I hung up because you gave me an important piece of a puzzle and I got excited."

"Cool! You know I like puzzles. Will you share?"

My initial impulse was to say no, but I had a lot of information bouncing around my brain and it occurred to me that chatting with an intelligent person like Amy might help me see something I was overlooking—or, perhaps, help me figure out who the hell she was.

"You ever heard of Mocha Mouse?"

"Of course. I'm on the way." She hung up.

Amy sat alone at a round table usually reserved for large parties. "Are you expecting more people?" I asked.

"I like having a little space around me."

"You don't think it's a little rude—"

"For god's sake, Jules, sit down. If a large party walks in we'll move."

She had a short fuse. I remembered her practically ordering me into her car after I left Margot's apartment. "You know, I don't get it— your anger."

"What the hell are you talking about?"

"This is the second time you snapped at me in the two days since we met. You would think that level of emotion would've required more of an investment of your time."

Amy rested her hand on my arm and smiled. "I'm sorry. I'm worried about Tanya. I feel like every minute we waste could be the difference between life and death for her."

She touched me. "So now you think she's alive?"

"We have to find her—either alive or dead. Until then, she'll never be at rest. Her family needs closure."

"Tanya's energy is calling you, but you can't tell if it's dead energy or living energy?"

Amy withdrew her hand from my arm. "Energy lives forever. In different forms, maybe, but it's always there. Anyway, back to the puzzle piece I gave you. What is it?"

"Margot inherited her father's wine collection two months before her husband, Doug, took off with Tanya."

"Cheating husband takes off with younger woman leaving millions in wine behind."

"Exactly. But I'm wondering if Doug knew the wine's value before he left. I'm not sure where it fits, but it's a piece of something. Anyway, I also discovered that Margot had some kind of relationship with Jeremy—the owner of the wine bar that used to be Doug's pub. Also, Margot is convinced her husband murdered Tanya, then killed himself."

Amy straightened up and thought about it. "You think Jeremy and Margot are having an affair?"

"Can't say. I don't know when Jeremy came along."

"But how is the stolen wine related to the missing woman?"

"Maybe she was just along for the ride with Doug."

"And then—her boyfriend came out here looking for her, and hired you." Amy looked around the room, then pretended to be interested in Mocha Mouse's beer list.

"Which *boyfriend* are you talking about?"

"Oh, stop it. You don't have to be psychic to assume Tanya had a boyfriend."

"She probably had a mother, father, brother, sister, dog, cat, and capybara too."

"Did Mom or Dad hire you?"

She had a point. "Eddie came out here from Newark. He'd been doing time when Tanya stopped keeping in touch."

"Why was Eddie in prison?"

"I didn't ask."

"What do you know about their relationship?"

"They grew up together, street kids from the Newark area."

We sat in silence while Amy resisted commenting on my investigative skills. "You're the professional, but it seems to me you don't know much about the subject of your investigation."

"You're the psychic who talks to Tanya's energy, you tell me about her."

Amy narrowed her eyes. "Why don't you admit I'm right instead of being a smart ass?"

"You sound like a woman with an agenda. What's your day job, by the way?"

Amy drummed her fingernails on the table. "I get the feeling you don't trust me. Just say the word, Jules, and I'll leave forever."

"So what's your day job?"

"I give readings. You know, the psychic stuff you think is bullshit."

"You make a *living* at this bullshit?"

"I earn enough. And maybe I have money— which would be none of your business. Now make up your mind, do want me to go away or not?"

I studied Amy's face for no other reason than the pleasure of it. Without a headband, her curly black hair parted naturally over her forehead, framing large dark eyes and a lovely brown face. "If you had said I didn't know enough about *Eddie*, the guy who hired me, I would've had no choice but to admit you were right."

Feeling validated, Amy smiled. "Maybe it would be worth going back East to see what you can find out."

"Yeah, I should go, like tomorrow." I don't think Amy believed me. "I even suggested to Eddie I should talk to some of Tanya's friends. But he didn't like that idea and told me so. In fact, he damn near threatened me."

"Your own client threatened you?"

"He apologized later with an envelope full of cash—so I accepted his apology."

Amy frowned. "So now he's okay with you poking around back East?"

"I don't know and I'm not going to ask. By the way, do you like cats?"

20

Having held the status of "neighborhood dive" throughout most of its existence, *Anagnostou's Taverna* now carried the *cool* mystique for having resisted the pressures of gentrification, remaining not the least bit trendy. The respect was such that younger folks of the professional class only cautiously patronized *Anagnostou's Taverna,* out of deference for the regulars old enough to remember Greektown having as many transient hotels as *gyro* stands.

Kalijero's retirement had facilitated his speedy entrance into this elite club and I found him sitting at the bar evidently telling a long, involved story to the bartender, who seemed quite amused. Gracing the wall behind the bar, a sunny Greek landscape needed touch-up paint. When the bartender noticed my approach, his amusement vanished.

Kalijero turned to me. "What the hell are you doing here?"

"Looking for you." I introduced myself to the bartender and offered my hand. He walked away. "Recent charm school graduate?" I asked Kalijero.

"What do you want?" he answered.

"I'm going to Jersey. I want to talk to that guy Cooper. The dirty cop."

Kalijero gulped down the last of his beer, put the glass down, shook his head a few times, then he mumbled something.

"Oh, c'mon, Jimmy! Why do you have to be like this?"

"You're gonna get yourself killed, Landau. It's one thing to snoop around where people know you. But go strolling into someone else's territory, acting like the cocky prick you are, and you're dead. It's that simple."

"I just want to talk to him! He sent Eddie to see you and you referred Eddie to me. It makes sense I should want to talk to him."

"Nothing makes sense in that world. You mention my name and he'll say he doesn't know who I am, because he doesn't know who you are."

"Then I'll tell him Eddie Byrne hired me. I'll give him Eddie's number so he can call and check. Holy shit, I'm trying to help them find Tanya—one of their own."

Kalijero started laughing and shaking his head again. "If Eddie's here to look for that broad, then she's probably involved in their operation. He didn't come out here just to find some girl—you should've figured that out by now. You're a dipshit romantic."

"Maybe you're right. But you know what, Jimmy? I'm going to Irvington, and I'm going to get as much info as I can, and if I get killed in the process, well, then that's just the way the cliché was written."

"So I'm supposed to *help* you get killed? Why not drink yourself to death like everyone else?"

"You used contacts to find out how dirty Cooper had become—"

"He's a cop, Landau. Go to his precinct and ask to speak to him."

I leaned back against the bar and looked at the molded rendering of a Greek temple hanging on one of the walls. Other walls were adorned with fake columns in the classical Greek style. Yellowing photos of Athens filled the area between the columns.

"Yeah, Jimmy, I knew I could just go to the precinct—"

"But you thought I could make it easier for you. You thought I might call up my old *pal* and have him meet you somewhere for a ginger ale."

"So what if I did? What's wrong with that?"

Kalijero didn't respond. I stood there for several more minutes refusing to believe he was content to let the conversation end on such a sour note. His anger was palpable, and probably as mysterious to him as it was to me. I thought about asking him what he was so pissed off about but decided to walk away. Just as I made a move, Kalijero chimed in with his own suggestion that I leave. I followed his advice, happy to let him think my departure was his idea.

Before heading out, I called in an order to Tasty Harmony. Despite Kalijero's bitterness, the *Taverna* had put me in a sentimental mood, which was why I decided to take Halsted Street all the way home. For those vulnerable to bouts of nostalgia, the old storefronts and façades of this storied street evoked romantic images of the poor, huddled masses playing out gritty urban fables, all while showing what it was really like to live in the big bad city. If Chicago had a heart, its aorta was Halsted, running south from Grace Street all the way to the Little Calumet River.

A white bag with my Bigboy burger waited at the front door. Once inside, I ate at my computer while checking the hundreds of flights to Newark. Why would so many people want to go to Newark? A ten-thirty departure the next morning sounded good. A few more mouse clicks and a cheap motel off the highway became my accommodation. I called Amy.

"You weren't kidding when you said you were going tomorrow," she said.

"It was your idea too. Now you want to talk me out of it?"

"No, no. I just—"

"Fine. Then come over and meet Punim. I can show you where everything is."

I left the door ajar and swept up a few months of fur balls from corners and under tables. Amy had sounded different, I thought, as I pushed the dark fluff into a dustpan. A half hour later, footsteps padded up the stairs. She appeared in the doorway wearing faded hip-hugging jeans and a gray open blazer over a black scoop neck T-shirt. A faint smell of roses followed her in.

"I love the open floor plan."

"Have a seat," I said, and walked to the bedroom where Punim lay on a window hammock awash in sunshine. I shouted, "You did say you liked cats, right?" No response.

Disturbing a comatose cat steeped in the warmth of a fleece bed could be risky. Disturbing a female cat with Punim's personality was just a bad idea. Nevertheless, I slipped my hands under shoulder and hip and carefully lifted her. A subdued growl resonated in my palms, becoming clearly audible by the time I returned to the front room. Amy sat on the couch, hands folded in her lap. She said nothing as I laid Punim on the opposite end of the couch, presenting her as one might offer a sacred relic.

I said, "Let's see if she wakes up on her own."

"Are you sure you know what you're doing?"

"Punim and I have been together—"

"No! The trip to New Jersey! Are you sure you know what you're getting into?"

"Of course not."

She paused.

"I hope I didn't push you into something. We are, I think, kind of friends, and I just want to make sure whatever you're doing—you would've done whether you met me or not."

Punim lifted her head, looked around, yawned, stretched. Then she got to her feet and walked toward Amy. I said, "Just act totally comfortable, like you own the place—she can smell fear."

Amy said, "Who am I to tell people what to do? You know what I mean? What the hell do I know anyway?"

"Here she comes."

Punim sniffed Amy's knee, climbed into her lap, then relaxed to Amy's slender fingers stroking her. The tender scene stunned me.

"Jules, are you listening to me?"

Deep breath. "I was already planning on going to New Jersey. I would be going back East regardless of whether or not you spotted me in the alley and wondered if I might be a ghost. You are absolved from any responsibility or liability regarding any harm that may come my way."

I walked into the kitchen and told Amy the litter was in a bag under the sink. From the fridge, I took out a plastic container and held it up. "Give her a heart or a liver or a kidney in the morning. The same in the late afternoon or evening. If they're small, give her two."

"Raw organs?"

"You ever see a wild cat cooking its food?"

Amy blinked a few times, then turned her attention back to her lap. Gently, she scratched Punim's head and then stroked the length of her spine, letting Punim's tail slide between her fingers before repeating the motion. On the few occasions visitors had attempted similar interaction with Punim, the aftermath included loud cursing and a drop or two of blood. Perhaps Amy's effect on Punim lent credibility to her claim of psychic powers. Maybe she really had a gift. Punim would know, after all.

I sat at the opposite end of the couch and watched a while longer. "Are you two talking about me?"

Amy didn't look at me, but I thought I detected the beginnings of a grin. "Do you think all that cash Eddie gave you might be—"

"Time out. I don't know this Amy. Suddenly, you really *care* about me?"

"I'm a human being, Jules. If I detested you I would never have bothered talking to you again."

"I prefer someone look at me when they say they don't detest me." She ignored my request. "She doesn't detest me! It must be love."

"Why are you so sarcastic?"

"You told me quite clearly not to call you for any reason other than my investigation."

"So you're either professional or romantic? There's nothing in between?"

"Okay. I'm glad you like me enough not to detest me. I'm glad you like me enough to be concerned."

Amy turned to me and smiled. Then she lifted Punim off her lap, stood, and softly laid her back down on the couch. "I have to go. Tomorrow afternoon, I'll start coming to take care of her."

I followed her to the door and thanked her for cat sitting. "Oh, here," I said taking the extra key off a nail behind the door. She closed her hand over the key, briefly engaging my fingers, then made the slightest gesture to leave before abruptly reversing course to kiss me warmly on the cheek. By the time her lips retreated from my face, my hand had found the small of her back. I pulled her tightly against me. Our mouths fastened, tongues explored, and loins gnashed with that erotic fire humans held fast until such moments.

As quickly as it began, so it also ended with Amy pushing me away. "No!" she said. "This can't happen." She walked to the top of the landing. "I'm sorry, Jules. Be careful over there and don't worry about Punim." I watched, stunned, as she disappeared down the stairs.

I hated mixed messages.

21

I had never been to the East Coast, and the iconic Manhattan skyline sparked a bit of excitement as the plane taxied on the runway in Newark. The feeling faded when my rented Ford Focus merged onto the Garden State Parkway, where the adjoining communities sprawled in patterns identical to any metropolitan area east of the Mississippi. At the Irvington exit, I caught a glimpse of my motel but continued into town. It didn't take long before another iconic image came to mind, one of urban decay. Abandoned buildings, broken windows, trash piles, shuttered shops, and gang graffiti gave Eddie's hometown a stunned, post-apocalyptic quality.

Here and there, I found reminders of civilization. On Springfield Avenue, outposts of major banks serviced the public on the same block as deserted warehouses, bars, strip joints, wig shops, nail salons, rent-to-own furniture outlets, and discount beauty-aid stores. And after discovering pockets of tidy communities proudly displaying the Stars and Stripes in their fight to maintain working-class respectability, I sensed a defiant entrepreneurial spirit still remained, representing a flicker of optimism within this forsaken piece of New Jersey.

I stuck to the major arteries, pulling over occasionally to peek down side streets, all of which looked equally depressing. By chance, I found the municipal building that housed police headquarters. I had planned on visiting the building the following morning, but remembered Frownie's advice to never put off an opportunity. After parking my Ford, I wondered if declining the extra insurance had been a mistake.

The sergeant behind the desk appeared absorbed in paperwork, but as I approached an officer, whose silver nametag read "Trujillo," he looked up, smiled warmly, and asked how he could help me. Above his name, the word "Valor" was written.

"I'd like to talk to Detective Cooper," I said.

Trujillo hesitated then leaned on his elbows. His eyes were now distant black dots under a furrowed brow. "May I ask what this is regarding?"

"I'm trying to locate someone."

"Someone in trouble?"

"I'm a private investigator."

"I could help you with missing persons."

"Thank you, but I'd rather talk to Detective Cooper first."

"I've been in this community a long time. I know a lot of people."

"Officer Cooper knows my client."

The sergeant's eyes bounced around my face. "Detective Cooper works out of a different location." Trujillo wrote something on the back of an envelope and handed it to me. "Here's the address. Do you know how to get there?" I shook my head. He took the envelope back and started sketching a map on the other side. "This neighborhood should be okay in the daytime. You can park in the area and walk. At night, only park in front of the building. If there's no space in front, leave and come back during the day."

After I thanked him and turned to leave, Trujillo said, "How well do you know Detective Cooper?"

"I hear he appreciates things that hold their value," I said and walked out, confident Trujillo's expression had not changed.

Cooper worked from a mini-precinct situated among dilapidated two-story homes, at one time comprising a charming middle-class neighborhood. Rottweiler-like dogs barking from numerous broken windows represented the only sign of life. The building itself, a one-level concrete rectangle, had all the charm of a vacated dry cleaners. The office was one large room. A plainclothes African American officer sat behind what may have been the Compaq desktop computer I owned in the early 2000s. His golf shirt fit tightly around biceps the size of cantaloupes. Slightly graying around the temples, he looked up at me through round tortoiseshell eyeglasses, then pleasantly smiled. "One moment please," he said in a surprisingly soft voice. After pecking out a few more letters and saving his document, he sat up.

"How can I help you, sir?"

"I was hoping I could speak with Detective Cooper."

The officer pursed his lips and drummed his fingers on the desk. "Well, I'll have to check his schedule. Does he know why you want to see him?"

"I'm investigating a missing person, someone I'm pretty sure he knows."

He nodded several times. "Okay, sure. So he'll know why you're here—but he doesn't know you personally?"

"Correct. But he knows people I know."

"Good. Can I have those names?"

"Officer Cooper is a police officer, right? Here to serve and protect on the public payroll?"

"Oh, no, no, no, of course. It's just that, like, you know, he's my boss, you know? And he likes to know who he's dealing with so it will make things easier if he knows a little bit about why you're here, that's all."

I watched a man who could break me in half with one hand squirm on a steno chair under the brunt of my glare. I almost felt sorry for him. I took a pen off his desk and wrote the name "Eddie Byrne" on a piece of paper.

The man took the paper and disappeared down a staircase off the back wall of the room. A few minutes later he returned.

"Detective Cooper was wondering if you could come back tomorrow morning. After nine o'clock, say?"

"I'll be there."

The Gala Festival Motel was a one-story, U-shaped, brown brick structure just off the highway. Two African American high school girls at the counter graciously welcomed me. One was taller and wore braided hair extensions, the other had a bob with a heavy side bang. The taller one told me my room had just been cleaned and that there was a hot tub somewhere out back. They both wore white blouses with a colorful badge depicting a torch in front of an open book.

From the doorway of my room, I surveyed the chasm running down the middle of the bed, then acquainted myself with the smell of chlorine bleach. The towels were stiff and the size of large washcloths. The only thing missing was a neon sign flashing on and off through the window.

It don't cost nothin' to talk, Frownie always said. *When you go to a new place, talk to anybody about anything. That's how you learn.* I walked back to the lobby and asked the girls what people did for fun in this town. They both giggled. The taller one said, "For you? Only one place we know about."

I thought I knew what they meant, but asked anyway. "What do you mean *for me*?"

More giggling. "White boys," the shorter one said. "Besides buying drugs, there's only one reason white boys come here."

"It's called 'Back End Up,'" the taller one said, and they both broke into peals of laughter. I couldn't help but join in.

"A strip joint?" I said.

"They cater to white boys from the 'burbs," the taller one said. "It's been here forever."

"What else?"

The laughing stopped. The shorter one walked over to the window, looked outside, and said, "Sir, it's getting kind of late and it's really not safe for you to be wandering around this part of Irvington at night."

"Except for Back End Up."

"Exactly," they said at the same time and then took turns filling me in. "It's all set up for white guys to feel safe. Lots of cops moonlighting as security. Some gangbangers too."

"Cops and gangbangers working *together* to protect white boys in a strip joint?"

Both girls nodded. "That's the way it's always been."

They watched me mentally digest the information until I said, "I know a guy who said he lives here. A white guy. What neighborhood would that be?"

They looked at each other. The tall one said, "No white guy lives in this town. Not since I've been alive."

"He's older than you. Maybe his family stuck around?"

Both girls looked mystified. The shorter one said, "I don't know any white people who live here. Maybe they do. But I've never seen them." The other nodded her head.

I said, "What are those badges you're wearing?"

"It's for academic excellence," they both said.

I congratulated them. The girls took turns thanking me and gave directions to Back End Up. From a convenience store, I bought a loaf of bread, grape jam, and a jar of peanut butter. I sat on the corner of the bed, eating and thinking. Despite the shabby furniture in a shabby motel, I saw no sign of roaches or ants. I attributed this to the motel's toxic approach to cleanliness. Cooper, a white cop, operated out of a mostly black town. This I knew. But thanks to a simple conversation, I also knew where white men went to spend money here.

22

The glow caught my attention at least five blocks from Back End Up, another large, nondescript cement rectangle but this one with a parking lot lit up like a football stadium. A man holding a radio transceiver to his mouth and wearing a dark windbreaker with the word "SECURITY" across the back, waved to me from the middle of the lot. He stood in an open space next to the last car in the row. After I pulled in, he welcomed me to Back End Up and pointed to another man standing twenty yards away, dressed identically, apparently waiting to escort me. As we walked, several other "SECURITY" men strolled the perimeter of the lot. On the corners of adjacent blocks, drug dealers and whores freely conducted curbside negotiations.

When we reached the sidewalk, I saw about a dozen men smoking cigarettes behind a roped off area in front of the club. My escort stopped, smiled, then gestured toward the door with an open arm. "Enjoy your evening, sir."

Before entering the club, I decided to hang out awhile with the smokers, all white men, ranging in age from early twenties to about seventy. Each maintained at least a three-foot buffer between himself and someone else. Personal space. Standing closest to me was a guy with black hair taped up on the sides, box cut, and spiked. He wore a tracksuit with the jacket unzipped enough to reveal a gold cross on a heavy chain. *Guido tuxedo,* I think his outfit was called. When he noticed me I smiled and said, "My first time here."

Guido Tuxedo blew out a plume of smoke and chuckled. "Undercover, huh?"

"What do you mean?"

"Nothin'. Yeah, this place is good for tit suckin' and ass grabbin' in a back room. More if you got the cash. Lots of Brazilian bitches. Watch out for the old girls. Still in decent shape but teeth all fucked up." Guido Tuxedo took a long drag, flicked the cigarette into the street, then returned to the club.

I observed the others a while longer, stoically puffing in their isolated worlds, then took one last look at Kalijero's picture of Cooper sitting at the table with his goons. When I entered the club, the world turned purple, thanks to a ceiling grid of canisters shining a spectrum of violet hues. The venue was shaped in a semicircle with sloping tiers leading to the performance area. I stood at the top tier where a row of corn plants blocked most of the view.

"Good evening," a smiling woman said, walking up to me. "There's a twenty-dollar cover charge and a two drink minimum." Although too old to be a stripper, she still looked amazing in a black bustier and matching miniskirt.

"Uh, okay, can I have a quick peek to see if my friends are here yet?"

Something about her body language set off a silent alarm because a young gangbanger in an oversized sleeveless T-shirt appeared from the top of an aisle and began wandering toward us. His shirt appeared to be red, although I couldn't be sure in the light.

I stepped between two corn plants and scanned the floor. On the stage, several topless women wearing thongs pole-danced beneath a blaze of lavender. Behind the bar, backlighting under a wall of mirrors emitted a purple aura around rows of bottles. Men leaned against the stage while another group of gawkers stood two deep behind them. I spotted a few semicircular booths on the first tier. One of the tables was crowded with men fitting the wiseguy stereotype.

"Sir," the gangbanger said, tapping me hard on the shoulder. The host stood behind him.

"Oh, god, I'm sorry!" I said. "May I sit over by those booths?"

"Twenty-dollar cover charge please," the woman said.

"Yes, absolutely." I fumbled with my wallet then gave her a twenty. She led me to a two-top on the fourth tier, not great for watching the dancers, but angled advantageously toward the booth, providing periodic views of a dark-haired man I hoped was Cooper. A few minutes later, a waitress appeared and I ordered a virgin strawberry daiquiri. While still assimilating my new environment,

Guido Tuxedo appeared from my periphery and walked up to me.

"Officer Dude," he said, "next time *overpay* the host and you'll get a better seat." Then he rapped his knuckles a few times on the table and joined the crowd at the wiseguy table. After he sat, several of the men leaned toward him, laughed, then turned to look my way. A moment later, half the table leaned in one direction and the other half leaned in the opposite direction, giving their boss and myself a good look at each other. He parted his hair in the middle and slicked it back like Spike, accentuating a prominent nose. I looked at the picture. It might be Detective Cooper, I thought and cursed Kalijero for his technological apathy.

The waitress reappeared with my $12 daiquiri in a twenty-ounce beer glass. I sipped and watched the wiseguys slap backs, pour drinks from a private stash, and basically act deliriously happy to be in each other's company. The celebratory buzz had an arrogant swagger about it—as if they owned the place.

The man I now decided was Detective Cooper from the photo waved to someone across the room. Minutes later, a dancer in a leopard print bikini strolled to within a couple of feet of the table. First, she posed seductively—hands on hips—giving the men a good, long gape, before starting a series of postures that blurred the line between superb athleticism and pornographic yoga.

Cooper barked a command. The men shoved their chairs back, which allowed the dancer to sit on the edge of the table before swinging her legs around and up in one fluid motion. Lying on her back, she gave the boss a direct view of her crotch. She raised her hips, undulated for several moments, then effortlessly maneuvered into various positions on her torso while the men stuffed cash under her G-string. Besides the eroticism, I couldn't help but appreciate the core strength required to perform with such physical prowess. Eventually, she ended up on her stomach and slid toward Cooper, who met her in a sensuous kiss and a prolonged groping session that would have earned an ordinary patron a speedy exit from the club.

After the tender moment ended, the dancer slid down and waved goodbye. High-fives ensued around the table along with more drinks and a general appearance of having accomplished something grand.

A gangbanger stood about five feet from Cooper's crew, scanning the stage and bar area. Our eyes briefly met. Had he been there the whole time? A bandana hung from his back pocket. I looked around the room and spotted several more gangbangers keeping an eye on things. The hostess escorted two guys wearing untucked polo shirts over corduroy slacks. She sat them near the stage. Eddie would've looked daggers into those boys, suburbanites slumming in the "hood." By age ten, Eddie had more street smarts than those boys would ever have.

"Another daiquiri?"

The waitress stood smiling, my required second drink already sitting on her tray. On her way back to the bar she passed a beautiful dancer in a black bikini walking toward me: tall, brunette, a body worthy of most men's fantasies. Her eyes left no doubt as to who was the object of her gaze. She pulled a chair over and sat next to me.

"Oh, no thank you," I said as politely as possible.

"My name is Candy."

"Candy, thank you but I'm not interested in a lap dance."

Candy pushed the hair off my forehead and said, "But it's already paid for. You don't want to waste their money, do you?"

The wiseguy table was one big toothy grin. Guido Tuxedo waved at me. "Enjoy!" he yelled.

"See?" Candy said.

She removed her bikini top, draped a leg over my thighs, then gracefully straddled me. This may have been a test. Undercover cops are not allowed to initiate sexual contact. I rubbed my hands over her breasts. Candy responded by pushing them against my face and shimmying for a good ten seconds before letting me up for air.

"Have you worked here a long time?" I said, sounding like a complete idiot.

She looked a bit taken aback. "Are you a *new* cop?"

I put my hands back on her breasts and rubbed her nipples. "Does that answer your question?"

She laughed. "Honey, every cop in this city has had their grubby hands on my tits."

She pressed her crotch against mine, gyrated as if *her* pleasure was as obvious as mine. Despite my original intention in coming to Back End Up, a culmination of events approached at a speed not experienced since my teenage years, and to my dismay, while fully clothed. Candy had the solution—which also gave me an idea.

"There are rooms," Candy said. "Fifty dollars."

"If I said I was a new cop, would I get a first-time discount?"

Candy didn't appreciate my comment. "I'm just trying to make a living."

"How about fifty bucks just to tell me the boss's name at the wiseguy table."

Candy continued gyrating. "I got lots of bosses."

"How about you take me to one of those fifty-dollar rooms? On the way, look at the table, then tell me who the boss is."

Candy seemed to ponder my suggestion. "Well, okay. But I gotta warn you, once we enter the room, I can't leave without my hard work being rewarded."

"If you let me get out my wallet, I'll pay you right now."

She laughed again. "Not here, sweetie. Let's go."

I followed her, noted she looked over at the wiseguy table and smiled, heard their laughter, disappeared into a dark corridor behind the bar, then walked through a door where my world became no bigger than the coat closet in my apartment. On the wall, a skinny, tall mirror. On the ceiling, a bare lightbulb. Candy dropped to her knees and began unbuttoning my pants.

"Wait," I said. "What's the boss's name?"

"No business *before* pleasure, silly."

I took her by the shoulders. "C'mon, stand up." She did as told. "I'm all business tonight." I took out my wallet and produced two fifty-dollar bills. "All I want is the boss's name and you're done."

Candy looked a little confused. "That guy is *the* boss. Cooper-the-cop, we call him—but not to his face."

I put the hundred bucks into Candy's hand and moved toward the door.

"Don't you want anything out of this deal?"

"Candy, you gave me all I needed for tonight," I said then walked out.

From the shadows behind the bar I surveilled the room. Cooper and his crew were gone. Pureed strawberry juice dripped down the side of my untouched daiquiri.

"How you doin', sir? Everything okay?"

The gangbanger's words startled me. "Everything is great. Thank you for checking in."

"Enjoy your evening."

"I will," I said, thinking only that I couldn't wait to get the hell out of there.

23

The next morning I awoke surprisingly rested, having learned that if I remained on my back in the crevasse of the mattress, a semblance of sleep could be maintained. For breakfast, two peanut-butter sandwiches, then off to meet the boss of Irvington.

I parked in front of Cooper's mini-precinct, still with a few minutes to kill. Although the sun had been up for at least three hours, the abandoned buildings and wandering, hollow-eyed dope addicts seemed to filter the light into a kind of duskiness. Staring through the windshield, I tried to imagine this neighborhood as the bleak backdrop through which Eddie trekked to school each morning. The thought of used hypodermic needles, tracked into the house from a kid's shoe, depressed me. I needed air.

Inside the precinct, the same African American man sat behind the metal desk. He looked at his watch. "It might be a bit early."

"Can I call you by name?"

The question took him by surprise. "Uh, sure. Sergeant Blake."

"Sergeant Blake, yesterday you said, *after nine.* It is now after nine."

Sergeant Blake looked at his watch again. "You are correct, sir."

He walked to the staircase at the back of the room and shut the door behind him. On Sergeant Blake's desk sat a business telephone system circa 1980. Nobody was calling or holding. The bare white walls seemed out of place without case charts or crime statistic graphs. A four-door vertical file cabinet caught my attention, then Sergeant Blake opened the door, a metal detector in his left hand.

"Detective Cooper will see you, Mr. Landau."

I walked to Sergeant Blake and held my arms above my head. "You looking for a weapon or a wire?"

Sergeant Blake didn't respond. "Okay, you're good to go."

A precipitous concrete stairway led me to a well-lit room resembling a plush home office, complete with wet bar, leather couches, and an HDTV taking up most of a wall. Sequestered at the other end of the room, the man I saw at Back End Up sat behind a beautifully preserved table of wooden planks. At the front of the desk, a gold nameplate with embossed black lettering said, "Lt. Landon Cooper." A tapered black shirt with purple stitching gave him a stylishly creepy look. A sign hanging from the front of the table said, "Entering a Drug-Free Zone."

"Old barns," Cooper said.

I stepped closer but kept my distance. The size of the table made him look even smaller and skinnier than last night. But his nose appeared larger.

"The desk. I can tell you like it."

"How can you tell?"

Cooper laughed. "Have a seat." He pointed to the chair in front of the desk. "Enjoy yourself last night?"

I pulled the chair a few feet farther from the table before sitting. "Nice little setup you have here. I don't think Kalijero ever had it this nice."

Cooper paused. "You know Jimmy Kalijero, huh? He's probably put in his papers by now."

"You're not in touch?"

"Why would I be?"

"You recommended Eddie Byrne seek him out."

Cooper looked up a bit and to his left. He stayed that way until a realization manifested as a smile. "Oh, you mean Eddie went to Chicago? That's what this is about?"

"Eddie hired me to find Tanya—"

"Just for the record," Cooper interrupted. "I didn't recommend nobody. I may have dropped Kalijero's name a few times over the years. But that's it."

Cooper still had a Chicago accent, but without the broad blue-collar inflection one might expect from a cop.

"Sorry. I thought you guys were good friends."

Cooper looked thoughtfully over my head. "I disappointed him. He took it personally. Fuck it. So what brings you to Irvington, Detective Landau?"

"Actually, I'm still just an investigator."

Cooper waited for more then took a breath. "So what can I do for you?" The irritability in his voice did not escape me.

"I'm getting lots of clues but I can't connect the dots. Eddie Byrne's kind of a mystery to me. He doesn't like talking about himself."

"Byrne. Even his name sounds like a pain in the ass. He hires you, but keeps secrets. What the fuck?"

"He's a challenge—"

"So you thought if you came here, you could find out more about him. Maybe dig up some info that might connect those dots for you. That makes sense."

"Thank you. You've lived out here a long time. How well do you know this kid?"

"Eddie? He's an odd one—but it's not his fault. I mean, he's just a product of his environment, you know what I mean? The apple-not-far-from-the-tree thing."

"Messed up family."

"Sure. And look where he grew up! Dumbass father refused to leave. What the hell kind of father would let their kid grow up in this town?"

"You were a patrol officer here?"

"Yeah, till I made detective. That's how I got to know Eddie. I tried steering him the right way but I was up against the whole culture, you know what I mean?"

"I'm not sure."

"The family. *His* family. The uncles and cousins. All into something. Low-level mob shit. Drugs, guns. Whatever can make a buck."

"He worked for his family?"

Cooper pondered my question. "Well, he kind of did his own thing. Ran around with other delinquents. But he was underage. So when we busted them, the worst they got was a night in the can or juvie hall. We tried to get him and his pals to flip on the uncles. But they were too deep in the culture. You don't ever rat someone out, after all. Never."

"Now Eddie's all grown up. Officially working for the family?"

"I don't know."

"What do you mean you don't know?"

"I mean I don't know. I *assume* he's still in the family biz. But unless we catch him doing something naughty, he isn't our concern. I can tell you this, though. I've told him many times that my door is always open if he needs someone to talk to."

"What were you thinking when you referred Eddie to Kalijero? You thought he'd take the case himself?"

"Like I said, I didn't *refer* him to Kalijero—exactly. I probably said out loud that if you're in Chicago, Kalijero would be a good contact, or something like that. I'm surprised Eddie even remembered his name. I would've thought Kalijero knew someone more experienced than you at this kind of thing."

"You don't think I'm the right guy?"

Cooper shrugged. "No disrespect. But the fact you made the trip here tells me you've lost the scent. So it's not just that you're wasting your time, but you could easily get yourself killed in the process. Right? And for what?"

I leaned forward, elbow on thigh, chin in hand, and stayed in "The Thinker" pose long enough to suggest a dilemma. "Yeah, I see your point. But while I'm here I'd really appreciate it if you'd let me pick your brain a little bit longer."

"Of course."

"Eddie's got a lot of cash. He swore it wasn't drug money. Should I believe him?"

"Yeah, I think you can believe him and I'll tell you why. Like I said, Eddie grew up in this dump. He didn't have a chance, but he learned to survive. He did what he had to do. But when his eighteenth birthday was coming up, I took him aside and told him it was time to clean up, otherwise he was going to end up in prison.”

“So you got him to reassess his life, take the straight road.”

“I did! And I’m telling you that kid had *everything* against him. Not just this town, but his family. All the cops knew his family had their fingers in all kinds of vice. It’d been going on for decades. Once Eddie was an adult, we would’ve popped him every chance we got, just to try to get to his uncles and cousins.”

“But he still ended up going to the slammer.”

Cooper sighed and shook his head. “Yeah, that was unfortunate. But it wasn’t drugs! He got into a fight and went a little too far with it. He should’ve stopped when the guy hit the ground. Had Eddie been a rat, they would’ve dropped the ‘aggravated’ part and made it simple assault. Pay a fine but no jail time. But Eddie’s not a rat.”

“Do you have any kids?” I asked, knowing Kalijero’s story of Cooper abandoning mother and child after the kid was born.

“No.”

“I get the feeling you kind of like Eddie.”

Cooper smiled. “You know, I’m one of those guys who can’t help but respect someone who was dealt a shit hand but tries to make the best of it. Sure, he got into some trouble. But he didn’t use or sell drugs, he wasn’t into armed robbery or putting himself in a position where an innocent might get hurt. Deep down, I think he's a good kid. He just didn't have any guidance."

I wondered what kind of guidance Cooper's abandoned child had. "Do you think Eddie's *only* reason for coming to Chicago was to find Tanya Maggio?"

"I have no reason to think he went there for anything else." Cooper sat up in his chair and cleared his throat. "Why do you ask?"

The sounds of commerce exuded from Cooper's head. Sprockets creaked. Meshed gears rotated and rattled. Industrial grease coated his eyes. "Well—I think I trust him. I mean, he probably carries a lot of cash because a guy like him might not have a good credit rating, right?"

Cooper pretended to think about it. "Yeah, you're probably right. And you know cash is part of the *culture* with families like his. They like to do everything in cash. They don't like banks."

Cooper pushed back his chair and walked to the bar. I guessed he stood five foot seven or eight. His distressed jeans added to a rakishly chic persona.

"You like scotch, Landau?"

"At nine-thirty in the morning?"

"Sure, at nine-thirty in the a.m.!"

He returned holding two tumblers with a couple of fingers of scotch. He sat back down then raised his glass. "You can thank the oak tree for fine scotch. It has to be aged in oak barrels. That's the rule. Here's to a long and successful career for Chicago's Detective Landau."

Cooper sipped then smacked his lips. I sipped then raised my glass and said, "Here's to Eddie finding Tanya."

Cooper didn't react. His eyes bounced around the room until he said, "Maybe it's better for Tanya that he doesn't find her."

"Why?"

"Look around this slum. Eddie belongs here but Tanya Maggio could do better."

"Maybe they'll go somewhere else. Together."

I carefully watched Cooper's reaction. "Eddie's not the type to leave. Irvington is all he knows."

"You knew Tanya pretty well."

"Nah. It's the company you keep, right? It's not hard to brand somebody around here. The die is cast early in life. But if you're smart in that trampy kind of way, *and* pretty, you can go far in life."

"When she took off, did you know she had left town?"

Cooper looked squint-eyed at his watch then back to me. "Not till Eddie told me."

"That was just a couple weeks ago, after he got out of prison. They hadn't spoken in a year. You didn't know earlier?"

"Why would I? I'd visit Eddie in the joint a few times a month. To make sure he was okay and that he knew I didn't forget about him. That kind of thing. Tanya was none of my business—unless Eddie wanted to talk about her. By the way, did you bring a firearm into the state, Landau?"

"Why do you ask?"

"New Jersey doesn't have a concealed-carry reciprocity agreement with Illinois."

"Thank you. I'll remember that if I ever decide to carry a gun."

"This is a dangerous town, kid. It's pretty stressful to be surrounded by violent gangs and drug addicts. You ever had a crackhead point a gun in your face, *investigator*?"

I cultivated a prolonged silence then said, "Sorry. I've been doing mostly birth parents and cheating spouses."

Cooper liked my answer. "Yeah, sure. You're still a young guy. It takes a while before you can get the kind of confidence for a scumbag world like Irvington. But you've got to know what you're getting into. A strange white boy snooping around this dump can get snuffed out pretty quick around here."

I pretended it all made sense. "If you don't mind, could you explain how a mini-precinct operates? What's the role in the community?"

Cooper leaned back. "I'm sure Kalijero filled your head with lots of lies. But I don't mind telling you that he doesn't know shit, sitting on his ass in Chicago. I developed a whole new way of policing this precinct. And I keep it real simple."

"Yeah, I agree. Kalijero and his like are out of touch. Old school. I'm gonna try to grab a flight tonight. Give me something to jam into Kalijero's snout."

Cooper gulped the last of his scotch. "We don't fight crime, we manage crime."

"That doesn't sound simple."

"There are innocents and there are criminals. You're one or the other. The precinct's job is to keep innocents from becoming victims of criminals."

I waited for the gag line. "And you do this by *managing* the criminals?"

"Correct. Guys like Kalijero will sit back, look at statistics, talk about how frustrated they are that murder and robbery rarely decrease, or if they do, only temporarily. In Irvington, we're asking the question: *who* is getting murdered and robbed?"

"Innocents or criminals?"

Cooper nodded. "I realize that's shocking to hear—at first."

"I expect Kalijero would love to know your criminal management technique."

"When you hear that a drug deal went south and some people selling or buying got killed—how bad do you really feel? Sure, you know the person was somebody's son or brother or sister, or mom or dad, but somewhere along the line a choice was made. Ultimately, you've got to take responsibility for your choices. But if an honor student happens to be walking by when the deal goes bad, and she takes a bullet to the head—well, that's unacceptable."

"And how do you prevent the unacceptable?"

"That's where management comes in. Irvington is what it is. Accept the fact we can't change it. The whole country would have to change for Irvington to change. The war on drugs, the war on poverty, the war on terror, they're all *rhetorical* wars, not meant to be answered with a victory or a defeat—"

"But meant to be managed."

"Exactly! And through proper management, society can benefit, even prosper."

"Sorry, but when I look around, I don't see much prosperity."

"That's because your view is skewed. Mobsters kill other mobsters, gangbangers kill other gangbangers, drug dealers kill other drug dealers or addicts. If they're all properly managed, an equilibrium is created."

We sat in silence. Cooper tried to gauge my reaction. I said, "It seems that the cornerstone of your management strategy would be keeping all parties happy—to maintain an equilibrium."

"Correct."

"And total cooperation requires total *participation*."

Cooper grinned. "And what are you suggesting, Detective Landau?"

I looked around the room. "Is this the Fraternal Order of Police lodge? Paid for with union dues?"

Cooper didn't like my question. "Do you have any idea how hard it is to get a good cop to stay here on what they make? No, of course you don't. Sergeant Blake, upstairs? I found him as a high school dropout. Helped him get his GED. Now he's working on a master's in criminology from Rutgers. He'd give his life to protect you, Landau. Because you're an innocent. He wants nothing more than to help those who *want* help. And most of those who want help around here are his black brothers and sisters. But they're stuck in this pit at the mercy of gangbangers and drug dealers."

"And the extra income for Sergeant Blake keeps him fighting the good fight."

"It's not just the money. They see the prosperity—"

"There you go again with the prosperity. Where's the prosperity?"

Cooper rolled his eyes, groaned. "It's relative to the environment! The expectations of Irvington's innocents aren't the same as what you're used to. They got a roof over their heads, heat in the winter, money for food, and we make sure their kids can walk to school unmolested. That's prosperity. What the gangbangers and dope peddlers do with their money we can't control."

"The white boys who come here to buy drugs—"

"They're criminals. If a white boy chooses to play in the ghetto culture and ends up dead in the gutter, it was his choice."

"Alive or dead, you still get your money."

My comment tested Cooper's patience. "It's not a perfect system, Landau, but that money keeps cops happy and on the job, it allows resources to be diverted elsewhere in the city, it funds scholarships for high school kids. The killing is a byproduct of the culture we manage. And I'll stake our statistics against any Chicago neighborhood any day— especially in the murdered-children category."

His last statement sobered me. Maybe he had a point. "But how do you get away with it? And why do you trust me with this information?"

Cooper laughed loud enough to startle me. "Who's hiding anything? The world is filled with open secrets. As long as statistics move in the right direction, nobody asks questions, everyone is happy—and the mayor takes all the credit and gets re-elected."

My host took another squint-eyed look at his watch then woefully described the forthcoming meeting-filled day—a necessary evil associated with managing crime. We shook hands. He wished me a pleasant flight back to Chicago.

24

Before getting into my car, I stood on the sidewalk scanning the neighborhood in search of prosperity. A woman carrying a bag of groceries approached from down the block. First one man, then another begged from her with an outstretched hand. She acknowledged neither, then sidestepped several more people sitting up on the sidewalk, leaning against buildings. When she arrived at the entrance of a three-story walk-up, a teenage boy departing the building held open the door. A couple of kids on skateboards raced down the sidewalk, skillfully maneuvering around the same panhandlers and transients. Just part of the scenery.

Cooper convincingly defended his crime management philosophy, despite the undercurrent of corruption running through every word. If Eddie wasn't working in his family's organization or Cooper's graft machine, what was he doing in Irvington? If he was involved in either enterprise, Tanya's decision to put this world behind her made perfect sense. But Eddie's lifestyle could not have been a secret. I still didn't know what had prompted Tanya to finally blow town.

As I drove my Ford Fiesta in the muted Irvington sunshine, Springfield Avenue's distressed storefronts and apartment façades reeked of Depression-era realism. Streams of people moved stoically down the sidewalks, walking into and out of various pocket eateries, thrift shops, convenience stores, and hair salons. Among the abandoned buildings, storefront specialty trades were surprisingly well accounted for with variations of tailor, butcher, seamstress, confectioner, and stationer. All had makeshift qualities—especially their cardboard signage—although they appeared to be going concerns. But it was a hardware store that really grabbed my attention. Something about its homespun appearance attracted me, charmed me, evoked a sense of permanence and reliability. An independent hardware store existing in the age of mega-houseware-homebuilding centers seemed quaint and defiantly utilitarian in the face of urban Main Street atrophy. I pulled over.

Above the store, a white rectangle framed "Hank's Hardware" in large block lettering. In the display window, an eclectic assortment of building and paint related items lay scattered. The front door of solid wood and thick beveled glass eased open with barely a touch then slammed shut on its own. Long and narrow like a shotgun shack, the store held rows of standard carpentry tools hanging in straight lines the length of the walls. All the tools had wooden grips, some with grooves worn in the shape of clutched hands. Paint-streaked cans and buckets of nails bordered the floor along the baseboards. Two long tables covered with every variety of nut, bolt, and screw split the room in half.

"Are you looking for anything in particular?" said a serious African American man approaching from the back, walking with a slight limp. He was large, but not fat, wearing brown slacks and matching vest over a white dress shirt. A sprinkling of gray in a full head of closely cropped hair complemented his neatly trimmed white beard.

"I was just driving by. I don't see many small hardware stores anymore. Are you Hank?"

His expression personified disdain and suspicion.

"What are you, some kind of sociologist? Slumming it today?"

"I'm a private investigator researching a case." I handed him one of my cards. "Have you lived here a long time?"

He stared at the card a moment then gave me a long, hard look. "You can call me Henry, and I don't remember you asking if it was all right to walk into my place and start asking me personal questions."

I shrunk back. "You're right. I'm sorry. My client grew up in this town and hired me to find his missing girlfriend. A white kid. Something about your store drew me. I'm gambling that the owner might have lived in the area a long time. So far, the only people I've spoken to have been kids or cops. I need to talk to a regular guy."

"I see," Henry scoffed. "You're looking for the nigger elder-statesman."

"I've never used that word in my entire life."

Henry looked at my card again, then back at me. Whether he thought about my words or thought about throwing me into the street, I couldn't be sure. Finally, he turned as if to walk away then motioned with his head for me to follow. At the back of the store, the room took an L-shape with the addition of a small nook just big enough to serve as an office. Several stackable chairs surrounded three sides of a card table. Henry sat in the maroon overstuffed chair that occupied the fourth side. An offer to sit did not appear forthcoming, so I took the initiative.

Henry surprised me by speaking first. "I've lived here my whole life—except two years in the army. You're looking for a white woman?"

"Yes."

"Where'd you get the crazy-ass idea I could help?"

"I'm taking a peripheral approach to investigating. Instead of going directly—"

"I know what 'peripheral' means, Landau." ·

"Sorry. I'm thinking the more I learn about my client's surroundings, the better my chances of figuring out what happened to his girl—"

"Why don't you ask your damn client about his life?"

"He's reluctant to talk about himself."

"He must be paying you well. Do you know what 'puerile' means, Landau?"

"I'm not sure."

"When an adult acts childishly, he's a fool, and only a fool would keep a client like that."

"Well, like you said, he's paying me well."

An African American man about Henry's age walked in. Without a word, Henry stood and met the man on the floor. Loud greetings prompted me to take up a position at the edge of the nook where I peered around the corner to see the two fused in a manly embrace, laughing. They exchanged small talk for a while before the man got down to business.

"Okay, Hank, I need your help. I'm pouring concrete for my floor safe . . ."

As the man described his project, Henry picked through the innumerable fasteners strewn over the tables, holding each one close to his face before placing it in his free hand or returning it to the table. By the time the friend stopped talking, Henry had the hardware ready.

"Push the anchor bolt into the concrete. Make sure to leave two to three inches of thread above the surface. . . . "

The man answered a couple of questions regarding support and stability, before the tone of the conversation lowered. I heard enough to guess that somebody was ill. With their farewell hug, I moved back to my chair.

"Good luck, my brother," Henry said loudly as his friend walked out.

Henry plopped into his chair, rested his elbows on the table, then buried his face in his hands. He didn't make a sound other than the air rushing in and out of his nostrils. Just as I was about to suggest I come back later, he lifted his head and said, "Is the white boy paying you cash?"

"He swears it's not drug money."

Henry leaned back and sighed. "So you want me to tell you something that will help Eddie Byrne find his girlfriend."

In retrospect, I should not have been that shocked. Where I grew up, I could've named all five people of color. "How well did you know Eddie?"

"I knew his father. A stubborn goddamn cracker. My family moved here from Newark after we lost our house in the riots. A couple years later, Burt and I both got drafted at the same time. Did our basic together. A lot of us came back messed up. Burt, more than most. We'd run into each other at the VFW. Didn't talk much, usually a nod and then mumble something."

I threw out an understatement. "I hear Irvington's changed a lot since the sixties."

A burst of deep, throaty laughter. "I bet you weren't yet even *conceived* in the sixties, Landau."

"I bet you're right."

Henry shook his head. "When I moved here, I was the minority. As the blacks moved in, the whites moved out—"

"I know about white flight. Same thing in Chicago."

Henry smiled. "All right then. Twenty years later, Burt is the minority. By the time Eddie's a teenager, his family is damn near a minority of three in their own neighborhood."

"Did you actually know Eddie? Did you talk to him?"

"No, I just saw him around. Watched him grow up as the white boy in the 'hood. I couldn't help but respect him from afar. I think a lot of the kids—even the gangbangers—left him alone after a while, just out of respect. Burt became known as the crazy white man in that house."

"You know where that house is?"

"Of course!"

I took out a photo of Tanya. "Did you ever see Eddie with this woman?"

He studied the picture. "Yeah, that's probably her. I never got a good look at her, just saw them walking past or something." Henry pushed his chair back and leaned over to open a small refrigerator sitting on the floor. I thought he was handing me a bottle of beer, but it turned out to be mineral water.

"Calcium," Henry said after taking a swig. "Mineral water is a good source of calcium. I bet you didn't know that."

"No, I didn't. What would cause Eddie's girlfriend to up and leave her hometown?"

"I didn't know her, Landau—"

"Humor me—please. Let's say she was an intelligent, introspective woman."

Henry took another swig. "Well, you've got to remember something. She wouldn't be just dating Eddie, she'd be dating his whole damn family. They're all associated, if you know what I mean. Connected to organized crime. *Peripherally* mobbed up, I would say." Henry laughed then drained his bottle.

"I heard Burt stayed away from that life."

"True. He worked manual labor, although he used his connections to score his own dope or whatever else he was into. His family did plenty of business with my black brothers who unfortunately chose that way of life."

"Tanya would've known the kind of life to expect if she stayed with Eddie. After he went to prison, she had a change of heart and took off. But she disappeared without saying goodbye, which makes me think she was scared of something. You think she had a reason to be scared?"

Henry shrugged. "I'd imagine if you hung around Eddie's element long enough, finding a reason wouldn't be that hard."

A long pause, then I said, "She knew too much about how business was run?"

"Yeah, maybe. Tell me, Landau. You said you talked to cops. Who did you talk to?"

"Detective Cooper at the mini-precinct."

Henry's eyes narrowed. "How the hell did you get to see him?"

"I had a name to drop."

"You thought he could help you find the missing woman?"

"I don't know what I thought. But I learned about his law enforcement philosophy."

Henry looked troubled. "I don't want to tell you your business, but you better know what you're doing."

"I don't give a damn that Cooper runs Irvington like a feudal lord and dirty money is the lifeblood of his precinct. Finding Tanya is what brought me here."

"Tanya's not here, right? You know it. Why should Cooper believe that's the only reason you're here?"

I tried to decipher what he meant. Then it hit me. "What? I'm a G-man?"

"If they think you're messing with them, you might not make it back to Chicago. I wouldn't hang around too long."

Henry's look burned a hole between my eyes, penetrated my brain. I doubted a man could have been more serious than Henry at that moment.

"If you wouldn't mind giving me an address, I'd like to make one more stop—on my way out of town."

25

If I dulled my vision, the block could have been any middle-class neighborhood on the Eastern Seaboard. Two-story wood-framed boxes, attic dormers, wide flights of stairs leading to large front porches. Only after sharpening my gaze would the peeling paint, water damage, cracked windows, and torn blinds come into focus.

An eight-foot privacy fence circled Burt Byrne's residence from one side of the staircase to the other. Boards standing vertical along the sides of the staircase reached almost to the second story, preventing a visitor from looking into the yard. Halfway up the steps, I saw two African American men passed out on Burt's porch. Empty liquor bottles lay scattered across the floor. None appeared to have labels. I stepped over the bodies. Ringing the doorbell provoked hysterical barking from the yard. The furious noise receded toward the back of the house, only to manifest moments later as three snarling German shepherds staring at me through the sidelights.

I retraced my steps back to the sidewalk, then loitered in the vicinity. Perhaps it was the "energy" Amy spoke of or maybe it was my keenness of history, but I sensed an uncanny quality about the neighborhood. Despite the gloom, the buildings themselves seemed, somehow, optimistic. Perhaps Amy would've claimed happier energy of the early-twentieth-century construction still embodied the framework—just waiting for good times to reappear.

A Dodge station wagon circa 1970 approached from the end of the block. Despite the relatively flat street, the vehicle conspicuously bounced, rolled, and swayed as if on a trampoline. The car slowed almost to a stop in front of Burt's house then slowly maneuvered into the driveway. The suspension bottomed out with a painful scrape. A man I assumed to be Burt Byrne stepped out of the car, holding a bag of groceries. Early sixties, six foot, dark circles under eyes, beer belly dammed up behind his belt. Upon noticing the unconscious visitors on his porch, he placed the bag on the hood, grabbed a wooden baseball bat from the backseat, then ran up the stairs shouting obscenities.

I looked on in horror as Burt raised the bat only to slam it down on the floor next to one man's head. The noise prompted the first signs of life, but not enough movement to prevent Burt from poking the men hard in their sides while continuing his verbal assault. Not until he started viciously kicking them did the two finally scramble to their feet and stagger off his property.

For several minutes Burt stood catching his breath, watching the derelicts shuffle down the sidewalk. When they were out of sight, he dropped the bat and walked back to the car to collect his groceries.

"Are you Burt Byrne?"

His look epitomized the same disdain and suspicion Henry displayed. "What do you want?"

"I know your son, Eddie. He hired me to find Tanya Maggio."

His expression turned incredulous, as if I had uttered the dumbest statement possible. "So what do you want from me?"

"I'd just like to ask you a few questions, that's all."

Without a word, Burt turned around and walked back up to the porch. I followed him to the porch's top step. A chorus of anxious whimpering replaced growling as Burt stood in front of the door, fumbling for keys. I couldn't think of what to say before Burt entered the house and locked the door behind him.

I held the doorbell button down, listening to the repeated chimes provoke the dogs into a frenzy of barking. Burt's footsteps approached with a heavy urgency. Instinctively, I stepped back, almost tripping on the bat, which I then picked up. The door flew open.

"Do you want to fuckin' die today?" Burt shouted as he advanced toward me.

I extended my arm, pointing the bat almost into his abdomen. His hesitation allowed me to negotiate my backward progress toward the stairs.

"I'm trying to help Eddie find his girlfriend," I shouted then pulled the bat away. "What's the big deal?"

"You're on my goddamn property," he said as I backed down the stairs lifting the lumber when necessary. "You don't tell me what to do on my own goddamn property!"

When I reached the sidewalk, I dropped the bat. Burt stood at the end of his driveway. "Okay, I'm off your property. Go ahead and beat the crap out of me." I stood with my arms behind my back, offering the most vulnerable of targets.

Burt gave me a queer, almost deranged look. In addition to the dark circles, his eyes were red and watery. His voice lowered, Burt said, "What is it you want?"

"I want to find out what happened to Tanya—"

Burt threw up his hands. "I don't fucking know."

"Why would Tanya take off without telling Eddie?"

For a few moments, Burt appeared to be thinking my question over, but I couldn't be sure. Then he said, "I don't get why I should I tell you anything. You just show up and think I'm gonna start talking to you?"

"I didn't just show up. Eddie hired me."

"He hired you to come talk to me?"

I should have anticipated this question. Too risky to lie. "He doesn't know I'm here."

Another demented look, eyeballs bouncing around. "Huh! And why is that?"

"He hired me, but I work on my own terms. I don't need his permission." Burt shook his head
176

then started back toward the stairs. *Think of something, damn it!* "C'mon, Burt, Cooper talked to me. And Henry the hardware guy talked to me. Don't you want to know what they said?"

Burt stopped, faced me with another moonstruck expression. "And why would I care what those fuckers said?"

"Truth, damn it! That's all I'm looking for. Where the hell is Tanya? Don't you want to know? For Eddie's sake, don't you want him to find out what happened to her? She's a human being that your son cares about. So I gotta learn about this whole world you all live in. You think I'd come here from Chicago—to this paradise of Irvington—just to fuck with you?"

I wanted to believe Burt's latest expression revealed the slightest acceptance of my last-ditch effort to salvage a conversation. When he turned and headed back to the house my heart sank, only to rise moments later when he motioned with his hand to follow.

On the porch, Burt pointed to one of three wicker chairs then held the door open and said, "C'mon, girls."

The image of German shepherds tearing my flesh had barely registered before the three dogs sat in front of their master, staring in silent devotion, ears back, tails sweeping the floorboards.

"Relax—sir. If I'm home, they're pussycats."

I handed Burt a business card. "Tell them I love animals so much, I don't eat them."

Burt stared at the card, mumbled my name. "Call her over," he said pointing to one of the dogs. "Daisy. Call Daisy over."

I did as told. Daisy approached cautiously and sniffed the back of my hand. I knew to avoid direct eye contact, and when Daisy lifted her tail higher, I knew I could slide my hand behind her ear for a little scratch. When she sat and plopped a paw on my knee, I knew peace would reign.

Burt kicked away a couple of bottles from the floor of the porch then pulled a chair opposite me. Daisy lay down at my feet. The other dogs lay on either side of Burt, who stared across the street, his expression now just the average scowl. His arms hung down the sides of his chair, each hand lightly stroking a dog's head.

I said, "Eddie didn't want me to come here and ask questions. I don't expect you to rat out your own son. But if there's something about his past that is related to Tanya's disappearance, I need to know."

Still staring straight ahead he said, "Eddie's been on his own a long time—I wasn't much of a father." Burt abruptly stood up, then disappeared into the house. The dogs turned their heads in unison to stare at the door until their master reappeared, holding a six-pack of Pabst. He handed one to me, sat back down to resume staring across the street, then cracked open a can.

"Eddie brought a hell of a lot of cash to Chicago," I said.

Burt gulped twice from the can. "You don't say."

I cracked open my can, pretended to take a long swig, but choked down only about a thimble's worth. "Didn't mean to shock you."

"It's a cash-and-carry world. Not much check writing around here."

It suddenly hit me that Burt spoke better English than Eddie. "You don't wonder what Eddie's selling for cash?"

"Too late to wonder."

"Drugs and cash are pretty well matched." Burt glared at me, then looked away.

"He's no dope dealer."

"Why not? You said he's been on his own a long time."

"Because he doesn't fucking sell drugs! Others maybe, but not Eddie."

Several moments of silence. I said, "But he's in the family business, right?" No response. "Eddie needs cash to go look for Tanya. Uncle Whoever gives him money. How do you know it's not drug money?"

Burt guzzled the rest of the can, belched, then opened another. "What difference does it make?"

"The difference is Cooper. He's the vice lord. He gets a piece of everyone's action, right?"

"So?"

"So it's all connected. Cash from strip joints, gambling, whores, crack. It's all part of the same pot."

"I don't know what the hell you're saying."

"A white boy in the hood. He's respected. He's gotta be working with Cooper. And since Tanya was Eddie's girl, she was probably plugged in, you know?"

"Ask your buddy Cooper."

It was my turn to scowl. "Sarcasm gives you away, Burt. You're angry Eddie works for Cooper and you blame yourself."

Burt shot up from his chair, startling the dogs. "Don't tell me what I am! I should throw your ass out of here. I don't know why the fuck I'm even talking to you."

"Cooper acted like he was Eddie's guardian angel, made sure Eddie kept on the right path. He said he knew Tanya only from a distance—as Eddie's sweetheart. That's gotta be bullshit. Did she run away from Cooper? Run from Eddie? C'mon, Burt, what do you think?"

Red faced, stomach falling over belt—a heart attack could not have found a more accommodating host. Burt took a deep lungful of air, then sat back down.

"Let's keep it simple," I said. "It seems unlikely Tanya could be Eddie's girlfriend but still have a life *unconnected* to Cooper."

Something about that chair compelled Burt to stare across the street. I leaned back, set my almost-full can of beer on the floor, and studied the face of a Vietnam veteran now hunkered down in Irvington, New Jersey. From his sixty-something face, I surmised a birth positioned perfectly in a ten-year stretch of Baby Boom arrivals, from which President Johnson plucked the unlettered, low-hanging fruit of American sons, and shipped them to a Cold War jungle. Just as the profiteering corporations loved a poor man's war, guys like Cooper knew how to exploit a local war on drugs.

"They were together too long," Burt said quietly. "She couldn't have helped knowing more than she needed to know."

From that simple acknowledgment, Burt appeared tragically helpless, yet somehow heroic. Up to this point, I had only assumed that the realities of Eddie's life might have played a role in Tanya's disappearance.

"Burt, I don't believe Eddie sells drugs. I really don't. But I have to work on the assumption that Tanya is running from something. And whatever that something is, Eddie's probably part of it."

Burt turned to me. For the first time, he didn't look angry. "He might not know what's going on. I always told him he couldn't trust that prick Cooper."

"Eddie says he went to Chicago to find Tanya. A retired cop friend thinks Cooper gave him the additional assignment of establishing inroads into Chicago for his drug empire."

Burt shouted, "I said Eddie is no dope dealer! He wouldn't do it, no way!"

"Okay, forget the drugs. What if Cooper financed Eddie's trip but wanted *some* kind of work done in return? Does that sound like Cooper?"

Burt nodded. "Yeah, Cooper would do that. Cooper would send Eddie off a cliff if he thought it was good for business."

Burt closed his eyes, leaned his head back. It seemed like a good time to call it quits. I stood and put another business card on my chair. "Thanks for your time, Burt. I hope you'll call me if something comes to mind."

I thought I heard an acknowledging grunt, but couldn't be sure.

26

Along with two peanut-butter sandwiches and a bottle of water, I parked on a corner intersecting Clinton Avenue, a couple of blocks from the mini-precinct. Despite the cars lining the street in front of the building, nobody entered or exited. I guessed the meeting Cooper had mentioned was in progress. An hour later, both sandwiches were gone. The sun beat down on the car. Weights hung from my eyelids. I opened the windows but the air was still. The drowsy spell would have its way, there was no going back.

Men laughed, car doors slammed, alarms chirped. Emerging from a hazy slumber, I started my car just as Cooper's crony Sergeant Blake joined another man in a large Buick. Their car pulled a tight U-turn and flew past me. I let them get half a block ahead then sped after them. Instead of staying on Clinton, they turned down a side street and meandered their way into an industrial park. The Buick stopped in front of a long structure in the shape of a top hat. In the middle of the building the warehouse towered high with three enormous bay doors flanked on both sides with standard one-story flat-roofed offices. I parked on the far side of an adjacent warehouse then walked toward the back of the top-hat building. As I got closer, I realized the lower level was twice as wide as the warehouse. The building now resembled a modernist style chair. I opened an unlocked wooden door on which the word *Office* had been sloppily painted.

The room was large, extending back to carpeted partitions lined up in front of a glass wall separating the office from the warehouse, and had a strange, overripe kind of smell, not unpleasant but not exactly desirable. I moved one of the partitions away from the glass and saw an elaborate network of steel tanks, hoses, valves, pumps, meters, and other obscure-looking mechanical devices. Two men in lab coats attended the machinery. One walked slowly around the equipment, stopping to check gauges and adjust dials, while the other added packets of powder or small quantities of liquids to one of the tanks. In the corner, a man sat next to a pile of wooden crates. Smoke drifted from a device he pressed against the wood.

"Miss your flight, Detective?"

Two men stood in front of the door. The guy holding a gun was Guido Tuxedo from Back End Up. Sergeant Blake stood beside him, arms folded.

"Weird. All the flights were full last night. Nobody gave up a seat."

I had failed to notice the glass door to a dimly lit hallway linking the office to the warehouse. A hulking figure approached.

"You got a gun under that jacket, Detective?" Guido Tuxedo said.

"I didn't yesterday. Right, Sergeant Blake?"

Sergeant Blake had no comment. His face looked as pleasant and unconcerned as when I first walked into the mini-precinct. The figure from the hallway pushed through the door. Middle-Eastern looking, he stood about six foot with gorilla shoulders and a chest like the front end of a Peterbilt truck. His smile disturbed me.

Guido Tuxedo said, "In such a small space, I'd feel better if I knew you were unarmed. I hope you don't mind if Ahmet pats you down."

"Guys, New Jersey doesn't have a concealed-carry reciprocity agreement—"

The smell of oregano arrived first, a moment before Ahmet stood behind me and executed a choke hold with his left arm while patting me down with his right hand. Despite finding me unarmed, Ahmet placed his right forearm against the back of my neck and applied pressure. My comical attempt to get a grip on his massive forearms was my last memory before I found myself sitting on the floor, leaning backward against someone's hulking stomach, but having no idea where I was. The oregano smell restarted my brain as the gorilla hands lifted me up by the armpits.

"Feeling better?" Guido Tuxedo said. He stood about a foot in front of me. Sergeant Blake remained at the door. "Now that we know you're unarmed, I feel better. Look, I'll put my gun away. Why don't we chat a bit?"

"Yeah. Let's be friends."

Guido Tuxedo frowned. "Playing the tough detective? You think you're in a fucking movie?"

I truly couldn't help myself. "I have to act tough or be a smart ass. Otherwise, what's the point?"

Guido Tuxedo looked confused. "Can't we just talk like men?"

"Okay. What's your name?"

"Mike."

Guido Tuxedo was now Mike. "Mike, your breath stinks."

A sudden ringing filled the room then everything spun in a mist of sparkling lights before the pain spiraled out of my ear and covered the top of my head. My knees buckled but I somehow remained standing.

"Turks are known to be hospitable," Mike said, "but not Ahmet. He just gave you a mild concussion without even trying. A concussion is a brain injury. Your brain should heal before you get another smack like that. Otherwise, you may never recover."

"Why don't you just put a slug in my head instead of scrambling my brains?"

"Well, we'd like to know who you're working for, then maybe we can discuss how you'd like to die."

"I told your boss Cooper everything."

"Everything? Why don't we believe you?" Mike held up my wallet then fished out a business card. "Jules Landau, private investigator. Landau. That's a kike name, isn't it?" They giggled. Even Sergeant Blake smiled a bit. Then Mike said, "Lucky for you it's not a Greek name," which brought down the house.

Ahmet's hands slid away from my armpits, allowing me to balance by myself. With the training wheels off, I clenched my right hand into a fist then swung wildly with everything I had. The sensation of Mike's lip splitting and smearing my knuckles with blood and saliva conjured an image of the collision like a still from a newsreel. I envisioned myself smiling with a kind of schoolyard bully satisfaction. For a long moment, I was a kid again, back on the playground, on top of the world. Then everything went black, although I felt hands gripping my shoulders, holding me upright, and then a dull throbbing on the right side of my head. A finger lifted an eyelid. My head erupted. I swallowed something then fell backward into a dark canyon.

A fixture of beveled glass crystals hung from the ceiling. The room tilted as I sat up and swung my legs over the side of the cot. I surveyed the room. Shelves of darkly tinted bottles. Toilet and sink in the corner. Metal folding chairs against the wall. I walked carefully to the door as the room toggled back and forth. Locked. I stumbled back to the cot.

Besides a slight headache, I had no qualms about lying on a cot in a strange room. In fact, I felt oddly content—a bit euphoric even—in a drowsy kind of way. Memories of the previous hours seeped in. They called me "detective," even though I'm an investigator. Lots of people called me "detective." They didn't know the difference but so what? Let them think what they wanted. I was in deep shit. What would happen next? I felt really cool, like in a movie.

When I opened my eyes, Sergeant Blake, Mike, and Ahmet stared down at me. A scab peeked out from the Band-Aid on Mike's upper lip.

"Ahmet gave you a chop to the temple," Mike said. "That's twice you've been clobbered in a short time. Your brain doesn't appreciate this. He hits you too hard, you're dead. Sometimes you think you're okay and then later your brain bleeds out."

"Thanks," I said calmly, my slight lisp becoming suddenly pronounced. "Thanks for not hitting so hard. I think you drugged me."

"You old enough to remember goofballs? We gave you something like that, just to calm you down—to help us talk."

Sergeant Blake grabbed the three folding chairs and the men sat in a row along the edge of the cot. I looked again at Mike's lip. Intense guilt ensued. "Dude, I'm really sorry for hitting you. God, I hate being like that. I'm not a bad guy, I swear. I don't go around hitting people."

"You want to make up with me, Landau? Tell me why you're here and we'll be pals."

A strong desire to appease took over. "Ask Sergeant Blake! I wasn't an asshole at your precinct, right? You and I got along. I did what you told me and I got to talk to Detective Cooper. We had a good conversation."

"Yes, you're a good man, Mr. Landau," Sergeant Blake said. "Detective Cooper liked you too. Now just answer Mike's questions and we'll all be friends."

"I reminded Detective Cooper I'm an *investigator,* not a detective—"

"Why did you come to Irvington?" Mike interrupted.

I started giggling. Unable to resist I said, "My health. I came to Irvington for the waters."

Mike tried to suppress his smile but failed. "See, it's just fun and games playing detective, right? You know fantasy worlds are a lot safer than the real world—right?"

"Jesus, relax," I said. "I'm just trying to help Eddie Byrne find his girlfriend—hey, Ahmet! Are we good? I deserved that whack on the head, dude." I offered my hand for a conciliatory shake. Ahmet didn't bite.

"What are you doing here, Landau?" Mike said.

Suddenly the question sparked a strange empathy—as if I *owed* them an explanation. I described Eddie's reluctance to talk—emphasized that he had every right in a free country not to talk—but framed my presence as a kind of peripheral approach to investigating, to see if some small detail would surface and inspire an insight. Mike whispered to Sergeant Blake. They stood then walked away to confer. I drifted into semi-consciousness, aware I was the subject of discussion, but still feeling really cool.

"What about the FBI?"

I opened my eyes to the men seated as before. I said, "I don't know any FBI."

"We know the Feds are watching Eddie," Mike said.

"Oh, no. He's not dealing drugs! Eddie's better than that."

"He's not dealing drugs," Sergeant Blake and Mike said at the same time.

"Then tell the Feds they're wasting their time."

"We need to know what you know, Landau," Mike said. "Like, why you came to this building?"

"Guys, I'm here to find out about Tanya, Eddie's girlfriend. Nothing else. Christ, I'm tired."

"You see anything in this building that's gonna help you find her?"

I was just too damn tired to talk. That oversized chemistry set in the warehouse had no relevance to Tanya. But Mike kept asking, kept insisting I knew what Eddie was up to. Maybe it was my fault, maybe I got a little nasty because I thought I heard someone throw a chair across the room. I kept saying I only wanted to sleep but then the hands returned to my armpits and I stood again, dangling like a marionette. "Hold him still," Mike said and Ahmet wrapped an arm around my chest then grabbed a handful of hair from the back of my head just before the first blow hit my mouth. The second followed closely and then another before I returned to the darkness.

27

My face throbbed. Mike and Sergeant Blake spoke casually. So many things I could've done with my life. History professor, antique dealer, lawyer, gemologist, park ranger, historic preservationist, geologist, linguist, bookseller, reporter, social worker, shop owner, real estate investor, arborist, or any other goddamn thing a white, upper-middle-class American male wanted to do. I chose private investigator, a path to lying on a cot and fearing that opening my eyes might provoke more violence. But to what end? Unless they were sadists, getting me to talk made more sense. If they had already used me up, I would've been re-homed somewhere in the Passaic River by now.

"I don't know. . . .What do you think the boss wants to do?"

"Depends on his mood . . ." Loud laughter. "And he knows that cop . . . could be tricky . . . attention he don't want . . ."

I sat up. Darts of pain pulsated around my face. The guys continued chatting, apparently unconcerned with my resurrection. ". . . Yeah, but things are better than they used to be. . . . I remember . . ."

My feet found the floor, provoking a glance. Games get boring when played too often.

I said, "You think I could get something to eat?"

Sergeant Blake took the cell phone off his belt, dialed a number. "Yep."

Moments later, Cooper walked through the door. "He's hungry," Mike said.

"Get him something. How about toast? You like toast, Mr. Landau?"

"Love it," I deadpanned.

"Good. Sergeant Blake, would you mind?"

Sergeant Blake walked out. Cooper sat in his chair. "How are you feeling, Mr. Landau?"

I walked to the mirror above the sink. Deep purple bruises blemished my mouth, cheekbone, and eye socket. "I feel just how I look."

Cooper grimaced. "I'm sorry about that. But this was your choice. Violence is always a choice."

"Whose choice was it to ambush me?"

"You chose to come to Irvington, right?"

"It's a free country, right? I'm being paid to find a missing woman, right? I'm doing my job, right?"

"A free country?" Cooper thought about it. "Well, Irvington's reality may not fit into your idea of freedom."

We sat in silence. Sergeant Blake returned with a plate of toast and several small packets of jelly. The three men watched me eat as if something of monumental importance hinged on the outcome.

"Anything else?" Cooper said.

"I want my wallet back."

Sergeant Blake left the room, returned with my wallet, then stood by the door.

Cooper said, "You'll find your wallet with everything intact."

I stood. "Before you leave," Cooper said, "tell me your impression—from what you've seen so far, I mean."

I gave my best *Are you kidding me?* look. "You really think I give a damn about some bum-booze distillery? A ghetto full of poor people happy as hell to buy your cheap hooch with no labels? That's what I call a captive audience. *I get it.*" I moved toward the door.

"Not just yet." Sergeant Blake stepped in front of the door. "I can't help but wonder if, maybe, later on, you might change your tune. I mean little things might fall into place and then you might get a different idea."

It had seemed too easy—that a guy with Cooper's reputation would just let me walk. I knew damn well private investigating could be dangerous, especially if organized crime was involved. But to disappear over bootleg booze?

"Why would I give a shit? I'm just trying to find Tanya—"

I looked at Sergeant Blake and then back to Mike and Cooper. As if choreographed, they both stood and walked to the door. Sergeant Blake opened it. Ahmet walked in and took a seat. Before the others left, Cooper said, "But can I take that chance? Relax a while. Let me think about it."

You didn't become kingpin by taking chances. Cooper knew a missing private investigator would attract little attention. He had everything to lose by letting me go and nothing to gain. After enough time passed some would say, *He knew what he was getting into.* Others might say, *He got what he deserved.*

Ahmet had moved his chair near the door, where he sat with his face behind a Turkish newspaper. I paced the room, noted the distance between the other chairs and Ahmet, then tried to calculate how quickly I could fold a chair before Ahmet recognized a threat—that is, if he bothered to look.

"Hey, Ahmet, I don't think they locked the door."

A guttural chuckle emerged from behind the paper. "You going somewhere?"

I put my hand on the back of a chair and lifted it a few inches off the ground. "Your boss doesn't like to take chances."

Another throaty laugh. "You have no chances."

The chair didn't fold as expected. I struggled with the seat, trying to stay calm. Anger at my ineptness replaced any inkling of panic. When I glanced again at Ahmet, he was already coming at me. I swung the chair in front of me just in time for Ahmet to pluck it from my hands, slam the seat flat, then throw it at my feet.

"That's what you wanted, no?"

I grabbed the chair and held it up, hoping to smash Ahmet's head with the heaviest part of the chair—where the legs, seat, and hinges folded together. Ahmet mocked me with his casual posture and smile, egged me on with hand gestures and words in his native language. I lunged toward him then retreated in a feigned assault. He flinched, I swung the chair at the side of his head. Ahmet blocked the blow with his forearm then cried out as blood trickled down his arm from where a rivet had torn his flesh. I jammed the chair into his stomach, which had no ill effect but allowed him to take hold and shove the chair back into my abdomen, dropping me to the floor. As I gasped for breath, Ahmet lifted me from behind in a crushing reverse bear hug. Adding a dash of humiliation, he leaned back on his heels then swung me around in clumsy pirouettes.

Helpless as I was, Ahmet's embrace afforded me enough physical stability to allow a rational assessment of my predicament, thus fostering a thought regarding the proximity of my feet to Ahmet's knees. I lifted my right leg as high as I could, then exerted every last bit of remaining energy in a downward thrust, crashing the heel of my shoe against Ahmet's locked knee. I saw and heard the "crack" of a baseball hitting the bat's sweet spot, followed by a primal scream as Ahmet took the path of least resistance, dropping to the floor over his shattered leg.

I sat a few feet from the writhing man, unaffected by the sight of Ahmet's right leg bent queerly at a ninety-degree angle below the knee. Slowly, I got to my feet then opened the door just enough to poke my head out. Ahmet's groans leaked into the empty hallway. A sense of urgency hit me but I couldn't leave yet, not without first taking care of Ahmet. The bedsheet from the cot tore easily into strips. Ahmet tried to resist, but with every move the pain discouraged his ambition. After tying his hands behind his back, I gagged him with a few strips then wrapped his mouth shut, tying the strip behind his head.

Once again, I poked my head out the door. The room was in the middle of a long hallway that I guessed ran the length of the building. One direction probably led to the office where I had entered. The other direction probably led to the lab where the front door was located. I took a last look at Ahmet, momentarily considered the magnitude of his discomfort, then closed the door.

Now outside the room, a feeling I associated with Amy's intuition directed me to turn right. I jogged down the hallway, enduring the throbbing pain bouncing around my face, but worried more about the few options available to evade someone appearing at either end of the corridor. About thirty yards from the end of the hallway, I noticed a single bulb illuminating the opposite side of the glass door. Beyond the glow, darkness. Ahmet had originally appeared from a dark corridor connected to the office. My spirits soared, although the emergence of Cooper, Mike, and Sergeant Blake from the shadows—about to push their way through the glass door—delayed an attempted dash to freedom.

I ducked into a doorless work space, then crawled under a utility table where several stacks of boxes offered refuge. The room had an earthy, dead plant odor, and the only light was whatever spilled in from the hallway. While approximating the progress of the three men chatting quietly as they walked down the hallway, I noticed several crumpled pieces of paper on the floor. I crawled over to one of them. The paper cracked easily and smelled like brewed tea. In poor light, the ornate handwriting and mysterious images brought nothing to mind. I moved closer to the doorway for better light and recognized a logo with five arrows splayed above and below a capital "R."

"Lafite Rothschild 1947," the yellowed label read. I grabbed several more scraps. "Mouton Rothschild 1945," "1982 La Mission Haut-Brion," "1978 Romanée-Conti."

On the table, tea bags steeped in a bowl of water. I grabbed a handful of paper from one of the boxes. Vintage labels laid out three to a page, waiting to be aged in tea. A small oven at the end of the table sat ready to bake in the appropriate antiquity. Hundreds of corks filled several other boxes. Scattered across one table were lead capsules, sealing wax, and rubber stamps with vintages and French estate names. The men's voices became louder. I ducked back under the table. They passed the doorway. Moments later, Ahmet's howls of agony raced down the hallway.

A fresh round of throbbing ricocheted around my face as I stood and bolted down the hall. Once through the glass door, I sprinted toward the glow of the office light where my adventure had begun.

Outside, the wet, cool air refreshed me, felt good against my face, prompted me to run faster. Not until I found my car and turned on to Springfield Avenue did I begin to relax.

28

Expressions of horror on their pretty brown faces reflected my battered appearance.

"I'm so sorry, mister!" the tall girl said. "We told you it wasn't safe for white men to walk around."

"Call the police," the other girl said.

"No!" I said. "I'm fine. Do *not* call the police. I'm going to rest awhile then go to the airport. Okay? Promise me you won't call the police."

Both nodded. Both were crying.

Once back in my room, I collapsed into the bed's crevasse. I relived running through the dark corridor before busting out into the cool air. All the doors had been unlocked, coming and going. Only a handful of people in the building. No security except a few cameras. Apparently, they had no fear of discovery. My presence had been a surprise. I drifted off, wishing I had a gun in my hand, then awoke less than an hour later, with a knowingness that I should get the hell out of town.

I ate another peanut butter sandwich, packed, gave each girl a hundred-dollar bill, then drove to the airport where security inquired about my face then disappeared for several hours with my IDs. Not until mid-afternoon did they allow me to pay an additional fifty dollars to book another flight.

I turned off all the lights in my apartment, preferring only the residual glow from the streetlamps. Punim strolled out of the bedroom then jumped onto the coffee table. She sat watching me with her tail wrapped tightly around her legs. She appeared well.

I swallowed a couple of aspirin then lay on the couch with two ice packs covering my face. In the background, an analysis of new information loitered, waited for integration with Tanya, Eddie, Margot, and Doug. Punim landed on my chest then stretched out across my torso. The barrel of my Glock stroked her back. I put the gun on the coffee table then rested my hand next to her belly. It was good to be home.

The three pairs of eyes were on me again. I smelled chemicals. A chloroform mask lay over my nose and mouth. The escape and reunion had been a dream. The disappointment ached.

"Wow, it's dark in here."

The familiar voice dissolved the men into the light of a gooseneck lamp. I removed the ice packs and sat up.

"That was a fast trip—oh, my god! What happened?" Amy's look of shock did not diminish her beauty.

"It's nothing, really. It only happens during a crime investigation. I think it's an immune system response."

She sat next to me. Her eyes jumped around my face. "You were badly beaten. It's not funny."

Amy stood then walked around the room turning on more lights. Punim jumped down and followed her to the kitchen. Amy dropped some raw meat into Punim's bowl then returned to my side on the couch. Pointing at the gun on the table she said, "Expecting someone?"

I grabbed the Glock, dropped it in the shoulder holster hanging from a hook next to the front door, then sat back down next to Amy. "You and Punim now BFF?"

"Don't give me that crap. What happened? Who did this to you?"

"Wine counterfeiters did this to me."

Amy stared a moment, as if confused. Then she surprised me with, "That makes sense."

"What makes sense?"

"Wine counterfeiting. It fits with what we know. You discovered the truth and got beat up in the process."

"Tell me how it relates to Tanya's disappearance."

"Wine is the theme, right? Margot's stolen wine. Doug married to Margot. Tanya disappearing with Doug. Which wine is real? Which is counterfeit? Maybe a blackmail opportunity?" Amy stopped to think about it some more. "Okay, there are dozens of possibilities, but I think you can say Tanya's disappearance is *somehow* related to stolen wine or wine counterfeiting."

Amy folded her legs under herself and waited for my response.

I said, "You seem awfully invested in my answer."

"I just want you to see what I see."

It hurt to frown. "I see Eddie coming here to find Tanya and find out about phony grape juice for—for his bosses. But I don't see it as simple as Tanya connected to the grape juice. I'm still going to assume there's another component involved. She was bangin' Doug, remember?"

"You don't have to be crude. You think Eddie is prospecting for new clients?"

"I think Eddie's more like a foreman sent to watch over an operation."

"So there's already a network here?"

"Perhaps. Can't see a street kid like Eddie selling a rare bottle of *Château Lafite Mouton* Rothschild B*lanc de Blancs Vin de Pays*."

Amy giggled. "Quite impressive, Jules."

I pointed to the beat-up paperback lying on the table. "My little wine book. Complete with phonetic translations."

Amy had a content, happy look. The kind that instilled confidence in men previously rejected. She said, "You stopped yourself from saying the name of Eddie's boss."

"There's no reason for you to know names."

"What difference would it make?" she asked.

"What you know could hurt you—and if you got hurt, I would never forgive myself."

Amy reached toward my face and may have barely brushed the bruised side of my mouth—I wasn't sure. "That must hurt."

"The other side feels fine," I said and bent toward her, expecting to feel the warmth of her lips against the undamaged part of my mouth. She shrunk back.

"Let's not," she said.

Misinterpreted signals? "You know, you didn't ask permission to kiss me goodbye two days ago—"

"I didn't think you'd respond by mauling me—"

"*Mauling* you? I seem to remember your body responding rather agreeably to my *mauling* you."

A pregnant pause. "Let's keep the focus on the investigation. It's important you talk about it while it's still fresh in your mind. Just relax and talk to me."

I lay back down, replaced the ice packs, then draped my legs over Amy's thighs. She didn't object. "I should confront Margot Daley about the bogus wine scheme. Or maybe not. Maybe I should talk about everything except the fake wine."

"I agree, don't confront her about the fake wine. See if she'll lead you somewhere first."

I changed the subject. "When did you first become aware of your energy reading or whatever you call it?"

Either Amy wasn't sure I was serious or was thinking about her answer. "It was a survival mechanism," she said, looking into the distance. "My father's unpredictable outbursts of violence. I learned to read his body language, so I knew when to hide until his anger passed. Eventually, I could tell his mood just by what I heard when he walked up the stairs to our apartment. Or how he put the key in the lock and opened the door. By the time I got to high school, I could check in just by thinking about him awhile and get a *knowingness* of what he was going to be like when I got home."

Amy looked at me. "I'm sorry," I said. "About the violence."

Neither of us spoke. Then Amy said, "How much trouble were you in? I mean—"

"As bad as it gets. So what? Investigating crime is dangerous. I know that."

"So your life doesn't mean anything to you?"

"I'm just saying that anyone who decides to investigate crime knows—or should know—it can be dangerous—as in life-threatening."

"You didn't answer. Does your life mean anything to you?"

I gave her a nice, long stare. "Does my life mean anything to *you*?"

"Yes."

"Why?"

She studied me. "Have you done anything about your depression?"

It hurt to laugh. "A depressed private investigator, how cliché! Unfortunately, I'm not much of a drinker. There's no bottle of bourbon for drowning sorrows while ruminating on missed opportunities."

"Depression is nothing to be ashamed of."

"Oh, Jesus Christ! If you're going to—"

"Of course your life means something to me! I *like* you. You're interesting. Probably a good person. But I don't think you're happy."

I stared at the ceiling, thinking of how to change the subject. Mercifully, Amy said, "Those guys that robbed you of Margot's money. How are you going to find out who they are?"

"She's going to tell me."

"Oh? She agreed to this?"

"Not yet."

I didn't want to talk anymore. Amy sensed my sentiment. She removed herself from under my legs and stood. "I should go," she said.

I sat up. "Thank you for your concern," I said and lay back down. The sound of Amy closing the door inspired a string of thoughts having something to do with her committed interest in the case and an illusory interest in me. Neither made sense.

29

Around two-thirty a.m. I left the couch, added ice to the cold packs, then collapsed on my bed where I remained until Punim's hunger patrol woke me four hours later. After feeding her and getting more ice, I returned to bed and stayed there until almost eleven o'clock, at which time I became conscious of the odor coming off my skin and clothes. I remembered Kalijero's comment about the stink of drug money rubbing off on those who profited. Counterfeit wine money smelled pretty bad too. Amy had been either very polite or very brave to endure such an insult on her olfactory senses.

I phoned in a lunch order then jumped into the shower. Standing under a stream of hot water, I thought about the beatings I had taken over the years. I'd become a candidate for premature brain wasting disease but took comfort in legally owning a handgun. I could always shoot myself when I started going off the rails. Around noon, three loud knocks told me Tasty Harmony had left a Bigboy burger outside the door. I ate then headed to Webster Avenue.

205

Forty degrees, low hanging clouds, and a stiff breeze eclipsed any symbolic harbinger of summer the approaching opening day at Wrigley Field represented. I stopped at *Pâtisserie Grenouille.* Brenda Gallagher and Jennie Adler were busy cleaning up.

"Looks like your morning rush is outlasting the morning," I said.

Brenda smiled weakly then walked over. She looked tired. "Yeah, it seems that way—what in god's name happened to your face?"

"I'm fine. It always looks worse than it is."

"You didn't answer my question."

"The morning rush getting longer. That's a good thing, right?"

Brenda sighed. "Oh, sure. It's just that I have less time to prepare tonight's items."

"Maybe you need more help."

"You know anyone looking for a job?" She sounded half-serious.

"I bet Margot's got extra time."

"Margot?"

"That was a joke," I said and Brenda forced an anemic laugh. "Did you ever know a kid who worked for Margot named Spike?"

Brenda was about to respond but stopped. "You're really not going to tell me how you got those cuts and bruises?"

"Answer my question and I'll answer yours. Did you know Spike?"

"Yeah. He ran around for her. She'd order a bag of croissants and Spike would come by to pick them up."

"When's the last time you saw him?"

Brenda thought about it. "It's been a while."

"More than five days?"

"Oh, definitely. Probably a couple of months."

"From your sour look, I'm going to guess you don't like him."

"He's just a punk acting real cocky, like he's a big shot or something. And he can be really vulgar with sexual innuendos. And that oily hair—he gives me the creeps."

"Margot said he was a college kid."

Brenda laughed then briefly put her hand on mine. "Right. A Mafia major. Why do you care about Spike?"

"Here's an abbreviated explanation: Margot's wine was stolen. After receiving an offer to buy back a bottle, she asked Jennie to call me on Margot's behalf. Would I accompany Spike in delivering an envelope of cash in exchange for the bottle? Easy payday. Margot drove Jennie to my office. Jennie brought me the envelope. I met Spike, got mugged, and relieved of the ransom money. It was a setup."

"Margot wanted you to get mugged and lose her money?"

"No, Spike double-crossed her. By the way, who's that old man I always see sitting by himself?" I pointed at the table against the far wall where the old man sat reading a newspaper.

"His name is Blackstone. That's what he goes by. He started coming in a few months ago. He's a nice old guy. Now he comes in almost every day and buys a couple of croissants." Brenda looked at her watch. "Damn. I need a quick smoke and then to get back."

I followed her outside. She didn't bother with a coat. Goosebumps covered her arms as she lit up. I bid her farewell and she thanked me for stopping by. Just as I stepped into the street she yelled, "You may want to ask Jeremy, the guy across the street who bought out Doug's place. I think Spike runs around for him too."

This time Margot used the intercom. "It's Jules Landau." A long ten seconds passed before she buzzed me through. This time her door was shut. I knocked. She took her time answering.

"You sure you want to let me in?"

"Don't be ridic—oh, my god! What happened to your face?"

"I fell and I don't want to talk about it."

Margot backed away from the door, closed it behind me, then walked to the chaise longue to lay down and stare out the window. I took my place on the love seat and waited. After a minute, I said, "So describe your situation when you first noticed symptoms?"

She flashed me an icy look. "You're suggesting I need a shrink?"

"Well, let's examine your behavior. Your interaction with me has been a continuous charade. I believe you may have issues with telling the truth."

Margot lifted her legs off the chaise to sit facing me. "My wine was stolen. I thought I could pay them off and that would be that."

"That gangster errand boy of yours double-crossed you."

"He stole the money not the—"

"You're in denial over that kid! Oh, that's right, he called you 'in a panic' after I got ambushed."

"Meaning what?"

"He's playing you, Margot! I told you he said, 'Fuck you, Margot,' right before I got knocked out. That kid's got 'future felon' written all over him. Even if he didn't know it was a twenty-grand bottle of wine, he knew I had an envelope full of cash. Maybe you didn't completely trust him—which is why you had me tag along."

"Don't tell me what I thought!" A nerve had been touched. "God, you men are all alike, always putting thoughts in my head. You think you know me that well, Jules? You don't know anything—and I want you off the case."

I laughed loudly. "What case? I've been hired to look for Tanya Maggio, remember? It's just that your damn wine keeps getting in the way."

Redheads had built-in emotion barometers measured in degrees of flushed skin. Margot said quietly, "Do you think Tanya's disappearance is connected to my stolen wine?"

I tried to sound ironic. "That could be possible."

"And exactly how was Spike involved in stealing my wine?"

"I'm not one-hundred percent sure. Which is why I need to talk to him. And what about Jeremy?"

"What about him?"

"Don't play stupid! You don't think he might be in on the scam?"

"No! Jeremy's helping me! He—he's keeping Spike close—to help me."

"Oh, yeah? When's the last time you spoke to him?"

She put her legs back up on the chaise and lay down. "We're regularly in touch."

"Maybe you know someone else who could find him?"

"Why would I?"

"Because four days ago when I asked what Spike knew about the meeting to swap the wine you said, 'Only that *we* asked him to exchange one package for another.' Who made up the *we*?"

"A friend—someone I asked advice from. And I don't like the way you're cross-examining me as if I'm some kind of suspect."

The best defense was a good offense. Margot was a natural. "Why can't you just admit that friend's name was Jeremy?"

"My god, you're a pain in the ass!" She stood up, walked to the kitchen, took a bottle of wine from the cabinet and poured a glass. "Yes, I know you barged in on Jeremy and so shrewdly confirmed we are friends. So what? There's some great conspiracy going on, is that what you're after?"

She paced the floor in front of the large sash windows that looked over the alley. I turned around in the love seat, leaned on the backrest, watching her.

"Margot, let me remind you of something. I just want to find Tanya. Everything else is none of my business. But I get the feeling you're involved some way over your head. If your stolen wine is connected to Tanya's disappearance—"

"Why do you think that? You've never said why you think that!"

"Did your husband know the value of your wine inheritance?"

"No! I don't know."

"You knew he had started stocking the pub with wine and he had Brenda as a wine mentor, right?"

She hesitated. "Wrong. I had no interest in the bar. I paid no attention to it. So I had no reason to think Brenda was teaching him about wine."

"Oh, I see. You were so sure Doug knew nothing about the wine's value that you didn't change the security profile at the storage facility after Doug left."

Margot didn't answer.

"I'll bet you a case of Lafite that the security cameras will show Spike or Doug taking your wine. Doug is dead but Tanya and the wine are still missing."

"Tanya is also dead, I told you that."

"Of course she is, although you won't tell me why you're so sure."

Margot returned to the chaise, put the glass of wine on the end table, and lay back down, dropping an arm across her forehead. "So what do you want from me?"

"I want a private chat with Spike."

Deep sigh. "Give me a few hours."

30

A copy of *Wine Kibitzer* sat on the coffee table in my apartment. I leaned back in the recliner and opened it for the first time. The magazine was divided into two sections. One dealt with consumption fraud, the other with collector fraud. An hour later, I called Paul from *Der Weingott* and asked him about wine equity trusts.

"They buy wine and wine futures," Paul said. "Then it's managed like any other Wall Street type of asset."

I thanked Paul then tried to recall the nuances of the previous hour. Margot toggled between resignation and anger. What did the anger represent? Things not going as planned? Maybe Tanya double-crossed Doug who was subsequently double-crossed by Spike? A case of wine probably weighed forty pounds. Tanya would've needed help moving ten cases around. My cellphone rang. It was Margot.

"Meet Spike at *Auvergnat*—Jeremy's wine bar—at two o'clock."

"I said a private meeting."

"Jules, he's just a kid. I don't think he should be alone."

"Goddamn it, Margot! What are you afraid of?"

"I don't know what—"

"Tell Spike to meet me at your apartment. Then you disappear for a couple of hours."

"No. I won't lie to that boy—"

"You want to know where I really got these big, nasty, black bruises? From getting the crap beat out of me—and all because of *wine*. Just a coincidence?"

Margot started whimpering. "I'm sorry. I—I can't . . ."

"How many people would even consider helping you, knowing you were full of shit? You want my help—for something. It's not just getting your precious wine. There's more you won't tell me. Only a reckless fool would hang around to see how it turns out. And you're damn lucky I'm one of those fools."

I listened to her sob a while longer then said, "Two o'clock at *Auvergnat Vin Bar*. But I'll tell you right now I'm not taking any crap from your pal Jeremy or that junior hoodlum. I'm usually a nice guy, but not always." I hung up then went out to buy a pack of zip ties.

Two waitresses setting up tables paid no attention to me standing among the paintings of sweeping Rhone sunsets and Loire Valley vineyards. Bruce and his pupil, Ted, were washing an endless supply of glasses. When he finally noticed me, Bruce picked up the phone. Seconds later, Jeremy appeared from behind the bar heading toward the dining room. Spike followed, sleepy-eyed, hands in pockets, chomping gum. Neither asked about my battered face.

I approached Jeremy. "Where are you going?"

"You want to talk, don't you?"

"In the office."

"No, I think we'll stay out here."

I pulled open my jacket to brandish my holstered pistol. I'd never done that before.

"Turn around and go back to the office," I said.

"I'm supposed to believe you'd shoot me right here?" Jeremy said bravely.

"No. I'm not going to shoot you. But I will pistol-whip you across the face and it will hurt and bleed a lot. Is it worth it?"

"I don't think you would do that," Jeremy said. Spike yawned.

I pulled the gun out and raised my arm. Jeremy stepped back, knocking into Spike. The bartender yelled, "Should I call the police?"

"If I'm arrested I'll tell them everything you and Spike are up to. And I'll make sure Detective Jimmy Kalijero follows up on all my leads." I held out my phone. "Give PD a call. Ask for Detective Kalijero." Dropping Kalijero's name had little downside risk.

Jeremy waved off the bartender, then said to Spike, "Just go to my office." Spike rolled his eyes then began trudging to the back like a stubborn little boy. The three of us walked through the kitchen, then into the little corridor that led to Jeremy's office. Jeremy unlocked the door, waited for us to enter, then closed the door behind him.

Spike sat at Jeremy's desk. I sat on the black vinyl couch and said, "I'd like to talk to Spike alone."

"Absolutely not. This is my office. Spike works for me."

"Just beat it," Spike said. "I don't need a scared little bitch hanging around."

Spike's slap hurt. I thought Jeremy might cry.

I asked Jeremy, "Why do you think Margot wants you to babysit Spike?"

"She doesn't trust you."

"She doesn't trust me or what Spike might say?"

Jeremy searched for an answer. "He's a kid."

"But he's a *tough* kid. Right, Spike?"

Spike gave me his rough-guy sneer-squint. Something about chomping gum gave people self-confidence.

"Just get on with it," Jeremy said. "What do you want?"

I looked at Spike. "Who helped you rob me?"

"Spike doesn't know—"

Jeremy's thin wrist twisted easily behind his back as I guided him first to his knees and then facedown on the floor. I pinned his arm with my knee, then took a zip tie from my pocket. Once I had both his wrists fastened together behind his back, Jeremy began shouting. That prompted me to shove my jacket sleeve into his mouth and hold it there long enough to extricate my arm before properly securing the gag. Sitting on the back of Jeremy's legs, I caught my breath while linking together a few more zip ties. Spike leaned back in Jeremy's steno chair and put his feet on the desk. I said, "Show a little respect. It's his office, after all."

"It's just laminate crap," he said. "My desk will be big old solid wood planks. Not this particleboard shit."

I smiled. "You mean like wood from an old barn?"

Spike nodded slowly with his eyes closed.

I returned my attention back to Jeremy. "This is for your own good," I said while fastening Jeremy's ankles together. "You shouldn't be conversing with criminals like Spike. Right now he's sitting at your desk, laughing his ass off."

Jeremy had lost the will to fight, preferring instead to focus on sucking adequate air through his nostrils.

"I'm not a barbarian, Jeremy. Relax while I chat with Spike and everything will be just fine." I crawled to the couch opposite the desk then climbed up. "Okay, where were we?"

"Dropping that cop's name was chickenshit," Spike said. "But I like your style, Landau. Maybe one day you'll work for me."

"Having fun playing gangster?" Spike didn't appreciate my laughter.

"Gangster! What a joke. It's business. And a guy like you could make a lot of money in this business. Trust me. I know."

"To be so cocky at your age, you must have a powerful friend watching your back."

"I lucked out. So what? I was born into this business. That's the best way to get in. Why should I go get an MBA when I can learn on the job from pros?"

"MBAs usually don't hurt as many people on the road to success."

"Nobody gets hurt that doesn't deserve it. Not where I work."

"The 'innocents' are unharmed."

Spike nodded. "Yep. That's how we work it. If it can possibly be helped, innocents don't get hurt. That's the goal."

Cooper was branching out all right, franchising his business model. Spike must have been expecting me. I kind of admired the punk, even though I didn't like him. He had a sort of smart-ass charisma I envied.

"Apparently, Margot and that guy on the floor are afraid of something you'll say."

"Yep."

"Why is that?"

"Because I know a lot."

"This being information about Margot, I'll betcha."

Spike grinned.

"You set me up the other night. You double-crossed Margot."

Spike shrugged. "I made my move."

"Who hit me on the head?"

"Just a guy needing some easy money. We only wanted to daze you with a thump to the back of the head. A mild concussion at worst. By the way, flashing your gun at the wine bitch there? Pretty amateur."

"Yeah, I know, but it worked. Golly, I could learn a lot from you. Do you know why I'm here?" Spike shrugged again. I took out a picture of Tanya. "You recognize this girl?"

"Yeah."

"You know where she is?"

"Nope."

"You know where Doug is?"

"Nope."

"He's dead," I told him. "He died last month in a car crash in New Mexico."

"No shit? What was he doing there?"

"I was hoping you'd tell me. Anyway, I was hired to find Tanya."

Spike perked up. "Find her? She's missing?"

"For quite a while now. That's the only reason I'm here. Anything I find out on the way, I don't give a damn. You're building a little empire of thugs? Good for you, but I don't really care." I leaned down toward Jeremy. "You hear that, Jeremy? I don't care!"

"What makes you think I know anything about Tanya?" Spike said.

"Well, you know about Margot's stolen wine. I'll bet you know Doug stole it. Tanya and Doug ran off together. Doug's dead. You have the wine."

Spike put his feet back on the floor. "You almost got it right. I took the wine using Doug's card—"

"Ahhh! You double-crossed Doug *first,* then set up Margot! I never thought of that. But—do you know what the wine is worth?"

"A lot more than the five grand I took off of you."

"What a greedy piece of shit you are! To think Margot worried about your welfare, and insisted I deliver the cash. She had complete trust in you—."

"I didn't think Margot would ever pay full price for her own wine, so I thought I'd squeeze a little money out of her before suckering in the big bucks. I didn't have to sell it back to Margot, after all."

I thought about how Jeremy fit into the story. What did Jeremy have that Spike needed?

"What do you know about wine, Spike?"

He smiled. "I don't know shit."

I knelt beside Jeremy. "I'm going to take my jacket out of your mouth. You have no reason to shout because we're all getting along. Okay?"

Jeremy grunted. I liberated my sleeve. "Cut me loose," he said. "Scissors in top drawer."

Spike tossed them on the floor in front of the desk. "Soon," I said. "Spike knows you through Margot. He must've made you an offer you couldn't refuse."

Jeremy said, "What does this have to do with that woman you're looking for?"

"I don't know. But while we're all here together, I might as well find out as much as I can."

"How do I know you won't go to the police?"

"And tell them what?"

Jeremy groaned. I cut him free. "Y—you said you knew what we we're up to—"

Spike cut in. "And when he lifted his hand you ran like a scared little girl. He played you."

I said, "I guess the cops might care if I could get them to question you about murder or kidnapping. But I don't think I have quite enough info."

"Murder?" Jeremy said. "You're crazy!"

"Shut up," Spike said. "What are you talking about, Landau?"

"Guys, chill. I'm sure the surveillance video will show Spike arriving then leaving with ten cases of wine worth a ton of cash. But dead men can't press charges. And although Tanya's body hasn't been found, the motive is pretty obvious, don't you think?"

"You're making up stories," Jeremy said. "I don't know anything about murder."

"But Spike might, which could make you an accessory. Are you connected enough to beat a murder rap, Spike?"

Spike had sobered somewhat. "You got nothing, Landau. But what the hell, I'll tell you. When Doug found out Jeremy was bangin' Margot—"

"Shut up!"

"It doesn't matter!" Spike shouted. "We didn't *kill* anybody, remember?"

"He's right," I said. "I'm just looking for the girl."

Spike continued, "When Doug found out about Margot and Jeremy, he became really pussy-whipped on Tanya. I'm thinking when I ripped off his wine and she realized she wasn't gonna get the big payoff, she probably dumped him."

Margot had shared some of his theory. I said to Jeremy, "You still screwing the woman you're screwing over?"

"I don't want to talk anymore."

"You're right. I don't need to know what your plans are for Margot or her wine—unless it has something to do with Tanya Maggio."

"It doesn't."

"You better hope not. Because if the cops stumble over some kind of racket while looking for a body, you're both in it up to your necks. I don't care who did the killing."

Jeremy got to his feet. "See? He's going to the cops!"

Spike deftly rolled a quarter back and forth over his knuckles. He looked at me then back to his knuckles.

"Jeremy, you are really annoying me," I said. "The police aren't paying me and I don't give a damn about rich people paying big bucks for fake wine."

"Fake wine?" Jeremy said, laughing. He almost looked happy. "Now you're definitely making stuff up. I'm not involved in anything—except what you know." He looked at Spike.

"Sorry, Jeremy," Spike said, "but you knew Margot's wine hadn't been verified as authentic."

"But I wasn't involved! I had nothing to do with it!"

I said, "It's not just about stealing expensive wine and selling it. It's also about selling fake wine back to the victim. Wine counterfeiting is a burgeoning industry. Right?"

Spike said, "Landau doesn't care that you knew where I was keeping the wine, and that you told me how to store it and that you would've gotten more money—"

"And I would've told you to go to hell! Even if I was only *suspected* of being involved in something like that, I would be ruined! All my years of training, all my accomplishments, worthless!" Jeremy sat shell-shocked on the other end of the couch. Spike continued rolling the quarter over his knuckles.

"You're going to cut Jeremy loose, right?" I said. "As long as he keeps his mouth shut? You're not going to pull some blood-in-blood-out crap as if you were a real Mafioso, right?"

Spike frowned. "I'm a businessman, not a terrorist."

"What about Daddy at corporate?"

Spike cocked his head. "What are you talking about?"

"I just spent two days in Irvington. All these bruises on my face? I barely escaped with my life. Don't pretend Cooper didn't warn you."

Spike gave me a long, hard look, then smiled. "Nope. That's not his style. He's into testing people, to see if they got what it takes. He'd let me deal with whatever came my way. No micro-managing. I gotta know—how did you figure it out?"

"An educated guess that you just confirmed. Lieutenant *Landon* Cooper. I have a feeling your first name is Landon, as in *Landon* Spike McFadden. But I won't tell anyone. You and Cooper both like desks of old wooden planks, and you both have this idea that corruption is cool as long as *innocents* don't get hurt. How sweet that your deadbeat father is now your mentor. Now tell me something. How did you find Margot as a mark?"

Spike rubbed his eyes with the heels of his hands. "Tanya told me."

31

Spike showed remarkable poise for a junior outlaw barely beyond a teenager. His cover having been effectively blown, he showed no panic or worry of consequences. Was his coolness a reflection of Cooper's backing or a sign of calculated intelligence?

"You have a wine tasting to prepare for, don't you?" I said to Jeremy.

He gave me a vacant look, stood, then left the room. Spike put his feet back on the desk.

I said, "So you're going to hang around and talk to me more?"

"If you want."

"What do *you* want?" I asked him.

"I want you to work for me one day."

"You think Jeremy's life would be worth two cents in Irvington knowing what you just told him? Knowing his state of mind?"

"All exaggerations. That whole thing about escaping with your life? C'mon."

"What do you know about Daddy, Spike? Just a nice guy who plays rough? You ever met Ahmet?"

"He's a goon, so what? But they don't clip people. Why would they?"

"Avoiding twenty years for fraud might get a few people clipped. When did Tanya tip you off on Margot's wine?"

"I don't know. Last Fall sometime."

"You worked at Doug's pub. Tanya shows up looking for a job. Hard to believe it was just a coincidence. I'm thinking maybe you had been in touch with Tanya. Did you know she was moving here?"

"I didn't know shit about her."

"Your daddy told me he only knew Tanya from a distance. And I suppose you didn't know anything about Eddie either."

"I grew up *here*, Landau, not that piss-pot Irvington. Cooper talked about Eddie and sometimes mentioned Tanya. I got to know Tanya after she arrived, but I never met Eddie."

This confused me. "Eddie never stopped by? Just to ask about Tanya?"

"Eddie Byrne's here, in Chicago?"

"You didn't know?"

"Why would I?"

"Because Cooper knows Eddie came here to find Tanya! Eddie *hired* me. That's the reason *I'm* here." Spike had no comment. I said, "I'm going to assume Daddy—"

"Stop the *daddy* shit or we're done talking."

"Sorry. Cooper knew Tanya at least well enough to direct her to where you worked. Didn't that make you think she had some kind of relationship with Cooper?"

Spike chewed on my words a bit. "Yeah, he told me she was coming. But all he said was that Tanya was Eddie's girlfriend. Eddie is Cooper's boy, you know. He probably knows all about your Irvington visit."

"Probably. But he paid me in advance, so I win no matter what. Why would Cooper lie about knowing Tanya?"

"You want me to call him and ask?" Spike took his cellphone off his belt and held it up as if threatening me.

"All of a sudden, you're a stupid kid. Great idea! Go ahead." Spike contemplated his next move. I don't think he liked me anymore. I said, "Why are you really talking to me? And don't say because you like me."

He returned the phone to his belt. "I like Tanya."

"So you knew her pretty well?"

"Eventually, I got to know her. I live in a big apartment Cooper rents. She moved in for a while."

"You had a thing for her?"

"Everyone did."

"What's Cooper hiding?"

Neither of us spoke until Spike said, "Let's get something straight about my old man and me."

"Please straighten me out."

"First of all, I don't work for *anybody*. Got it? This is about setting up my business. Making money. Yeah, he's helping me, but it's just an investment for him. I never had a dad. He told me he feels some responsibility. So he wants to help—help his guilty conscience probably. But what do I care? If he'll help me make it in business, I'll take it."

"You and Cooper are all about career, opportunity, networking—I get it. Now what about Tanya? You think she might have dumped Doug and then he lost it? Maybe choked her to death then dumped her body before splattering his torso all over the dash of that nice BMW when it hit the tree?"

Spike winced—a sign of weakness that wouldn't serve him well in the mob world. "I don't know. I can't see it—but I don't know."

"I bet Tanya stayed in touch with Cooper."

"She didn't talk to me about Cooper."

"How about you tell me why Tanya tipped you off on Margot being a good mark."

Spike's grin exuded unyielding admiration of a self-acknowledged shrewdness. "I was working for Doug and Margot when she inherited the wine. Doug had told Tanya he thought it might be worth some money. Tanya mentioned it to me, so I talked to Jeremy. When Jeremy told me its true value, I told Doug, but Doug acted like he already knew."

"But what brought Tanya to Chicago in the first place?"

"Who knows? She's not a dumb broad, that's for sure. We're all businessmen—"

"Cooper is a goddamn criminal. What did he say that prompted Tanya to leave New Jersey and dump Eddie in the process?"

"I don't fucking know! Why are you such a prick?"

"Dude, you gave it all away as soon as you admitted Tanya fingered Margot."

Spike cursed loudly then dropped his feet back to the floor. "I want to find out what happened to her. That's why I'm still sitting here instead of telling you to fuck off. But I gotta think of my future."

"You're afraid Cooper will cut you off if you start asking questions about Tanya?" Spike didn't answer. "Okay, I'll shut up. But your relationship with Doug Daley. How did you end up working for him?"

Spike stood, stretched his back, shoulders, neck, then plopped back down in his chair. "I always pictured a bar as a place that would be my hangout—for my crew, you know? Like they all have a place to chill, talk business. And I wanted to know how to run a business like that. I was already Doug and Margot's little helper. I liked this neighborhood and when Doug opened the bar, he hired me. I don't know why, I guess I bullshitted him pretty good, told him how I wanted to learn and all that crap people like to hear from guys my age."

"I have a hard time picturing you serving people."

"Yeah, well, Cooper gave me some money to help convince Doug to let me be like—his assistant. And he was okay with it and he kind of got off on knowing what I was up to, that I had connections to guys like Cooper and all that. I thought Doug's blood-and-guts magic tricks were cool. He was pretty good at it. We got to be friends. Then Tanya shows up." Spike leaned on his elbows, head resting in hands.

I said, "Did it seem strange she would suddenly leave New Jersey?"

Spike waited a few seconds. "Cooper said he wanted her to help me start my business. Doug got another little payout for hiring her. To be honest, I thought Cooper wanted her to spy on me and that pissed me off, but she turned out to be cool. I don't think she gave a shit about business. I think she was just happy to be out of Jersey."

"So you became good friends? More?"

"When I make a lot of money, I'll get babes like her. But I knew about Eddie, so I wasn't gonna mess with that. I just really liked Tanya. And she seemed comfortable around me. She never talked about Eddie. She got really nervous whenever I mentioned him. She didn't want to talk about Cooper neither. I knew she had secrets but I didn't care. Then Cooper called me, said he wanted to fly me out there to talk about some kind of new business opportunity."

"You met with Cooper who told you about making fake grape juice."

"Doug was pissed about Margot banging Jeremy. I told Doug we should heist Margot's wine. I'll even do the stealing, I told him."

"Of course you did. Did Doug go for your plan right away?"

"He wanted to think about it."

"Meanwhile, Doug had been hitting on Tanya."

Spike groaned. "Yeah. That was tough to watch."

"Doug and Tanya take off together."

"That pissed me off. I never saw her again. A few weeks later Doug calls me to talk more about the wine. Now he's really hot to steal it. I talk him into sending me the access card and password to the wine storage place."

"You think the wine is the only reason Tanya stayed with Doug?"

"I don't know. Didn't matter. I was still pissed he took off with her like that."

"And you taught him a lesson by getting Margot's wine and keeping it."

"Something like that."

"Remind me when the heist went down."

"January."

"And where have you been stashing Margot's *stolen* wine all this time? Or am I to believe you already sold it to some Gold Coast chump?"

"I'll keep that card facedown for now."

"Speaking of cards, you got a business card, businessman?" Spike handed me a card with "Secondhand Furniture Dealer" over his name and phone number. I laughed. "You'll go far in this business. But what was the plan? Where were you supposed to meet Doug after you stole his wife's wine?"

"I don't remember, somewhere in the city. But I told him Margot moved the wine somewhere else. He figured it out later that I screwed him over."

Something seemed off. When you run away with a lover, it's usually far away. Spike read my mind. "You think maybe he never went to New Mexico?"

"Yeah," I said, handing one of my cards to Spike. "Something like that."

32

Driving to my office, I thought of one more question that needed answering. Brenda picked up on the first ring. She sounded harried.

"I'm getting a large delivery," she said. "What's up?"

"Do you remember Doug ever asking you about the value of a Mouton vintage?"

Brenda laughed. "Oh, yeah, a 1945 vintage. I told him to forget about it, although he picked a good year. Costs hundreds of thousands just for one case. Why?"

"You helped me close a circle," I said and told her I would explain later.

The office door pushed into three days of bulk mail lying on the floor. I imagined a device automatically pushing the recycling box under the mail slot whenever I left the office.

With the footrest extended, I sat eating from a bag of Chilean grapes and pondered the state of my investigation. There was a disconnect between people I had assumed were inextricably connected. Apart from having Cooper and Tanya in common, Spike and Eddie had no obvious link to each other that included a connection to bogus wine and Tanya's whereabouts. Clearly, Cooper was juggling Tanya and the two junior gangsters, but to what end? Men dropped like flies around Tanya. Spike's concern for her well-being exposed a flaw in his hoodlum ambitions—cold-blooded bastards like Cooper had no humanity. Finding Tanya required exploiting this flaw. *Things that held their value.* I popped a few more grapes into my mouth, then reclined the backrest about ten degrees. Paintings. Precious stones. Fender guitars. Fermented grapes. I guessed valuing wine had to do with taste bud arrangement or something. My buds didn't know Mouton from Manischewitz. My cellphone vibrated with Kalijero's name. A bad taste from our last conversation still lingered. "Landau Investigations."

"Still in New Jersey?"

"Who's calling, please?"

"Let me guess. You're pouting. Is that it, Landau? Someone talks a little rough and you get hurt like a little boy?"

"I'm sensitive, so what?"

"Sensitive people don't belong in this business. That's so what."

"Well, I've been sensitive in this business for ten years including two solved—"

"Murder investigations. Good for you."

"What do you want, Jimmy?"

"You back in town?"

"Yes."

"That was quick."

"I can learn a lot in two days."

"You want to share what you learned?"

"All of a sudden you're interested?"

"I've always been interested. And I need the money."

"What money?"

"You forgot the deal we made a week ago? I'm your *consultant*."

"That's right. I forgot. You work for me. Why shouldn't I fire you for being an asshole?"

"Because I'm valuable. I was a cop—"

"For forty years. Of course."

Silence. "Well?"

"I stumbled across Cooper's operation. A high-tech still churning out phony wine and fake labels of legendary vintages to sell to rich folks."

"And Eddie's here to find rich suckers?"

"He's here to find Tanya."

"You still think that's the *only* reason he's here?"

"I'm not sure about wine scamming—Eddie told me he doesn't know anything about *stealing* wine. The thing is, Cooper's protégé is the kid he abandoned, Spike. And it was Spike's idea to boost Margot's wine and sell it back to her. He's the same kid who led me into the ambush down at the Oriental Theatre."

"You're saying Eddie and Spike *aren't* working together?"

"They've never met. They're only peripherally aware of each other."

Kalijero mulled this over. I pictured him staring into the distance, fiddling with his gold Parthenon pendant necklace. He said, "That Cooper is a crafty son of a bitch. A smart son of a bitch. Knows how to play all angles. And he's dangerous. Right?"

My turn to mull—particularly the duplicitous tone of Kalijero's *Right?*

"How would I know if he's dangerous?"

"You said you spent two days in Irvington."

"It's a dangerous town. I knew that before I left."

"Yeah, but you said Cooper runs this dangerous town—"

"You asked if I was back from New Jersey. That was bullshit. You knew I was back."

"Oh, did I? C'mon—"

"Goddamn it, Jimmy! We talked about this. You said you were looking into connections Cooper had in Chicago. I thought probably a cop or ex-cop. Don't play games with me. What do you know?"

"I know you disappeared then re-emerged with your face looking like ground beef. I didn't know this before but—"

"Who is it? Who's the contact?"

"I don't know names, only acknowledgment that there's a lot going on behind the scenes, Landau—"

"Tell me what you know—"

"Shut the fuck up and listen! My contact says the Feds are all over Cooper. And he also knows they don't give a shit about some smart-ass private investigator. They'll watch everything you do, take what they can use, then shrug when your bloody corpse shows up in the trunk of an abandoned vehicle."

I pressed the speaker button, laid the phone on the desk, then closed my eyes. I thought of Spike's disbelief that Cooper and his pals hurt people. Maybe a G-man could take him aside and straighten him out about that.

"Landau? You still there?"

"Why aren't the Feds working with Irvington or Newark police?"

Kalijero either cleared his throat or laughed. "Corruption too deep-rooted. Not worth taking on. Easier to nab him for interstate fraud."

"Capone got popped for tax evasion."

"Exactly. And you should assume Cooper told Eddie about your Irvington trip."

"Thanks, Detective. Can't wait to see how much you'll charge me for that brilliant piece of insight."

"Your sarcasm is bullshit."

"I can't help it."

"You ever thought about talking to someone?"

The question sounded extraterrestrial coming from Jimmy's mouth. "Have I thought about what?"

"Talking to someone."

"Talking about what?"

"About why you're so damn sarcastic! Sarcasm masks depression."

Suddenly, I'm having tea with the March Hare. "I've never been happier! Look in the mirror, Jimmy, and give advice to that weather-beaten puss."

"You know how damn reckless you are! You got a death wish, Landau. It's not normal."

"Normal people don't become private investigators. So what?"

Kalijero shouted, *"Vlaka!"* which I didn't take as a Greek compliment, and then the call dropped.

33

"Eddie can't come to the phone," said a woman's voice, flattening the letter "a" into authentic working-class drawl.

"Who is this answering Eddie's phone?"

"Gina."

"Okay, Gina, can you ask him to call Jules Landau right away?"

"Yeah, sure."

A woman answering Eddie's phone unsettled me. Scenarios of Eddie's relationships with women came to mind. Despite the evidence of Tanya bedding down with Doug and James, I had only pictured Eddie with Tanya, as if they belonged together through some grand cosmic plan. Call me a romantic. I recognized my prejudice. Frownie had warned me about emotional appeal. *Schmaltzy sentimentalism*, Frownie liked to say, *distorts your thinkin' and can get you dead*. Frownie knew best, but my gut told me the underlying motivation that put me on this case was a Jersey boy seeking reconciliation with his Jersey girl.

An hour later I called back. The same woman said, "I dunno when he's comin' back. He's over near the printers."

"The what?"

"He said somethin' about meetin' friends at the printers. They was gonna get dinner."

I hung up, thought a while about her babbling, then drove to South Dearborn Street, a neighborhood of enduring brick structures that once housed Chicago's printing industry but now provided lofts for an eclectic mix of professionals and artists. Persevering through the decades of change were restaurants and bars whose adherents boasted of eating or drinking at places called Blackie's or Louie's sometime in Chicago's storied past. And it was in one of those venerable eateries that I spotted Eddie sitting alone in a booth, a waitress having just set a plate of food before him. He positioned his hands around an enormous sandwich. When he lifted it off the plate, I slid into the opposite side of the booth and said, "How the hell are you?"

"Oh, hey," he said. He put the sandwich down without taking a bite. It looked like shredded pork.

I said, "How's it going?"

Eddie's half-smile looked forced. "Yeah, it's going okay. I mean, I was hopin' to hear from you. But I didn't wanna keep buggin' you or nothin'." He repositioned his hands around the sandwich and took a bite.

"Who's that chick answering your phone?"

Eddie grinned. "Nobody special."

"You let nobody special answer your phone?"

"I forgot to bring it with me. She answered it."

"You got a girlfriend now?"

He didn't want to talk about the girl. He didn't want to talk about anything. Even at our first meeting, he spoke only if someone twisted his arm.

"Last time we talked, you said you had nothing to do with stolen wine."

Eddie stopped chewing. "That's right. I don't know nothin' about that—or sellin' drugs."

"A kid named Spike set me up to get robbed of that wine-ransom money. You know him?"

Eddie looked at me then put the sandwich down and wiped his mouth. Then he took a long, slow sip of beer before wiping his mouth again. At that moment, I hated his guts. He said, "Why would I?"

"Go fuck yourself."

"Oh, c'mon, Mr. Landau. What was that for?"

"Cooper is Spike's mentor. And his biological father."

"I'm sorry. Okay, I've heard of him. What's the big deal?"

"You came here to find Tanya. What else did Cooper want you to do?"

"Nothin'."

"Cooper didn't expect you to get in touch with Spike? You weren't supposed to see how the fake wine business was coming along?"

"No."

I stared at Eddie, watched him carefully rearrange his hands around the sandwich. "Actually," I said, "it's possible you're telling the truth. Spike said he didn't even know you were in town. But that's what I don't get. Why would you *not* be in touch with Spike?"

Eddie's brows projected low over his eyes. He took an angry bite. His chewing accelerated like a piston, then stopped. After gulping down the mouthful of pork, he said, "What did Spike tell you?"

"Relax. He doesn't know where she is."

"How do you know he ain't lyin'?"

"Doesn't matter. Cooper must've told you Tanya worked with Spike at that bar."

"By the time I got here, it wasn't that bar no more."

I thought I was hearing things. "Cooper didn't know the bar went out of business?"

"I guess not."

"Spike wouldn't have told him? What bullshit. You sound like a fucking idiot. What's Cooper hanging over your head, Eddie?"

"Mr. Landau, you don't know anything. I mean, you don't get what's goin' on—"

"Really? Where have I been the last few days?"

"How would I know?"

"Irvington. I had a nice long meeting with Cooper. He's a good storyteller. A natural liar. A seasoned criminal. Since you're not curious where I got these bruises, I'll tell you. It's from getting the shit beat out of me by Cooper's pals. Isn't it kind of weird he didn't tell you I was snooping around your backyard? He knew you came here to find Tanya, but he didn't tell you she worked with Spike? You think Cooper really cares if you find her or not?"

Suddenly subdued, he said, "He wants me to find her."

"Why?"

Eddie pushed aside his plate of uneaten food then covered his eyes with his hands. His lips pursed as if struggling with horrible pain. Suddenly, I saw a pathetic little boy, unsure what to do.

"Eddie, you love this girl, don't you?"

His chin quivered. He bit down on his lower lip. I told him again that he loved Tanya. He began nodding slowly, then with more emphasis while keeping his eyes covered. He stayed this way for a full minute before lifting his head and wiping his eyes.

"Before I got out of jail," Eddie said, "Cooper came to visit. You're right. He was sendin' me to Chicago to get with Spike. He wanted me and Spike to put this wine scam together. Create a business. He told me Tanya went there too, to work with Spike at the bar."

"Why didn't Tanya tell you she was leaving?"

"She knew I'd freak out that she started workin' for a scumbag like Cooper."

"So you get out of jail and go see Cooper about making the move."

"He gave me a bunch of money. Then he told me the bar closed and Tanya had disappeared. But he still wanted me to meet with Spike and do the wine scam business."

"Why didn't you?"

"Once I got here, I told Cooper I can't do nothin' until I find Tanya. It's true. I can't concentrate on nothin' else. Sometimes, I think I'm goin' crazy."

"He knew how close you two were. He had to have known you were going to look for her, right?"

Eddie didn't respond, just stared into the abyss of the condemned.

"I'm going to guess Cooper gave you a bunch of cash before you left." Eddie nodded. "Holy shit, Eddie. You're *paying* me with Cooper's money! You think he's just gonna let you hang out in the Windy City with a load of his money?"

"I just gotta find Tanya."

I tried to get my head around Eddie's self-absorbed mindlessness. He knew guys like Cooper didn't become rich and powerful by tolerating such blatant insubordination.

"Maybe Cooper did something that prompted Tanya to leave town," I said. "Did you ever think of that?" He looked at me then away. Despite already knowing the answer, I asked, "Why the hell didn't you tell me all this from the start?"

"I ain't doin' you no favors tellin' you stuff you shouldn't know."

I shouldn't know? There was more he wasn't telling me—for my own good. What a sad sack. When I stood to leave, he said, "You're not gonna ditch me 'cause it's Cooper's money, are you, Mr. Landau?"

"No, Eddie, I'm not gonna ditch you. To be perfectly honest, I kinda like the idea of Cooper's hard-earned swag providing my staff of life." And it was true.

34

I lay on the couch, right arm draped over my eyes, Punim curled on my stomach. At times, ideas surfaced when I stopped trying so hard, just hung out in the alpha waves or something. How would Amy describe my disposition? *Rummaging through themes of the investigation's consciousness,* perhaps. Look at the periphery. Who were these people? Spike the gangster, the businessman. Doug the pub owner, wine connoisseur. What did others see? Doug the clown, the loser. Doug the magician.

I sat up quickly. Punim's claws dug in as she leapt off, scratching thin lines of blood on my torso. I reached for the phone shouting cat-directed obscenities.

"Johnny Bail Bonds."

"Jules for Johnny."

"Hold, please." Irish tin whistle music, then, "Hey! You okay?"

"Cops nowadays got all kinds of databases. And I bet Sheila knows how to use them."

Laughter. "She just might."

"New Mexico vital records. Someone named Doug Daley killed in a car wreck. Find out whatever you can."

The darkened bay windows and flaking paint gave a Victorian spookiness to Margot's apartment. As I stood staring from the end of the block, it occurred to me I had never seen Margot outside her home.

The post-dinner crowd occupied every table at *Pâtisserie Grenouille.* Margot sat alone, reading a hardcover book. Without lifting her head, she used a fork to cut off a bite of pastry and bring it slowly to her mouth. Brenda fluttered among her patrons, never losing her smile. I wondered if Margot had apologized to Brenda or if they both feigned ignorance of a strained friendship.

I meandered around the area, staying within eyesight of the Pâtisserie's window. Across the street at the *Auvergnat Vin Bar,* dapper North Siders learned how unoaked vessels differed from stainless steel as they swirled and sniffed Bordeaux reds and Alsace whites. Would they know the real thing from a fake? I leaned against a haloed streetlight. Despite the banality, the Hollywood imprinting of my youth provoked a trench-coated image with fedora and cigarette. I then saw a ten-year-old staying up late to watch an old movie with his father. On the television, usually an urban black-and-white world of detectives, spies, or gangsters in the thirties and forties, both decades well within Dad's living memory. The din from *Pâtisserie Grenouille* broke the spell as Margot walked out.

I kept a full block between us then ducked around the corner when she reached the door to her apartment. A minute later, I re-emerged to see Margot staring at me down the sidewalk. "You gonna stand there all night or do you want to come in?"

Professional investigator or amateur sleuth—a perception easily blurred. When I approached, Margot said, "Next time stand in the shadows and not under a streetlight."

"You're assuming I didn't want to be seen."

She walked past me to the stairs rolling her eyes. Once inside, Margot flicked a switch that illuminated several lamps, transforming the apartment into her mustard-yellow refuge. Then she assumed her customary position on the chaise longue and stared out the bay window. I remained standing.

"Two visits in ten hours. I should be flattered."

"I'd like to see the newspaper article—about Doug's car crash."

"You know where it is."

I walked to the writing desk, opened the small drawer, noticed the .38 revolver, then reread the article. Margot watched my reflection in the window. I put the article back in the drawer then sat on the love seat.

Margot said, "Christ! So say something already."

"The article isn't dated."

"It was in February."

"Just a couple of months after he disappeared with Tanya."

"Yes."

"Do you have a death certificate or a coroner's report?"

Margot sat up for a moment, glanced at me, then fell back. "Did you see the car? I don't think an autopsy was necessary."

"I'm just curious about the date on the death certificate."

"What's with you and dates? Why don't you just say whatever the hell it is you're implying?"

I stared at Margot's profile. "Was it last fall that Doug found out about you and Jeremy?"

"I guess. I don't know for sure."

"Later in the year—around Thanksgiving—Doug hits the road with Tanya."

Margot closed her eyes. "Sure, whatever."

"But he stayed in touch with Spike. Together they decide to rip off your wine."

"It was Doug's idea, I'm sure. He talked Spike into it."

"This morning I wagered a case of Lafite the security cameras showed Doug or Spike liberating your ten cases of Mouton from a high-tech storage facility like The Vintner's Treasure. Over two million dollars, walking out the door. Did you ever bother to look at the surveillance tape?"

"I don't—I don't care anymore."

"You think you can just *not care anymore* and suddenly everyone leaves you alone? You're now free to lay on your chaise staring out the window, watching the seconds of your life tick away? Is that it?"

Margot swung her legs off the chaise and sat facing me. "And why the hell do you care so much?"

"Admit it. Doug never went to New Mexico with Tanya, they were here the whole time."

"How much to get you to leave me alone? Tell me how much, damn it!"

"Not gonna happen, Margot. Now that you've been cornered by the truth, you want to buy your way back to fantasyland."

Her neck flushed first before spreading to her face and ears. She stood, walked to the kitchen, began opening and closing cabinets until she found a long-stemmed glass. From another cabinet she took a bottle, filled the glass with red wine, then sat at a small round table in the kitchen. She sipped, looking deep in thought, as if I had taken money and left as she suggested, problem solved.

"You didn't answer my question," she said. "Why do you care?"

"I don't give a shit about your wine. It's finding Tanya I care about."

Margot laughed. "You've spent all this time making things so complicated when I told you from day one Tanya is dead."

"But from day one you've been lying to me. And you've refused to say how you know she's dead."

Margot took a large gulp. "I don't even like the expensive stuff," she said. "Just give me a nice pinot noir, and I'm happy." She refilled the glass. "You really want to know why I'm so sure Tanya is dead?" I didn't respond. Margot took another healthy gulp. "Because I killed her."

35

I waited for the punch line but Margot offered only a catatonic gaze at an empty wine glass. The implication of her confession permeated all previous thoughts, prompting a hard reboot.

Finally, I said, "Uh, you mind expanding on this theme?"

Margot glanced at me, looking bored. "A few weeks after Doug ran off with Tanya—about mid December—they came over, ostensibly to try to keep things amicable. Of course, that was a lie. He wanted to talk about the wine. He claimed I purposely kept the wine's value a secret. He reminded me that legally, we were still married. He started threatening lawsuits and claimed he could prove I was having an affair before I got the wine and god knows what else."

I waited. "Then what?"

"We argued. I killed her with that gun you undoubtedly saw in the drawer."

"And why would you leave the murder weapon in the drawer instead of throwing it in Lake Michigan?"

"Because I don't know how long I can live with knowing I took someone's life. In the meantime, if someone wants to investigate, here I am. Anyway, you have your answer. Tell your client to stop wasting his time looking for Tanya."

"Do you really think I'm gonna walk out of here without knowing the circumstances of you *killing* her?"

"What difference does it make? She's dead. Call the cops if you want."

"Where's the body?"

"I don't know."

"I should call the cops and tell them there's no body and nobody has reported her missing. You're a real nut job. I don't believe a word you said."

"They wouldn't leave it! They kept pushing me! That little bitch kept saying how they were going to take everything in the courts if I didn't give them half of the wine. Who the hell was she? That little street tramp coming to my house, thinking she's so smart and clever, like she had something on me."

"So you let Tanya push enough buttons to provoke you to shoot her?"

My comment pushed a button of its own. Margot shouted, "What do you know? You're so smug with your detective pomp! So cool, so full of yourself. They pushed me! I was scared. Doug trained her, told her all the things to say—very *personal* things! Tanya pranced around acting like she owned the place, like she owned me. And you know what was weird? I saw right through her. I knew it was all an act, that she was really a sweet girl Doug had convinced to go along with his scam. It was Doug talking through her. When I pulled the trigger, I was shooting Doug."

"So you lost it. You took the gun out of that drawer and shot her."

Margot stood, then walked back to the longue. I followed her and took my place on the love seat. She said, "You're having a hard time thinking me capable of such violence." I didn't answer but it was true. "I'm surprised an experienced detective like you isn't more cynical about such matters. You know, *the dark side* all people harbor."

"I'm plenty cynical, but I'm not the grizzled, disillusioned veteran just yet. Don't worry, I'll get there."

"Do you have dark secrets, Jules? Things you've done that you would never want anyone to know about? Things that would ruin your reputation?"

"My reputation isn't worth ruining. You want to tell me the dark secret that made you a murderer?"

Margot didn't answer.

"Okay, so you shot Tanya, then what? How did Doug react?"

"He screamed, took her into his arms. I fell to the floor and curled up in a ball, begged for it to all be a dream. At some point, I crawled to Doug, begged him to forgive me. I told him to take the wine, take anything, just don't tell . . . He didn't say anything. Just held her. There was blood . . ."

Margot pulled her knees to her chest, wrapped her arms around her legs. "I don't know how much time passed. I lay on the floor and just kind of surrendered to whatever was going to happen next. I'd never felt that way before. Without saying anything, Doug got to his feet and started opening closet doors. I walked over to him and asked what he was doing. 'I need blankets,' he said. Tears dripped off his face. He really loved her."

"So Doug wrapped her up and carried her away?"

"I helped him put her in his car. After that, I don't know where he took her. I don't want to know. A few days later, he calls. Says he wants the wine. I gave him an access card and password—"

"Spike had volunteered do the stealing, but you didn't know anything about Spike being involved, did you? You really didn't know Spike decided to keep the wine for himself."

"Doug didn't realized it right away either. He called me, angry saying I changed my mind about giving him the wine and accused me of hiding it somewhere."

Johnny Bonds called me back to verify what I already knew—nobody named "Doug Daley" had died in a car crash last February in New Mexico.

"Your own husband started blackmailing you," I said. "Get his wine back or else. Someone called to set up an exchange of wine for ransom. It didn't occurr to you Spike was behind it?" Margot didn't respond. "I guess you weren't cynical enough. You didn't see *the dark side* Spike harbored. Where's Doug hiding now?"

"I don't know. At first, he called periodically to threaten me. I guess when he figured out Spike betrayed him, he stopped all communication."

"What if you called him to set up a meeting?"

"He doesn't answer the phone. He's the only one who knows where Tanya's body is and he wants to keep it that way. So what's next for you? Collect the rest of your money and on to the next case?"

"Nothing's changed, Margot. I'm still looking for Tanya."

"But I told you—"

"Nobody's dead if there isn't a body. And if I want to find Tanya's body, I need to find Doug."

Margot looked as if she might vomit. "Why don't you just turn me in to the police and get it over with?"

"Why would I do that, Margot?"

"Because I killed somebody."

"You've got it backward. Are there witnesses to the shooting? The fact Doug knows where to find Tanya's body condemns him, not you."

"But you know the truth. Could you live with yourself knowing you let a murderer get away?"

"The only truth I need is confirmation of Tanya's death. Everything else is only so much talk."

36

Lying on my back, staring out my bedroom window, watching a curtain of mist hover a few feet above the buildings. I sat up. Wall-to-wall clouds, forty-something degrees. Springtime in Chicago.

Margot settling her neck over the chopping block exhibited naiveté. People got away with murder all the time. Doug guaranteed deflecting murder charges away from Margot when he carted off Tanya's body. But Margot believed in Truth—a potential prison in itself for those wanting to live in a just universe. The puzzling part was not Margot shooting Tanya, but Doug so readily taking care of the body. Through Doug's shock and grief, his thoughts turned to blackmail? I fed the hungry cat then grabbed the phone.

"If you wanted to find Doug," I said to Spike, "where would you look?"

"A graveyard."

"Pretend he's alive."

"I'd pretend not to care."

"You should care. He's got info on you."

"Bullshit. He's got nothing."

"How about that fortune of stolen wine, dumbass?"

"He knows I'm connected. He won't touch me."

"Are you a businessman or *Cosa Nostra*?"

"It's perception that matters, Landau. The way you carry yourself. You know that. What about Tanya? If Doug's alive, does that mean Tanya's alive?"

"I need to find Doug in order to find Tanya. Are you getting it now, Professor?"

Spike sighed through his nose. "So what do you want?"

"I'm not sure. Just tell me more about him. Anything."

"What makes you think he's still in Chicago?"

"Because that's where the double-crossing son of a bitch with his stolen wine is."

"You think he's laying low, making a plan?"

"With millions of dollars' worth of wine at stake, wouldn't you?"

"So what's he waiting for?"

"It doesn't matter. Since you know where the wine is, I would suggest embracing the following scenario: one way or another, you will be contacted and asked questions. It may get uncomfortable."

Spike laughed. "You think I should be afraid of Doug Daley? He doesn't have the stomach."

"A couple of million bucks can change a person. Why not consult with Cooper?"

"Because I don't need Cooper."

"Of course. Asking for help would show weakness. Then take the initiative and call out Doug. Make him an offer."

Another laugh. "I'm supposed to pay off Doug when I've got what he wants? Only a pussy would do that."

"Compromise! It happens all the time in business."

"Only losers compromise."

My turn to laugh. "Do I gotta teach you to be a gangster? It's about *perception*, remember. Make him an offer *appearing* to want compromise. Then after you get him in your sights, you get *physical* with him until he agrees to take both of us to Tanya."

I didn't know what pained Spike more, agreeing with my plan or the idea of twisting someone's arm. "I'll think about it," Spike said.

"What's there to think about? You want to find Tanya or not?"

"Yeah, yeah, yeah, but—"

"You disappoint me, Spike. Get the word out! Isn't that how the system works? Let the street know you want to make things right with Doug. It'll get back to him. You pull this off, Cooper will be impressed, that's for sure. You'll be on your way."

Spike's ambivalent grunt almost provoked more career-path advice from me. But people can change. Who was I to discourage a young criminal's dream?

The last time I spoke to Kalijero, he'd insulted me in Greek and hung up. He owed me an apology.

"Jimmy, it's time for you to show me the value of your forty years of cop work."

"I don't have to show you anything."

"Yesterday you were so concerned about my well-being. I was really touched. Today, I'm nothing but a cheap whore."

"A cheap whore has more sense than you."

"Okay, that's settled. But you need to help me get some info out on the street."

"I need to?"

When will I learn? "I'm *asking* you. Think of it as more billable hours. You said you needed the money."

"Use your contacts, Landau. That's what private investigators do."

"Exactly! I'm using you and your forty valuable years of cop contacts. You're the best bang for my buck."

Kalijero had no retort for an idea so brazenly well-reasoned. "Okay, Landau. What's the word you want on the street?"

Kalijero's sarcasm was unmistakable and stung my confidence. "First a little background: Margot Daley said her husband is still alive. Margot said she shot Tanya dead in front of him and Doug carted her off—"

"You believe this?"

"Not until I see a body. But here's the message: Spike wants to make things right with Doug. Split the wine fifty-fifty. Meet him at—at *Pâtisserie Grenouille*. Have him call you or one of your contacts to set the day and time."

"How about Sunday, high noon?"

"Fuck you, Jimmy. We're talking over a million bucks' worth of wine."

"Bullshit."

"Doug gets five cases of Mouton Rothschild. Do a little research if you think it's bull."

Kalijero paused, then said, "Okay, I'll try to get the word out. Just don't be surprised if Doug doesn't get the memo."

37

Despite the temperature, I cracked the window and sat listening to the din of Halsted. The neighborhood appeared dull and washed out under the clouds. The traffic sounded muffled too, as if the city's volume had been turned down. Even the pedestrians appeared to walk with a heaviness in their stride.

Eddie answered on the second ring. I said, "Where are you? We need to talk."

After much throat clearing, Eddie responded quietly with, "What happened?"

"Don't worry, dude. Nothing big. Just want to give you some info—but not on the phone. Maybe I'm paranoid."

Eddie gave me a Lakeview address about a mile from my apartment. "No kidding? You get tired of roaches and syringes?" Eddie didn't respond. I said I'd be over in a few minutes. He hung up without saying goodbye. Bad manners, like his dad.

The address was a two-story graystone on a quiet tree-lined avenue, as virtually removed from the South Jackson Street crud as one could get without living in suburbia. Eddie sat on the top step

260

of the front stoop, playing a game on his phone. I sat on the next lowest step.

"Nice place," I said.

"Gina's dad owns it," he mumbled, still focused on the game.

"Good investment."

"He grew up in this house. Kept it in the family."

Eddie continued playing until he said, "Damn it!" then put the phone down.

"Doug Daley isn't dead," I said.

His face lit up. I didn't recognize him. "Then Tanya's probably alive?"

"I don't know. Spike stole a lot of pricey wine from Doug. Now we're trying to lure Doug someplace, to talk with Spike about splitting the wine. I thought you could use some of your contacts to get the word out that Spike wants to make things right. But he's going to have to tell us where Tanya is if he wants the wine."

"I don't got no contacts. Not here."

"Ask Cooper."

Angry Eddie said, "Ask him what?"

"Tell him you're helping Spike dump some pricey wine on a rich chump named Doug Daley. You want to get the word out, and set up a meeting. Cooper will think you're following through on the reason he sent you here."

Eddie snapped at me. "It's not like you make a call and everything just happens! It's not some stupid movie."

"Tell Cooper that Doug knows where Tanya is. He wants you to find Tanya, right?"

Eddie straightened up. His face relaxed a bit. "Yeah," he said. "That might work."

Neither of us spoke. Across the street, a young couple packed their Volvo with luggage. On the porch, two small kids wearing blue hooded sweatshirts with Cubs logos laughed while jumping up and down.

"It's coming to an end, Eddie," I said. "We're getting closer to the truth."

I thought I heard the slightest chuckle. "Yeah," he said. "I know."

An abstract grayscale mix of shapes reflected off the windshield of the gray sedan parked across from my apartment. The four concentric circles on the grille held no special significance until the driver's side window lowered. We stared at each other. I extended my arms, holding my palms up with a bewildering look. Amy smiled weakly, then stepped out of the car. We had spoken on my return from Irvington, but watching her cross the street in tight stretch slacks and a black cable-knit sweater temporarily eclipsed all memory of why she approached.

"Ooh. Your face is still a mess," Amy said.

It took a moment, but I remembered what she meant. I considered suggesting we go upstairs, but something about her posture discouraged me. "You look like you want to tell me something."

Amy sat on the second stair of the building's stoop. I sat next to her, but not presumptuously close. She said, "I was thinking about our conversation the other day. Maybe it would be best to confront Margot Daley directly about the wine counterfeiting and how it relates to Tanya's whereabouts. You know, get right to the point."

"Fake wine is irrelevant to Margot."

"Oh, yeah? Why do you say that?" Something about her words sounded staged.

"Margot's wine was stolen—an inside job, it turns out—but she doesn't know about the wine counterfeiting. Figuring out why Tanya left her old New Jersey home in the first place will tell us a lot."

"Margot was betrayed by someone who conspired with her husband?"

"A kid named Spike who then betrayed Doug and kept the loot."

"Margot still insists Doug killed Tanya?"

"She's an unreliable narrator. Nobody is dead until we find a body."

Amy leaned back, as if to take a good look at me. "You seem kind of uptight. "

I leaned back, intentionally imitating Amy, as if to take her all in. "Why are you always showing up suddenly? Why don't you just call me?"

"Because I prefer talking face-to-face. I was going to give you five more minutes before driving off. I was just about to leave after I finished reading the paper."

"Why do you need to *see* me? Am I special?"

"Just tell me to get lost if that's what you want! What are you afraid of?"

She had a point, but even tough guys like me needed their secrets. "Margot admitted Doug's not dead," I told her.

Amy looked like she wanted to yell at me again. Instead, she nodded her head a few times then said, "He orchestrated his own death in a phony car crash. Interesting. Did she concede anything else?"

Her choice of the word "concede" struck me. "Like what?"

"Oh, c'mon! Something about Tanya?"

"She didn't tell me what Doug did with the body. Which is why we have to find Doug."

"Maybe I can help—"

"That's right! You said you have a friend in law enforcement, the one who told you where Margot lived."

"You think I'm lying."

"I think you followed me to Margot's house."

Amy laughed. "What else have I lied about?"

"Not knowing Tanya Maggio had a boyfriend who hired me."

More laughter, only more intense. "Anything else?"

"Give me time. I'll think of something."

Joining in her third spasm of laughter had not been my intention, but the genuineness of her amusement captured me. Amy said, "What about Spike, the guy who stabbed Margot in the back? Is he involved in counterfeiting wine?"

"Excellent investigatory work."

"You could've told me this."

"It's more fun to watch you figure it out."

Why did Amy put up with me? I wanted to think she hoped to be my girlfriend one day, but I also wanted to think I would one day play third base for the Cubs. Maybe she was just a rich, pretty psychic who would come around every now and then to try her hand at private investigating.

Amy said, "So you want my help finding Doug or not?"

"Something tells me my answer is irrelevant to your actions."

Amy's expression became trance-like. No doubt wheels spun, cogs meshed, levers pivoted, but I had no idea what it all sounded like inside her noggin. She said, "I think you're right. Tanya was running away from someone. Maybe your client."

"I didn't say that."

"You implied it."

"Eddie Byrne still had several months to do in prison when Tanya hit the road."

"Anyone else in Irvington worth running away from?"

"You ever been to Irvington? I wanted to run away as soon as the plane landed."

"How would Doug Daley benefit by pretending to be dead?"

I played along. "What better hiding place than a grave?"

"But hiding from what? Spike has the stolen property." Amy's features broadcasted a catalogue of coded emotions.

"What?" I said probably louder than I should have. "Just say what you're thinking."

"It seems odd you didn't ask Margot why she went along with this charade."

I didn't want to tell her about Margot's murder confession. "Until we find Tanya, everything else is a waste of time. You psychics are all alike. You know I'm not telling you everything but you won't come out and say it. How about we focus on finding Doug and then we can discuss all the things I'm not telling you?"

Without waiting for a reaction, I stood then walked up the stairs. Once inside my apartment, I lay on the couch and ransacked my brain, trying to figure out how Amy knew Doug supposedly died in a car crash.

38

My head ached with unorganized data. Keep it simple. Tanya's relationship with Cooper was probably the key. No doubt, a slime bucket like Cooper tried getting into her pants. That alone would be worth running away from New Jersey. Her decision to tell Spike Margot's wine might be valuable, was probably meant to enrich herself and Doug while letting Spike do the dirty work.

A few hours earlier, Kalijero had said he would get the word out. On the street, news traveled at the speed of sound, a perception based purely on Hollywood portrayals. Kalijero's forty years of contacts plus a sprinkling of Amy's psychic dust, inspired my vision of an illicit whisper campaign covering the city like summertime ozone. When a few more hours passed with no call, Kalijero's sarcastic "Okay, Landau" played repeatedly until I could stand it no longer.

Kalijero answered the phone saying, "You're still such an amateur, Landau."

"Well?"

"Yes, son, I got the message out. But this could take time. Or maybe it won't work. You're betting

267

Doug Daley is connected to the street like a career hoodlum. Only you know why this could be true."

"Doug's connected to the dark side through Spike whether he knows it or not. With millions at stake, it seems like word has to get back to him. And what about that Chicago cop connection Cooper has to help him expand business?"

"What? I never said it was a cop."

"You were looking into the possibility."

"There are a lot of possibilities in this case and none of them give a damn about you."

"Care to explain what you mean—a little bit?"

"You know what I'm talking about! Lots of groups want to see Cooper in prison. You're not in one of those groups. You're on your own, getting paid by one of Cooper's lackeys. When I say you're on your own, I mean it. To the good guys, you're just a clown walking into a hornets' nest. If you get stung to death, it's your own damn fault. But they'll thank you for leading them to the nest."

"A few days ago you said you felt a little responsibility for me since Frownie died. Later you suggested therapy for my recklessness. Suddenly, you no longer feel the love. If I die you don't get paid, you know."

Ten seconds of angry mumbling in Greek. "Even if I wanted to watch your back, I don't have enough details. I'd find out about you in the morning paper."

"Just promise to come down and identify my corpse."

"I'll bring the flowers to your funeral since no one else will be there. Go take your cat for a walk."

Kalijero hung up. Punim slept peacefully on the window hammock.

Perhaps Brenda fell in love with Doug Daley gradually, over a period of time, enough time to allow the obscure chemical reactions to open her heart to another's subtleties. On the way to *Pâtisserie Grenouille,* I stopped at an animal shelter called Furry BFF, to get a packet of information. At the Pâtisserie, the light-lunch surge had already peaked. The old, white-bearded Blackstone sat at his usual table. I grabbed a two-top that Jennie had just cleaned, then took the packet out of the folder. "Congratulations!" the introductory page began. "You're taking the first step in establishing an enforceable compact to provide a legally sanctioned arrangement for the care and sustenance of your pet should you die or become disabled. . . ."

Brenda interrupted my thoughts. "Hi," she said then set down a tall, caramelized pastry with custard oozing out the bottom. She took two forks from her apron pocket then sat. "You look serious," she said.

"I'm setting up a trust for my cat."

Had I not spoken with a straight face, Brenda might have simply giggled instead of screeching with laughter. In response, I could only muster a sympathetic grin which proved the antidote to Brenda's glee.

"Oh. I'm sorry—"

"It's fine. I suddenly realize how funny that must've sounded."

"Well—I don't know. If you love your pets, you want to make sure—hey, is something wrong? Besides your bruises needing to heal?"

"I'm fine."

"Hey! I just remembered something. Tanya wanted to organize a catch and release, spay and neuter program to help control the feral cat population. We both loved cats. That was another reason I liked her."

"That's another reason I hope we find her in good health."

She pushed a fork across the table and said, "Eat." I cut out a gooey chunk. Brenda eyed me suspiciously. "Too rich?"

"Why do you say that?"

"By how long it's taking you to swallow."

"I have an unsophisticated palate."

"You never told me how you got those bruises."

"I'm hiding something underneath them."

Brenda frowned. "You wanna wear that *canelé* home with you?"

"I got roughed up a few days ago."

Brenda closed her eyes and sighed. "What about that circle I helped you close? When you asked about Mouton Rothschild?"

"Oh, yeah. Well, you verified that Doug knew the value of Margot's stolen wine."

Brenda assumed an exaggerated slack-jaw. "Margot had Mouton Rothschild *in her collection?*"

"Ten cases. 1945."

Brenda sat up and leaned back in her chair. Her eyes glazed over. "I can't believe it. And Doug stole it? And Spike helped him? And—Doug is dead, so where's the wine?"

"Brace yourself. Margot says Doug's not dead. Spike has the wine." Several days ago Brenda learned the man she loved was a murder-suicide suspect, today she found out he's not dead. I watched her digest the information through a series of beastly expressions. "I'm sorry," I said. "This must seem like a nasty joke."

"That girl! Tanya. You don't care about the wine, you want to find Tanya. She might be alive too?"

Brenda not dwelling on Doug pleased me. "I need a meeting with Spike and Doug. Doug gets his share of wine, I get Tanya. Where do you think a dead man like Doug would spend his days while trying to get his wine back?"

Brenda's face reflected the strangeness of the question. "I'm not sure I really knew him *that* well.

And you're not telling me *why* Doug and Margot want the world to think he's dead."

"Brenda, do me a favor and trust that everything will be revealed to you. But for now, try to be a little psychic. Pretend you're Doug. You're owed millions and you're not going anywhere until you get it. Where would you hang out?"

Brenda considered my request. "He was the calculating type. He would've had everything planned out. And I don't think he's one to hide somewhere. He needed to be around people."

"Maybe he's hiding in plain sight?"

Brenda studied me. "Yeah. You may be right. Maybe Tanya is hiding with him?"

Mentioning Margot's murder confession seemed pointless. "Maybe," I said. "But someone could recognize him."

"Who's looking for him besides you?"

She had a point. The cops were not involved.

"I have contacts trying to arrange a meeting between Spike and Doug here at the Pâtisserie. I hope you don't mind."

Brenda touched my hand. "Nah. That's okay. The more I learn about the guy, the less I like him."

39

The implication of the man keeping pace in my periphery escaped me until I reached for the car door and a hand gently but firmly took my wrist. I flinched, braced myself, then turned to see round tortoiseshell eyeglasses on a brown face.

"Hello, Landau," Sergeant Blake said.

Three days ago, that same face had a view of my battered body lying on a cot as he casually discussed business.

"What a pleasant surprise," I said. "Ahmet's knee safely on the mend, I hope?"

Sergeant Blake didn't respond but maintained a benign hold of my wrist. "Let's talk a bit."

"Let me guess. You're here to tell me to stop picking on three-hundred-pound Turkish wrestlers?"

The sound of air violently exiting Sergeant Blake's nostrils accompanied the twisting of my arm to the threshold of dislocation. "I give you credit for still being alive," Sergeant Blake said into my ear, still maintaining his soft-spoken tone. "When I walked out of that room, I assumed Ahmet would've snapped your neck like a chicken bone. As easy as separating your arm from your shoulder. But I'm glad you made it out alive. Wanna know why?"

"Because you like me?"

"Because we're both looking for Tanya. However, I did tell Ahmet I would bring him your head in a bag. So your chance to disappoint Ahmet depends on your cooperation finding Tanya."

I grunted an affirmation. He let up on the torque. I said, "Maybe if you tell me why—"

A slight turn of the wrist dropped me to the ground. "You like walking that fine line, don't you, Landau? Detached arm. Attached arm. Disconnected neck. Connected neck. Don't worry about why. Worry about *me*. Any information you get on Tanya's whereabouts, you tell me. Say, 'Yes, Sergeant Blake. I understand.'"

I said the magic words. Sergeant Blake released me, threw one of his business cards down, and said, "Sometimes it takes a little pain for guys like you to understand the greater good at play. Live to fight another day, and be thankful."

"Do you really think I'm going to call you?"

"Damn, Landau! Can't you trust me on this? I could've broken your bones and left you here to squirm. But I didn't!"

From my knees, I laughed. "I should *trust* you! Okay, I see the logic. Thanks, Sarge."

Sergeant Blake stared at me while he adjusted his glasses. "Okay," he said, then walked away.

My shoulder ached. From my car, I watched Sergeant Blake walk casually down the street next to the parked cars lining the curb. He stopped at an older sedan and placed his hands on his hips. Then he spent a minute examining the front and rear fenders' proximity to the adjacent cars. He fished a key out of his pocket, opened the door, then, after numerous back-and-forth maneuvers, freed the car.

The elevated status of my 1983 Honda Civic to a more conspicuous retro-cool could prove problematic when trying to remain undetected. I tried staying at least thirty yards behind Sergeant Blake as he drove east on Webster. At Lincoln he turned north. Busy Lincoln Avenue worked to my advantage. The street was fairly wide and getting a car or two between us required little effort. Once past Diversey, it occurred to me who might be the target of Sergeant Blake's next visit. The closer we got to Lakeview, the more I wondered. I took the phone off my belt.

"Who knows you're living at Gina's house?" I said to Eddie.

"I don't know. Nobody. Why?"

"Sergeant Blake just paid me a visit. I'm following him up Lincoln. We're almost at Belmont. If he turns on Addison, you should expect a visitor. Anything you want to tell me?"

"I don't care. He's just one of Cooper's bitches."

"We're through Roscoe, approaching Cornelia. He wants to find Tanya pretty damn bad."

"He wants to scare her, so she'll go back to New Jersey. And he's here to check up on me."

"Just scare her? Or do something worse because she knows too much?" Eddie didn't respond. "Approaching Addison," I said. "No turn signal. We're going through. Talk later."

As we continued northbound, it dawned on me that I didn't know what Cooper thought of Spike's million dollar wine scam or even if Cooper was aware of his protégé's newly acquired assets. Cooper would be quite angry if Spike did not plan to share the spoils with his mentor-daddy.

I called Spike. "Cooper knows about your big score, right?"

"Huh? He knows I'm in the game."

"Does he know you ripped off a fortune of wine?"

"Why should he? It's my business—"

"Blood is untouchable. Is that it? Daddy feels guilty for abandoning you? He won't care if you go rogue? If you really think Cooper won't expect a piece of that action, you're a fool who won't last long in this *game*."

Spike's laugh, sounded forced. "What do you want, Landau?"

"Sergeant Blake's in town. And he's not in a good mood. I'm following him northbound on Lincoln. We're almost at Argyle. Any chance we're headed in your direction?"

Silence. "So Sergeant Blake is in town. I was in that area—"

"He just pulled over. He's calling someone. Or maybe he's answering the phone."

"What block are you in?" Spike said.

I looked around but couldn't see a number. "I don't know."

"Is there a building at the corner with a red awning?"

"Yes."

"Yeah, I guess he might be looking for me. I was just there."

"Where are you now?"

"Jeremy's office at the Vin Bar."

"Stay there!"

Front wheels spitting gravel, I pulled a tight U-turn. Four-cylinder Honda versus eight-cylinder sedan. Did Sergeant Blake realize how far west we had angled on Lincoln? I cut over to Western and headed south to Clybourn, which slanted directly to Brenda's Pâtisserie. I parked across the street from the Auvergnat Vin Bar, arriving with time to spare, thanks to my masterful navigation.

Since the tables had not been set up with bottles, glasses, and menus, I assumed a tasting had not been planned for that evening, although Jeremy stood at the bar, flawlessly attired in black apron, black jacket, gold stickpin of grapes, and silver saucer hanging around his neck. He was preoccupied with a piece of paper he held in one hand while staring at the wine racks behind the bar. I absconded to his office where Spike sat behind the desk in a steno chair, feet up, looking cocky as ever. A quick appraisal of the room deflated my spirits. "No closet?"

Spike dropped his feet to the floor. "Just throw your jacket on the couch."

"I'm looking for a place to hide. I want to hear what Sergeant Blake has to say when he shows up."

"I'll tell you what he says."

The desk's modesty panel reached almost to the floor. "Don't take this personally," I said as I pushed Spike backward in his chair. "But I don't really trust you." I crawled under the desk and sat, hugging my knees against my chest.

Spike stared at me. "What the hell is wrong with you?"

"I'm surprised Jeremy still lets you hang around."

Spike chuckled and rolled the chair closer to the desk. "You should've figured out by now that I own a stake in this place."

"You or Cooper?"

"Doesn't matter. Jeremy can't stand me. But then he thought about it a while—"

"And visions of dollar signs on Mouton Rothschild bottles started dancing in his head."

"Remember, he knows where the wine is," said Spike.

I let go of my legs to see if they could rest comfortably on their own. They couldn't. "That doesn't worry you?" I asked.

His face lit up. "It's the 'keep-your-friends-close-but-keep-your-enemies-closer thing." Spike turned his attention out the door. We heard Sergeant Blake's voice, then Jeremy asking questions. They spoke casually.

"They know each other?" I said.

Spike didn't respond. He walked to the door and shouted, "Hey, Blakie-baby!" before sitting back down and pulling himself to the desk, his knees now inches from my head.

"Have a seat," Spike said. Sergeant Blake closed the door but chose to stand directly in front of the desk. He wore the traditional wingtip style shoe.

"Has Eddie been to see you?" Sergeant Blake said.

"Eddie's here to find Tanya."

"So you *did* talk to Eddie?" the cop asked.

"Eddie's looking for Tanya. Trust me."

Sergeant Blake shuffled his feet. "Eddie's head seems to be in a different place. If he talks to you about Tanya, you need to tell me what he says. He was supposed to get together with you—"

"Yeah, I know. We were gonna team up, but guess what? He wants to find Tanya first."

"I want to find her too. But your father gave Eddie a lot of money to come here and help you start setting up the business. If he has some other plans—well, that's not good. And don't let him influence you."

"Influence me? I don't need Eddie. Cooper could've sent me that money to get the business going. And don't call Cooper my father. Yeah, we're blood but he didn't raise me."

"If you want him to trust you with money, you can't have secrets. You didn't think we'd find out about the wine you scammed? There's a lot of money in wine. But if you go cutting deals behind our backs—"

"Yes! I *hate* secrets. Why did Tanya take off? What did you and Cooper do to her?"

"Goddamn it!" Sergeant Blake shouted, stepped away a moment, then reversed path. "I don't have that kind of involvement with her. You'll have to ask your father if something happened between them."

"Tell me the truth. Cooper was hitting on Tanya, and that's why she's running?"

"I don't know anything about that."

"Sure you don't. Just give me a hint."

"Tanya asked for some more challenging work. Cooper asked if she wanted to come here and help you start the wine operation. You know that."

"Yeah, but she wasn't into it. She was just happy to get away."

"Do you want to be a part of your father's organization or not?"

"Just because we're blood-related doesn't make him my father! He had nothing to do with me growing up."

Sergeant Blake stepped away again. He paced a bit then said passionately, "Spike! Wake up! You're in the catbird seat! Just go along with being Cooper's son if it makes him happy! That's called *ambition.* You could be at the top one day if you just go along with things—and don't make secret deals."

Silence. I imagined the two locked in a staring contest. "Jesus!" Spike said. "You're really pussy-whipped on Cooper, aren't you?"

Poor Sergeant Blake. Did he ever imagine verbal abuse by a mobster's son would be part of the job description? I heard the door open. "You know how to get in touch with me," Sergeant Blake said. "If you find out anything about where Tanya might be, I need to know immediately."

40

"Move!" I said. Spike pushed back his chair. I emerged from under the desk. Spike stared at the floor. I said, "Does Jeremy know Sergeant Blake?"

"That lying bitch."

"Did you hear me?"

"Sergeant Blake likes wine. He and Jeremy bullshit about wine."

"Sergeant Blake seems pretty invested in you. How long has he been around?"

"Always. He's Irvington."

"You don't think he's here to *kill* Tanya, do you?"

"He's here to check up on me and Eddie, idiot!"

I had become completely desensitized to Spike's blindness. "But what if Tanya knows too much? She was *working* for Cooper while Eddie was in prison."

"Sergeant Blake's not a killer, and he's too close to Cooper. They would contract out for something like that."

Spike had not seen Sergeant Blake's inhospitable side, but he was probably right. "You wouldn't know anything about him, being the teacher's pet. He acts like your guardian. I bet keeping you on the wide and crooked path is part of his assignment. That whole catbird speech. He was trying to tell you not to let pride get in the way of ambition."

"I don't need a goddamn father."

"You're missing the point. Cooper could have called you himself and said all that shit Sergeant Blake said. Sending a messenger is Cooper's way of emphasizing the opportunity you have. The way I see it, Eddie has a decision to make. If he runs away with Tanya, then you're the number-one son."

Spike walked to the couch and sat, letting his head fall back over the top of the sofa. I took the desk chair and put my feet up. Spike said, "So what do you think Eddie's gonna do?"

"If he can, take the money and run away with Tanya."

"What's wrong with getting the hell out if that's what he wants?"

"Because you don't just *get the hell out* of this business. And if you don't know that, your future is less than promising—blood relative or not."

"You're all caught up in the Mafia thing. That's not us. Capone wasn't Mafia, you know."

"Oh, sure. Capone was just a businessman. If he had only paid his taxes on all that income, the Feds wouldn't have given a damn. And if you had told Sergeant Blake about your plan to split the wine with Doug in exchange for Tanya's whereabouts? I'm sure Cooper and Sergeant Blake also wouldn't have given a damn."

Spike put his hand over his forehead. I watched him awhile then stood to leave, purposely pushing the chair with the back of my knees so it bumped against the wall. Spike's hand remained in place, as did the rest of his body.

Lincoln Avenue seemed more alive, now that the fog had given way to partly cloudy skies. Or maybe the mist had lifted from my brain. Either way, after driving past Argyle Avenue, the red awning of the two-story stone building at the end of the next block beckoned me. Across the canopy's fringe, white capital letters spelled "LEGERDEMAIN," and hung over a blackened window with the words "LEGERDEMAINIST SUPPLIES." On the side of the building a wooden staircase led up to a second floor apartment. Despite the fifty degrees of late-March, an air conditioner in the transom above the apartment's door hummed loudly.

The door opened to a comfy, wood paneled room lined with shelves of small, unidentifiable items. Labels such as, "Fire Magic," "Money Magic," and "Stage Magic" revealed the store's function. A smiling, white-bearded man with yellowish crooked front teeth walked through an open doorway behind the counter. It took a moment, but I recognized him as Blackstone from *Pâtisserie Grenouille*. Suddenly, the place reeked of cliché— an old wizard's magic storefront, a backroom where he donned a purple cone-shaped hat adorned with stars and moons and practiced the Black Arts. At any moment, I expected an owl to land on his shoulder.

"Greetings," he said in a nasally voice, a bit higher than I anticipated. He leaned over the glass counter, resting on his elbows. "How may I assist you?"

"What does 'Legerdemain' mean?"

The smile vanished. "Literally, 'light of hand.' Today we know the word as 'sleight of hand,' or trickery."

"I've never known the word."

"Why would you?"

"Of course, it takes a legerdemainist to know a legerdemainist." Blackstone didn't respond. "Why not just call the place Magic Shop?" I asked.

Delayed response. "*We* know the word. Those that need me, find me. A curious passerby wastes my time."

The brightness of his eyes suggested premature aging. "I'll try not to waste your time. How long have you worked here?"

"I bought this place about a year ago."

"I'm wondering if you know a guy. He liked special effects, bloody stuff." I recalled Doug from Brenda's description: six-foot, fit, chiseled features, white-streaked grayish hair.

Taking it all in, the man stroked his beard just the way one expected a wizard to do. "Did he have a daughter?"

I took out a picture of Tanya. "This is what she looked like several years ago."

A quick glance then, "They often came in together."

"No kidding? When was the last time you saw them?"

"Hard to say."

"Did you get to know him? What did you talk about?"

He looked me over. "What're you, some kind of detective?"

I showed him my investigator's license. "I've been hired to find the young woman."

He seemed neither impressed or put off. "She's missing, huh? Why would I know anything about that? Disappearing women is not part of my act."

"I didn't mean to imply—I'm just gathering information. Any little tip that might tell me something. Like, what kind of stuff did he buy?"

"As you said, he liked grisly illusions. Razor blade slice bloody wounds, spike through tongue, needle through hand, knife through arm. Sometimes he bought, other times he just wanted pricing."

"What about her? Did you talk to her?"

He shook his head. "Nope, she just waited for Dad."

I suppressed my impulse to give a cursory explanation of their relationship, then remembered what brought me back to this neighborhood. "How about a young guy named Spike?" I described a skinny kid with slicked back hair. "He's friends with the other two. Did he ever come in here?"

"Lots of kids come in here looking like that."

His answer surprised me. I thought Spike appeared atypical for his age group, but what did I know? I pretended to suddenly recognize him. "Hey, I know why you look familiar. From that French Pâtisserie on Webster."

Blackstone straightened up, walked out from behind the counter, then leaned back against the glass case. "You go there often?" he said, no longer looking very old or very wizardly.

"Occasionally. You're friends with the owner?"

"No. You?"

"She also knew the man and—his daughter."

"And now you've made a connection between the man, his daughter, Brenda Gallagher, and myself."

"I'd say I discovered a coincidence—unless there's something you're not telling me."

"I understand. A good investigator should always be suspicious. By the way, how did you happen to find my shop?"

"Yellow Pages."

"Really? Among the dozens of display ads for magic stores, you chose to visit one with a simple listing."

"And how do you know I haven't visited every store with a display ad before I came here?"

He grunted a laugh. "Hard to believe."

"Perhaps. Well, I hope I didn't waste too much of your time." I dropped a card on the counter and walked out, wondering how much time I should waste on the wizard knowing Brenda's last name.

41

The wizard's overt distrust of non-legerdemainists—as if protecting a secret society—annoyed me for its clannish pretension. If he really wanted to hide something, it made more sense to act friendly and open. His Yellow Pages comment screamed that he knew his shop was chosen for a reason. I drove a few blocks then pulled over and dialed Brenda. It rang once before call-waiting beeped Kalijero.

"We get our meeting?" I said.

"Jules?"

My first name coming from Kalijero's mouth sounded bizarre. "Jimmy?"

"Yeah," Kalijero said through an exhale.

"Everything okay?"

"Huh? Yeah, listen. You gotta really watch your back now. Word is, someone flew in town to shut someone's mouth—for good. Probably on Cooper's order."

"Cooper's muscle already talked to me."

"You're not listening. Nobody's talking to nobody. You're just dead. There's no discussion."

"You think I'm that someone?"

"You pissed off a lot of people—who was this guy? What did he say to you?"

"A Cooper clown named Sergeant Blake. He's here to find Tanya, but hopefully not harm her."

"What's your thinking?"

"Well, maybe she knows too much."

"Stay away from Sergeant Blake."

"I just want to find Tanya, get her with Eddie, and my job is done. Be honest, Jimmy. If the bad guys really wanted me dead, what chance would I have?"

Pause. "Not much."

"Then what's with the dumbass advice? And what's so important about my life that—"

"That's what I'm talking about! You don't give a damn if you get blown away. You're fucking depressed, Landau!"

"I was talking about Cooper, Mommy! Why is it worth sending a hired gun halfway across the country to kill me? Just because I know Cooper is making bum wine?"

"It's the skirt, idiot. They don't want you to find her. And if they figure out where she is before you do, they might get you out of the way first."

"Cooper must think she's alive. But why would Margot lie about killing her?"

"That girl's got everyone damn scared."

"Except Eddie, who hired me."

"You think Eddie's stupid enough to cross Cooper?"

"Love conquers all, Jimmy."

"You sound like a real *malaka* sometimes."

"Why?" I said, with the assumption *malaka* was not a compliment. "Eddie blew off Spike in the wine-scam business. Tanya is the only other reason he'd be here."

"You don't think it's blood-in-blood-out with these guys?"

"Probably. I don't know. They're not Sicilian. Maybe it's more *Mafia light*."

"You joke too damn much. But, listen, I'm gonna have a procedure done. I'll be in bed for five or six days. Highly sedated. So I don't know how much help I can be."

"What's the matter?"

"It's no big deal. I'm just telling you so you know."

"Okay. Thanks for telling me." Brenda beeped on call-waiting. "I got another call—"

"Take it." Kalijero hung up.

"I couldn't get to the phone earlier," Brenda said. "But I'm glad you called because it reminded me of something I forgot to tell you this morning."

"Pray, do tell."

"Yesterday, we were talking about Spike. And later in the afternoon, I stepped out for a smoke and saw him hanging out across the street, just kind of wandering up and down the sidewalk. I didn't think too much of it, but an hour later he's still out there."

"Did he know you spotted him?"

"I don't think so—or he didn't care. Anyway, I got busy in the kitchen for at least another hour, and when I came out, Margot was sitting at a table, eating and reading like she does. I got curious, so I stuck my head out the door and saw that Spike was gone."

"He would've had a clear view of Margot leaving her apartment and walking to the Pâtisserie."

"Exactly."

"Interesting. Hey, how does that old guy who likes croissants know your last name?"

"I keep business cards on the counter so a lot of people know my last name. Why?"

"Just curious."

"So what do you think?"

"You mean about Spike? I'm wondering if he's smarter than I thought."

"Really? Why do you say that?"

"It's complicated but for now—"

"Trust everything will be revealed to me. You said that a few hours ago."

"I'm sorry—"

"Hey, it's okay! I trust you know what's good for me. I gotta go."

I couldn't tell if she was being sarcastic or not. Either way, she spoke the truth.

From Brenda's parking lot, I sat in my car and stared at Jeremy's black Porsche in the dusky light of early evening. The idea of Sergeant Blake and Jeremy knowing each other troubled me. It seemed odd that Spike wasn't equally troubled. Jeremy stepped out of the Vin Bar attired in the sacred garments of a master sommelier, and began grooming in the Porsche's side view mirror. He had a date. Perhaps he was scheduled to meet with the Mystical Potentate of the Vintner's Temple or some other secret sanctuary reserved for worthy nobles of the grapevine. In the meantime, I called Margot.

"Has anything gone missing from your apartment recently?" I asked.

"Who is this?" Margot said.

"Sorry. Jules Landau. Does Spike have a key to your place?"

"I don't know. Back up. You asked if I was missing something?"

"I think Spike staked out your place yesterday—waiting for you to go to Brenda's café."

"How do you know?"

"Brenda told me."

"I see. Is she working for you now?"

"We're friends. So what? You should change your locks, Margot."

"What do I have worth stealing?"

"That baby grand is probably worth 10K, right?"

Exhaled sound of disgust. "I'm fairly certain my piano was not stolen."

Jeremy climbed into his Porsche. "Well, double-check just to make sure. And I meant it when I said you should change your locks. Gotta go."

I followed Jeremy east on Webster about three miles until he turned south on Clark Street and wound his way to a Gold Coast neighborhood on East Lake Shore Drive. He turned into one of the storied neo-classical limestone and brick buildings, then handed his keys to a valet. Having my 1983 Honda Civic parked by a man wearing a jacket, tie, and white gloves would be a first. I gave my key to the valet. He looked confused. "I'm the millionaire next door," I said.

"Who are you here to see?"

"I'm with Jeremy—the *Auvergnat Vin Bar* guy in the black Porsche."

The man sort of nodded then said "Eighteen" to another man who opened the elevator. I sat on the leather bench all the way to the eighteenth floor while admiring the Persian rug and my reflection in the beveled mirrors. The door opened into a hallway wider than many North Side streets. Directly across on the other side of the hall, a crowd socialized in what I believed the wealthy referred to as the drawing room. I approached cautiously, but nobody seemed to notice or care about my presence. On closer examination, the guests appeared quite varied in affluence, age, and grooming habits. Connoisseurs in Italian suits chatted with evenly tanned former beatniks. Hipsters in tight jeans, ill-fitting sweaters, and chunky jewelry mingled with the bulging biceps of athletes.

Tables of wine bottles and long-stemmed glasses lined the perimeter of the room, although some tables had only a large, glossy photograph of an opened wooden crate displaying a few bottles of a hallowed vintage. I found Jeremy standing toward the rear of an eclectic group, listening to a British gentleman dressed in an old fashioned single breasted tuxedo with satin lapels, lecturing on wines sold from various French river valleys. It seemed odd that Jeremy, the vin master himself, would be among the audience instead of out front leading the discussion. A bushy white beard, wispy and windblown, caught my eye. When I saw the beret on the shiny head, I recognized Blackstone from the magic shop. He stood in the back of the group, stoically watching the lecturer interact with his fans. I got the feeling he wasn't listening as much as waiting. I navigated through the crowd, trying to position myself closer. When I reached the outer edge of Jeremy's right periphery, I heard a British accent assigning distinctions such as immortality, one-hundred plus points, and alternative investment. I snaked my way to the display where a lustrous photo of several 1945 Mouton Rothschild bottles dignified the table. Then I squeezed my way back through the crowd until I reached the hallway. From there I called Spike.

"He's *already* looking for a buyer?" Spike said. "He's trying to screw me even faster than I thought he would!"

"I get the feeling you're not surprised."

"Seriously, Landau? With that kind of money at stake?"

"When I called you earlier, you said Sergeant Blake might be looking for you at the magic shop. What were you doing there?"

"I was just checking something."

"How do you know about that place?"

"Doug would send me there to buy stuff for him."

"The old guy remembers Doug and Tanya coming in."

"I don't remember any old guy." I described the bearded man. "Nope."

"You want to tell me what you were checking?"

"No."

"If it was related to Tanya, you wouldn't be playing goddamn games, right?"

"You hurt my feelings." The call dropped.

Back at the party, I stood just inside the doorway and scanned the room for gray-haired, GQ-looking guys who might be Doug Daley. Why would Doug be at this party? To see if Spike was using Jeremy to sell the wine behind his back?

Gradually, the group around the tuxedo man thinned enough for Blackstone to hobble up to him. They chatted for a bit before the man raised his arm and signaled to someone with his index finger. A minute later, Jeremy approached. Tuxedo Man quickly introduced him to Blackstone, then excused himself. The two new friends walked to the edge of the crowd and found a gap along the wall, where they stood ensconced in their own little world.

What could this odd-looking pair possibly have in common? Did Blackstone have a few million in cash he wanted to hide in vintage wine? Jeremy handed the man a small book. He looped his cane over his left arm, held the book with both hands, then began paging through it. Occasionally, he stopped to read something. Jeremy watched and waited. Blackstone seemed to be in no hurry, despite his one-man audience. Finally, he closed the book, handed it back to Jeremy, and smiled. They spoke a bit more, shook hands, then the old guy hobbled through the crowd and out the door.

Jeremy waited a bit longer then made his way through the crowd, passing within a few feet of me on his way out. He had that spacey look of joyful preoccupation. After the elevator doors closed, I stepped into the hallway and pushed the down button. By the time I reached the valet station, Jeremy's black Porsche was pulling away.

The curtain of mist that had greeted me upon wakening once again dangled over the city, engulfing anything taller than a standard brick mid-rise. As I drove home, I couldn't help but think that

Doug had been present at the party, or maybe his interests had been represented by an agent lurking among Jeremy's crowd of admirers. Then it occurred to me that perhaps Blackstone and Doug had some kind of alliance. He had, after all, admitted Doug and Tanya often came into the magic shop.

42

My phone rang around five a.m. "Get over to that building with the red awning on Lincoln," Spike said.

"Yes, you woke me."

"Dude, get over here. Jeremy just pulled up." The call dropped.

Half asleep, I threw on some clothes, dropped a chicken heart in Punim's bowl, then stood outside my apartment, trying to remember where I parked my car. To the east, the first sign of light diffused through the cold, clear air that had replaced yesterday's fog. Ice water coated the city. The idea that Chicago would one day be warm seemed more remote than the Cubs playing baseball in October. I turned onto Lincoln, pondering the significance of Jeremy showing up at the magic shop. Had he struck some kind of deal the previous night with Blackstone? Maybe they were meeting again to finalize something. Why would that demand my presence?

When I arrived, Spike stood on the sidewalk across the street from Legerdemain, leaning against the window to a Bosnian restaurant, arms folded. He seemed not to notice my approach. As far as I could tell, he was staring at the illuminated window above the shop, grinning the way one did when taking pleasure in another's misery.

"I'm here," I said.

"Look at the window, tell me what you see."

Initially, I saw just a bare white wall before a man quickly walked past the window, then returned in the opposite direction, stopped, laced both hands behind his head, then walked about erratically, coming into and out of our line of vision.

"Can you feel the panic?" Spike said.

"That's Jeremy? What's he doing?"

"He's looking for Margot's wine," Spike said gleefully.

I needed a moment to audit his words. Up to this point, the wine had existed more in a virtual state than a tangible one. The implication that ten cases of Mouton Rothschild had been stored in a dreary little apartment maybe thirty yards from where I stood, brought with it a sense of awe.

"That's why the air conditioner was on!" I said. "To keep the temperature cool." Spike looked at me and nodded enthusiastically. "But how did you know when Jeremy would come and get it?"

"After you told me he had found a buyer, I had a feeling he wouldn't wait until the morning to check on his fortune. No way he was getting any sleep. So me and my amphetamine salts have been waiting in my car all night."

"You moved the wine."

"Don't worry about the wine, just stick with what you're supposedly good at. Like setting up a meeting with Doug. How's that meeting coming along?"

Spike's brash sarcasm staggered me. He knew more than I realized and the cheeky prick wasn't afraid to shove it in my face. Why was I taken off guard? The idea he could make me uncomfortable in my own investigation rubbed at the blister covering my usually dormant susceptibility to violence.

"What's that supposed to mean?" I said.

"I mean, for a crack detective, you don't seem to know shit. You're supposed to be *plugged in*, remember?"

The slightest hint of mirth settling upon Spike's face was all it took for me to land my fist squarely below his left eye, dropping the little bastard to the sidewalk. I sat on his chest and raised my fist again, only to hold it in check, aware that another blow could turn a fairly harmless black eye into a fractured socket or cheekbone. Instead, I put my hands around his neck knowing full well I wouldn't strangle him, but would still receive great satisfaction feeling my fingers pressed against his throat.

"Having fun playing gangster?" I said. "Did you know guys like Cooper actually have people beaten to death? Not just one slug to the face, but one after another after another, until your face is a swollen, bloody pulp and your brain is like an overripe peach."

The apartment window went dark. I dragged Spike around the corner by the back of his jacket and sat him up against the wall.

"What was that for?" he said.

"Don't you know? In the gangster world, most of us gotta earn respect. We don't just get it 'cause Daddy says so. You gonna give me some respect now and quit fucking around?"

Spike touched cheekbone. "You're a fucking asshole."

I sat down next to him. "Maybe that old man—his name is Blackstone—and Doug are working together?"

Spike pretended he had to think about it. "Yeah, maybe."

"We both know Jeremy's going to call you and tell you he's found a buyer for the wine. He's going to try to convince you to tell him where it is. You're going to play along, set up a meeting with the old man, and then we're going to find out how he knows Doug. Sound like a plan?"

"You're still a fucking asshole," Spike said, which I took as a kind of grudging acknowledgment.

"Yeah, I know. Put some ice on your face."

Punim watched me from her window hammock. The pet trust had to be funded. A caretaker had to be assigned. A trustee had to be designated. I sat staring at the trust papers on the coffee table. A feeling of stagnation spread over me. Waiting for a call after invoking a sublime telegraph service to get the word out only aggravated my awareness. For all I knew, Kalijero hadn't done a damn thing with his contacts. No doubt he hid information from me. Only Eddie really knew whether Cooper wanted him to find Tanya or not.

I moved the coffee table closer to the couch then lay down with the knuckles of my right hand resting in a bowl of ice. Out the window, I saw a hint of blue in the atmosphere, which meant the sun lurked just under the horizon. As a little boy, I thought the sky reflected blue off Lake Michigan. Back then, I knew as much about the optical phenomenon of scattering sunlight as I knew about Newton's laws of knuckles colliding with cheekbones.

I couldn't shake the feeling I had underestimated Spike, perhaps to the point where he had co-opted my investigation. Considering his relationships with Cooper and Doug, what he knew and what he decided to tell me gave him a power difficult to resist. But what was his ultimate goal? To make a lot of money or find Tanya? As my

knuckles transitioned from cold to burning, I
thought about my surrender to violence, how
Frownie would've said punching Spike in the face
showed weakness, not strength. The fact Spike
could influence my behavior revealed who was
really in charge. Twenty minutes later, I removed
my numbed knuckles from the ice, returned to bed,
then drifted off, wondering if Spike was a bona fide
hoodlum prodigy.

43

The phone rang about nine o'clock, rousing me
from an agitated slumber. I anticipated Spike calling
to tell me about a meeting with Jeremy and
Blackstone. Instead, Amy said, "Do you think Spike
is also connected to Eddie's boss?"

I yawned. "Why would I think that?"

Amy's irritation transmitted loud and clear.
"Eddie came here to check up on the wine
scamming biz, remember? Maybe Spike was his
contact."

"Eddie doesn't care about the wine. He wants
to find Tanya, which means we need to find Doug."

"You keep saying that, but Eddie and Spike
have other things in common, so why not broaden
the focus?"

"Why are you so invested in this case?"

Amy cursed loudly, startling me. "I told you this days ago! Tanya Maggio's energy is calling me. And I'm really sick of your attitude—"

"Okay, I'm sorry. Tell me what you think."

"Eddie and Spike work for the same person. Maybe Eddie was sent here to straighten Spike out. Instead, he gets in touch with you because he wants to find Tanya. His decision to blow off the wine thing is a statement. He's breaking away from his boss and his old life."

Amy's insights into Eddie's life added to my feeling of insecurity begun by Spike, although it bothered me less since she had the unfair advantage of psychic abilities. Sufficiently deflated, I surrendered.

"The boss is a guy called Cooper who referred Eddie to a cop I know. That's how Eddie found me. Spike is Cooper's biological son and was supposed to have been Eddie's contact. What you said about Eddie breaking away from his old life appears to be true."

My candidness took her off guard. "Okay," Amy said pleasantly.

"But I got something else. A Cooper goon named Sergeant Blake is in town to find Tanya."

"Anything new regarding Doug's whereabouts?"

"Spike has a possible lead. I'm waiting for a call."

I could almost hear Amy thinking. Then she said, "Yesterday, I asked you if Tanya could be running away from someone—"

"Cooper is an authentic slimeball. But why wouldn't Eddie tell me Cooper scared Tanya away?"

"Maybe Eddie doesn't know."

Another good point I should've already deciphered. Eddie wouldn't be aware of what took place between Cooper and Tanya during Eddie's stretch in prison. A scumbag like Cooper trying to coerce sex from Tanya seemed too easy to be the whole story of why Tanya left town.

I said, "Eddie is sure Cooper *wants* him to find Tanya. That tells me Cooper isn't afraid of anything Tanya has to say."

"But *why* would Cooper want him to find Tanya?"

"To make a choice?" I said. "Run away with her or bring her back in?"

"But Eddie's got to know that bringing Tanya back might be dangerous for her—if they think she's a security risk."

Silence. "True. Either way, the little rat loves her. No way he's taking chances with her life. They're gonna run." I shrunk back from our new rapport. Was Amy now a full partner in my investigation? "Tell me about your friend in law enforcement."

"I want to help you find Tanya! Can't you just accept that and trust me?"

"Trust is a two-way street, yeah?"

Amy swore loudly again. "He works undercover. Okay? That's all I can say—and I'm not even supposed to know that!"

My initial reaction was to believe her, then I thought how easy it would be to create a fictional undercover contact. The issue of trust felt tiresome, if not pointless.

"I'll let you know about a meeting with Doug," I said.

"I hope so," Amy said, although I didn't think she believed me.

Sitting on the couch, the idea of an association between Blackstone and Doug nagged me as I watched March's late morning sunlight traverse the windows overlooking Halsted. Figuring out their connection would be purely guesswork, but thanks to Amy's influence, I decided to recognize the feeling as intuition and embrace the two being in cahoots as my working theory.

As the noon hour approached without a phone call, my misgivings over Spike intensified. I dialed the *Auvergnat Vin Bar*. Jeremy answered.

"Yes, I was wondering if you could help me find a bottle of Mouton Rothschild 1945—"

"Who is this?"

"Jules Landau—"

"Oh, god! What do you want?"

"Have you spoken to Spike lately?"

"Why?"

"Believe it or not, I think I found a wine buyer who also might know Doug's whereabouts. What do you think of that?"

Jeremy hung up. Minutes later, Spike called and said, "What did you say to Jeremy?"

"Why the hell didn't you call me after Jeremy called you?"

"What do you think I'm doing, douchebag?"

I fought the urge to call this brat every vile blasphemy ever catalogued—and then cultivate a few more. The anger spread through my gut then migrated north, settling around my heart. I always felt my heart was my weak spot, my Achilles' heel. Anger would destroy my heart.

"Whenever you're ready, pal," I said.

Spike gave me a near north address on Wabash. "Seven o'clock. Wait inside."

I hung up. If he had more to say, I didn't care.

Chiseled into the archway was a five-pointed star inside a crescent moon. The symbols blended with the building's ornate domes to emit a flavor of occultism, evoking an era when architecture embraced Islamic imagery. The enormous oak doors opened to a vast corridor of black-and-white square tiles running straight through to the opposite end of the building. The heavy masonry of granite walls and fifteen foot ceilings struck me with a sense of timelessness. Egyptian pyramids came to mind.

Apart from the faint sound of indistinct voices, the hall was quiet. I strolled along the wall, looking at portraits of aristocrats dressed in elegant nineteenth century suits, each with a red sash falling across his chest and a gold starburst attached to the collar. All had the title "Supreme Magus" embossed on a plate at the base of the frame. A couple of middle-aged men walked in, both dressed in black cutaway frocks, red waistcoats, and top hats. They nodded at me as they passed then entered the stairwell halfway down the hall. A few more men dressed like the previous two entered and then more arrived until a steady stream of antiquated fellows filed down the corridor and disappeared into the stairwell.

Besides the increased murmuring, the hallway returned to quiet. I looked at my watch. Quarter past seven. I whispered a string of curses. It was likely Spike's plan that I stood alone and self-conscious in this esteemed hallway of sublime grandiosity. All at once, the murmuring stopped. I walked to the stairwell landing. One floor below, the slightest sounds of human activity came from behind arched double doors. I walked down the flight and listened. A gong sounded.

I put my hand on the latch, pushed down, then slowly opened the door. With its barrel vaulted white ceiling, the room seemed like a palatial auditorium. Steep stadium seating bordered three sides of a rectangular checkerboard floor. Maybe two-thirds of the seats were filled. At the fourth side, a huge stage of red carpet, red curtains, and a single red upholstered high-back chair drew the attention of the attendees. I stayed in the standing room area behind the last row, and watched. A few men glanced at me. None appeared concerned that an infidel stood in their midst.

A bearded man appeared stage right and walked to a stand-up microphone. Around his waist he wore a white apron with blue trim and embroidered designs. On his head sat a black, high crown fedora with a feather tucked into the trim. Something about him struck me as familiar. The man began waving his hands wildly, as if swatting imaginary flies. Then he shouted, "Off with you! Off with you! Away, away!"

The room erupted as a single voice in an unidentifiable language. I noticed an older man standing about four feet from me. He had a relaxed, pleasant look on his face. I stepped closer to him and whispered, "What did everyone just say?"

The man smiled, then leaned into me like he was an old friend about to share a funny punch line. "Anna dimgalbi, kia urgalbi." He laughed and was about to say something else when the guy onstage started shouting again in the mystery language. I smiled and nodded at my new friend then descended a couple of tiers, just close enough to recognize Blackstone as the man on the stage babbling in a strange tongue.

While once again struggling to reconcile Spike's mastery over me, another man appeared from stage left. He circled the chair, stopped, then circled the chair again, this time walking backward in the opposite direction, before stopping in front of the chair and facing the audience. Blackstone prompted the man to repeat an oath in which he vowed to devote his lifeblood to the Ancient Craft. His voice didn't have the nasally aspect I remembered from talking to him in the magic shop. I watched, somewhat disengaged from the symbolism of the ceremony itself, but present enough to remember my original goal to question Blackstone regarding his relationship with Doug. As I made my way down toward the stage, Blackstone crooned on about rings of brilliant light collecting in one's heart and nourishing one's soul. A huge banner proclaiming, "Magick: The Discipline and Artistry of Inducing Metamorphosis" unfurled across the top of the stage.

The audience stood and cheered the initiate, who smiled broadly and waved like a pageant winner. The celebration continued for several minutes before dissolving into a kind of gentleman's reception. Long tables of cakes and sparkling grape juice were set up on the floor. Onstage, several men had joined Blackstone in engaging their new comrade in lively talk. Then Blackstone excused himself and disappeared stage right. Most of the other attendees remained standing at their seats or drifted toward the refreshment tables.

"Thinking about joining?"

I turned and looked into a smiling face standing a bit closer to me than I preferred. "I thought I'd check things out, meet some people. You know the guy on the stage who ran the show?"

"That's Blackstone. Kind of a weird bird. But likable."

"What do you mean weird?"

"Oh, nothing really, just takes it more seriously than most. But we need a guy like that."

"Why is that important?"

The man thought about it. "A connection to childhood innocence, I guess. Once magic gets in your blood, it stays there. That's just my theory."

"And Blackstone's really into the ritual, huh?"

"Oh, yeah. He made sure the ceremonies still use the archaic Coptic Egyptian. You could say he literally lives and breathes the Ancient Craft." The man laughed. "He made a deal with the Masons who own this place. They let him live here in a little studio apartment in exchange for taking care of the place."

"Really? I guess you're probably not supposed to know that."

The man frowned. "Everyone knows. It's the door at the end of the hall when you go back out. It's where the Venerable Sovereign lived in the old days, like a priest's rectory."

The ease with which this fortuitous gift arrived almost made me suspicious. I asked my new acquaintance what sort of magic he practiced and he gave me an enthusiastic, detailed description of his birthday party performance. I pretended to be interested until I looked at my watch and excused myself.

44

I milled around awhile, observing the scene near Blackstone's apartment. The only real threat of discovery seemed to come from the occasional guest crossing the hall after exiting the auditorium. I put my hand on the knob and rattled the door, surprised it was just a hollow wood veneer with no dead bolt. It appeared almost comical surrounded by the granite and brick wall.

The space between the jamb and door gave my credit card easy access to the latch assembly. Typical of cheap locks, the bolt was slanted inward, allowing me to easily force it back. Once inside, I relocked the door, turned on the light, and immediately understood why security was of little concern. Despite the belief Blackstone lived in the studio, there was little evidence to suggest it was anybody's actual home. The mattress on the twin bed was bare, the fridge contained only a pizza box, and there was nothing in the way of cooking utensils to be found. A phone-booth-sized closet devoid of clothes had a curtain for a door. The only signs of human activity were basic toiletries in the bathroom. There was, however, a rather large dresser.

I opened the top drawer and saw what looked like a pile of tiny firecrackers, several boxes of condoms, a bottle of black powder, a roll of electrical tape, and strands of copper wire connected to tiny pipes. I opened the second drawer and caught a whiff of nail polish remover. Scattered about were a few small plastic bottles of clear liquid, several quart-sized bottles of red liquid, and what appeared to be a .38 revolver. I picked up the pistol. It felt lighter than expected and looked like it had been painted black. The hammer wouldn't move. When I pushed the cylinder release, nothing happened. It was a very safe gun.

An exuberant voice assaulted me as I stepped out of the building. "Did you see that? Wasn't that some crazy initiation shit?"

It took a moment for Spike's appearance to break though the chaos clogging my neural pathways. The shiner I gave him that morning was at its peak of ripeness.

"What do you really know about Blackstone's relationship with Doug?" I said.

"Did you see all those old fucks dressed up like—"

"How much do you know?" I shouted.

"Whaddya getting all pissed off for? I just wanted you to see him dressed up, playing wizard.

It's good to know the kind of guy you're dealing with. Now let's go to the meeting."

"So there is a meeting?"

"Yeah, dude, nine o'clock at Jeremy's office. It's eight-fifteen now."

"Hang on. How much does Jeremy know about Blackstone?"

Spike lit up. "Only that he wants to buy some expensive wine!" His sudden giddiness bordered on bizarre. He stared at me, anticipating a reaction to match his delirious glee.

"Okay," I said. "But I've gotta make a call first."

Spike ran to his car then, for some reason, waited for me to pull the Honda behind him. I left a message at Margot's apartment, then followed Spike into the left lane on busy Wabash. I called Amy.

"I'm on my way to the *Auvergnat Vin Bar*," I said. "An old man wants to buy Margot's wine."

"Buy it from whom?"

"Jeremy, the owner of the bar."

"Listen, there are things you need to know."

"Hang on." I pulled on to a side street. "I should know you're a Fed, right?"

Amy forced a laugh. "Why would you say that?" That she could have been so genuinely caught off guard surprised me.

Spike's number vibrated on my phone. "When you came over the night before I went to Irvington. That was just to cover your FBI ass, to make sure I would've gone to Irvington *without* your suggestion. You didn't care about my safety—"

"I *did* care—"

"Calm down, I get it! I was already warned by a cop friend that the Feds were all over Cooper and that whatever happened to some puny private investigator was irrelevant."

"You're not irrelevant—"

"And all that psychic stuff? Just bullshit?"

"I'll explain later. Who's this old man?"

"He has some kind of relationship to Doug," I said.

"Fine. Go to the meeting. I'll explain more later."

45

Once in *Auvergnat's* parking lot I called Margot again and left another message. Spike waited for me next to his car.

"Where the hell did you go?" Spike said.

"Bathroom."

Spike didn't appreciate my response and turned to his Mr. Mobster-Tough-Guy attitude—which pissed me off. "You got somethin' you wanna to tell me?" Spike said.

I threw it back at him. "Listen, *sonny boy*. I don't gotta tell you nuttin' about nobody."

I walked into the *Auvergnat Vin Bar* without checking to see if Spike followed. Business was brisk. A few couples waited on benches for a table to open. I waved at Bruce the bartender as I breezed past, and didn't bother knocking before I entered Jeremy's office. Blackstone sat on the end of the couch, leaning forward with both hands on the handle of his cane. Jeremy had been sitting behind the desk but stood when I appeared.

"What are you doing here?" Jeremy said. The old man looked at me but didn't move.

"I'm sorry. Isn't this where the Sacred Order of Fermentology meets?"

Spike walked in and sat at the opposite end of the couch. "Hi, Merlin," he said.

"What is Landau doing here?" Jeremy said.

"Landau is still looking for Tanya," I said.

"This is a private meeting that has nothing to do with a missing woman," Jeremy said.

"I have a theory," I said, leaning against the wall, "that the missing *wine* is related to the missing *Doug* which is related to the missing *woman*."

Jeremy looked at Blackstone then at Spike. "What's he talking about?"

Spike got up from the couch and walked to the front of the desk. "Here's the deal," he said. "Merlin here tells us how to find Doug, then maybe we sell him some wine." Blackstone stared at the floor.

"How would Blackstone know anything about Doug?" Jeremy said.

"You slimy rat-bastard," Spike said, sounding effectively unhinged. "First, you try to sell the wine behind my back? Now you insult my intelligence?"

I thought Jeremy might faint. "I found an investor with Mr. Blackstone," he said, his voice wavering. "For my wine trust. I swear that's all. I don't know anything about Doug."

I said, "You mean not since you and Spike ripped off the wine Doug wanted to steal from Margot, and that you're now trying to sell behind Spike's back."

"Don't listen to him," Jeremy said to Blackstone. "Everything is legitimate."

"What do you say, Merlin?" Spike said. "You know where Dougie is?" It seemed Blackstone moved just enough to glance at Spike, but I wasn't sure. "Don't feel like talking, huh?"

"He doesn't know Doug!" Jeremy said.

"Doug Daley was a customer at the magic shop," I said. "Tanya used to accompany him."

"That doesn't mean he *knew* him," Jeremy said.

"Well, Merlin?" Spike said. "Did you *know* Doug?"

Blackstone straightened himself up on the couch and said through his nose, "He was a customer."

"You didn't sound as nasally onstage," I said. "A special microphone?"

"Get rid of Landau and let's do business," Jeremy said to Spike.

Spike looked at me. "Well, Landau?"

"There's no business-doing until Blackstone tells us how to find Doug."

"Oh, goddamn it!" Jeremy said. "Blackstone just wants to buy the wine! He doesn't know where Doug is!"

"He's investing in your trust *and* buying the wine?" I said. "That's one profitable magic shop."

"So what price did you get us?" Spike said.

Jeremy squirmed in his seat. "I told you on the phone."

"I forgot."

Blackstone chimed in. "Twenty-five hundred. Per bottle."

I waited for Spike's reaction. He looked horrified. "So ten cases of twelve equals three hundred grand," Spike said then looked at me. "He's practically giving it away!"

"You're getting screwed," I said.

"That's a fair price!" Jeremy said.

"The wine is worth eight times that," I said.

"What it's worth and what people will pay are two different things!" Jeremy said. "I'm the expert! I know what people will pay for wine!"

In the doorway, Margot stood emotionless before her conspirators. We all noticed her at the same time. I said, "I hope you don't mind I invited Margot."

Spike flashed me a *What-the-fuck?* look.

"Margot, meet Mr. Blackstone," I said. "He wants to buy your wine! Isn't that wonderful?" Jeremy rushed to Margot and started whispering in her ear. "Oh, was there something your boyfriend neglected to tell you, Margot? Like he's trying to sell your stolen wine?"

Margot stepped away from Jeremy. When Jeremy tried to close the gap, she shoved him hard in the chest then angrily whispered something back.

Blackstone rose from the couch. "It seems the details have not been taken care of," he said.

"I think it would be better if you stayed," I said. Time to act tough.

Blackstone's eyes widened and then he smiled just a bit. "And I should assume you will prevent me from leaving?"

I pretended to think about it. "I suppose. Although the idea of fighting an old man disturbs me."

"Leave him alone, Landau," Jeremy said.

"Yeah, let him go if he wants," Spike said.

"Really, Spike? Suddenly you're a lovable gangster?"

Spike's face reddened. "Fuck you! You want to make the guy a prisoner?"

"Spike's right, Jules," Margot said. "Is this why you begged me to come here? To watch you beat up an elderly man?"

I shut the door then stood defiantly, hands on hips, holstered gun clearly visible, and said, "Nobody moves, nobody gets hurt." Nobody laughed. "Sit down, old man."

"You're just a punk," Blackstone said.

I walked to Blackstone, then shoved him hard in the chest. He fell backward on to the couch. Despite his contorted expressions of pain, I thought he landed rather nimbly for an old man. Jeremy got in my face, started shouting. A quick thrust to his gut with the heel of my hand sent him to his knees. Margot stood, staring in horror. She shouted, "What kind of man are you?"

"Oh, relax," I said. "I didn't hit him that hard."

"Landau," Spike said, "you need to chill out."

"Okay, everyone," I said. "I'm sorry to have been such a prick, but two grave injustices have been perpetrated upon my friend Margot, and it's time this maltreatment comes to an end."

"What are you doing?" Margot said.

"Landau," Spike said, "this wasn't part of the game plan."

Jeremy got to his feet, then stumbled to the chair behind his desk. Blackstone seemed calm, even resigned.

"The people responsible for Margot's predicament are present in this room," I said. "Yet here she stands, stoically accepting her fate. Margot, Jeremy wants to sell your wine for twenty-five hundred bucks a bottle. What do you think of that?"

"Jeremy's an idiot," Margot said.

"Is that because the wine is worth more like *twenty thousand* a bottle?"

Spike looked at Margot. Margot nodded. Spike said, "What about it, Jeremy?"

"Nobody would pay that kind of money!"

"I don't think Blackstone believes that," I said. "What about it, Blacky?"

Staring at the floor, Blackstone said, "Good wine is an asset. A solid investment."

"But why would Jeremy settle for one-eighth of the wine's value?" I said.

"I should call the cops and have you thrown out of here," Jeremy said.

"Jeremy needs a pile of cash so he can attract investors for his wine equity trust. You're probably thinking, *He has ten cases of Mouton Rothschild! What does he need cash for?* Well, cash is the truest of liquid assets. Cash has no authentication requirement like great works of art or rare wine. Jeremy's problem is that he's a wine *expert*. And because he's a wine *expert*, he has reason to believe the wine could be fake."

"That's a lie!" Jeremy shouted. "To work as long and hard as I have to become a master sommelier, only to risk my reputation by selling counterfeit wine? I'd die first!"

"What do you think, Margot?" I said. "I mean, it's *your* wine after all."

"My father was a highly regarded wine connoisseur," Margot said. "He was also one of the most respected cardiac surgeons in the country. His integrity was impeccable."

"It's not possible Dr. van Bourgondien was conned somewhere along the way?" I said.

"What are you getting at, Landau?" Jeremy said.

"A magazine called *Wine Kibitzer*. Each year they devote an issue to the latest wine scams and rehash the most significant scams of the previous years." From the breast pocket of my jacket I took out a page I had ripped out of the copy Paul from *Der Weingott* had given me. "Here's an article about Dr. Thomas van Bourgondien, who three years ago filed a lawsuit in federal court claiming he was sold ten cases of counterfeit wine—Chateau Mouton Rothschild 1945."

"It was never proven," Margot said.

"He dropped the lawsuit," I said.

"Dad's health was deteriorating. He didn't want to spend the money so late in life."

"Are you finished, Landau?" Jeremy said. "Spike, let's talk privately."

"The possibility of selling phony wine made Jeremy nervous. That's why you settled for the reduced price. Asking twenty grand a bottle would've brought too much attention and scrutiny. But three hundred thousand for ten cases—that doesn't raise an eyebrow in your world. And the price was low enough so Blackstone could resell it for, say, five grand a bottle, and also make a tidy profit."

Jeremy stood, walked to the couch, then extended his arm to Blackstone. "C'mon, I'll walk you out."

"Let them leave, Jules," Margot said.

"He doesn't need your help, Jeremy," I said. "This strapping young buck could knock a skinny boy like me aside with no problem. But that would give away his secrets, right, Blacky?"

"Christ almighty!" Margot said. "What are you talking about? What secrets?"

"Whaddya say, Blackstone? You want to do it or should I? Tell those secrets, that is."

Blackstone's face clouded over. He stared first at me then took turns locking eyes with the others. "Go ahead," he said scathingly. "I don't want to ruin your fun."

"Jeremy, take off Blacky's beret and then take a pinch of that latex bald cap."

Jeremy gawked at me a moment then put his hand on Blackstone's shoulder. "C'mon, let's get out of here."

Blackstone swatted Jeremy's hand away. I rushed over, knocked off Blackstone's beret, took a pinch of his scalp between thumb and forefinger, then stretched the latex an inch or two. An elbow to the stomach dropped me to the floor.

"Hello, Doug," I gasped. "It's nice to finally meet you."

46

Spike glowed with joy. Margot appeared either detached or astonished. Jeremy did a walking dead imitation back to his desk, then sat like a dejected little boy.

Doug took out his fake teeth. "Okay," he said. "Get over it already."

"Here's some acetone to remove the adhesive," I said and tossed a small plastic bottle at Doug's feet. "C'mon, get rid of that cap and beard, let's have a look at you."

"Damn it!" Spike said. "I really thought you were dead."

"Working at the magic shop was a nice touch," I said. "I have a feeling you've had this Blackstone character around for quite a while."

Without a word, Doug picked up the bottle, removed a few Q-tips from his pocket, then calmly applied the liquid to the edges of the latex before carefully peeling off the cap, liberating his white-streaked gray hair.

"What did you do with Tanya?" I said.

"I don't know what you're talking about," Doug said.

"Landau knows," Margot said.

"Knows what?" Spike said.

"Margot killed Tanya," I said. Spike's and Jeremy's initial expressions were of the incredulous variety, almost smiling as if waiting for the punchline. Spike stepped toward Margot. I didn't like his posture. "Keep your distance," I said, grabbing his arm then shoving him back. "What did you do with the body, Doug?"

"Go fuck yourself," Doug said.

"Boring!" I shouted then removed a pistol tucked into the small of my back, the pistol I found in the dresser drawer of Doug's room at the Masonic lodge, the pistol I now pointed at Doug.

"Put it down," Spike said, producing a gun of his own and pointing it at me.

I laughed. "Really? You're gonna shoot me?"

"Put it down. We can beat the info out of him if we have to."

"Ach! You're such a buzz-kill." I put the gun in my jacket pocket and at the same time removed a tiny plastic tube that I tossed near Doug's feet. As Spike put his gun away I slipped my hand back into my pocket, gripped the pistol, then aimed it at Doug through the jacket material and pulled the trigger. A sharp crack sent everyone into momentary cardiac arrest. The exploding squib smeared a gooey, red mess on the carpet in front of Doug, splattering droplets over his shoes.

"No way!" Spike said. "You faked her out!"

I said to Margot, "You still think you killed Tanya?"

Margot's gaze bounced between Doug and the crimson mess on the floor while she reconfigured the facts since last December. Her facial expression remained mostly benign, although the twitching, narrowing, and blinking of her eyes betrayed some kind of ongoing calculation. Finally, she bristled, "*You son of a bitch!*" bolted at Doug shouting, "*Bastard!*" then threw herself upon him, wrapping her arms around his skull and turning side to side as if attempting to twist his head off. Doug struggled to repel the attack until Margot grabbed his beard with one hand and an eyebrow with the other, eliciting a ghastly scream as the latex base of the fake hair tore at Doug's skin. He dropped to the floor and tried to roll her off. Somehow, Margot ended up lying on his chest while still maintaining her hold on his whiskers. But the move had been advantageous for Doug since he now had the leverage to twist her fingers backward, forcing Margot to relinquish her grip, and allowing Doug to shove her away. The two lay panting on the floor. Could this marriage be saved?

"Time for angry sex?" Spike said.

"Fuck off," Doug said, pushing himself up then falling back on to the couch. "Crazy bitch."

I walked to Margot, helped her up, guided her to the other end of the couch, then sat between them.

"All better?" I said. "Got it out of your systems?"

"Tell me, Doug," Margot said. "Those tears. After faking her death. How did you get yourself to cry like that?"

I took out a thirty-millimeter plastic bottle of clear liquid and handed it to Margot. "Some type of mentholated liquid. Actors use it to make their eyes water." Doug had nothing to add. I said, "Margot has no fear now since she knows she didn't kill Tanya. So why don't you tell us where she is?"

"I don't know where she is," Doug said.

"What the fuck, Doug?" Spike said. "I'll tell you where Margot's wine is if you tell us where Tanya is."

"I said I don't know!" Doug said loudly. "She moved out a week ago—to room with someone from the bar and don't ask me who it is because I have no fucking idea."

"How sad!" Margot said. "Did she break your withered little heart?"

I gave Margot a *you're not helping!* look and said, "What exactly was your relationship with Tanya?"

Doug sat up, the embodiment of helpless resignation. "It was nothing real," he said.

Margot leaned forward, looked around me at Doug. "Not real?" she said. "Pretending I killed her so you could squeeze money out of me was not *real*? Threatening to ruin my life was not *real*?"

"Her feelings! She didn't have *real* feelings for me—not like that."

"Not like what?" I said.

"I cared about her—"

"You're obsessed with her," Margot said.

"Hey!" Doug shouted, taking his turn to look around me at Margot. "You were screwin' Jeremy before I ever met Tanya, remember?" We all glanced at Jeremy, who had no discernible reaction. Doug then said quietly, "I was out of my head. She wasn't afraid to use sex to get what she wanted. And she could be incredibly cruel."

"Oh, god!" Margot groaned. "Are we supposed to feel *sorry* for you?"

"Did you know somebody from New Jersey was looking for Tanya?" I said.

"She seemed nervous, like someone was after her. She kept saying she wanted to disappear. *Disappear from what?* I would say. *What are you afraid of?* She would never answer. When that little shit Spike stole the wine, Tanya hatched this crazy idea of getting Margot to shoot her. If Margot thought Tanya was dead, she would say so if questioned, which would help Tanya disappear. I thought she was kidding. Then I thought she was nuts. But she kept pushing me to try it."

"I guess I should be flattered," Margot said. "You didn't think I was stupid enough."

"I didn't think you were *crazy* enough. It was Tanya who saw—"

Margot jumped up and looked at Doug with a loathing I could only describe as feral. "You told her things about me—"

"But she went along with your little game, right?" I said. "After you wrapped her in blankets and carried her out of Margot's apartment, then what? What was the plan?"

The four of us watched Doug fold his arms and let his chin fall to his chest. It occurred to me Doug wanted to be a part of this investigation, that he needed some kind of closure. Otherwise, why wouldn't he just walk out? Maybe he was relieved now that the charade was over.

Doug lifted his chin and said, "I was going to call her when I got the money from the wine. The money would let her get away and start over somewhere else."

I smiled, looked around expecting the others to reciprocate their joy in how simple things had suddenly become. But all I got was blank stares. "So call her!"

Doug didn't like my tone. "Don't give me orders, Landau."

"Does anyone care where the wine is?" Spike said.

"Give Margot her wine back," Jeremy said.

"I stole the wine from Doug," Spike said. "What about it, Doug? You want your wine back?"

"Give it back to Margot," Doug said.

"And give her back the five grand you took after knocking me out," I said.

"What? That wasn't me—I didn't hit you."

"I got cracked on the head because you're a lying, selfish little prick! You can all talk amongst yourselves about who gets to sell bogus wine. But Doug needs to set up a meeting—"

"We still don't know if it's fake!" Margot said.

"Your dad filed a lawsuit," Jeremy said. "He must've had a reason. Some idiot paid half a million for wine owned by Thomas Jefferson. He's suing too."

"So who cares?" Spike said. "As long as there's a dumbass who thinks it's real, then it's real. It's all fermented grapes."

"Listen to me, Doug," I said. "Tanya's boyfriend Eddie is looking for her. He hangs with a lot of nasty people from New Jersey who want her found. And there are others looking for her. Lots of potential *motivations* involved here, Doug—"

"You're being *paid* to find her," Doug said. "Why should I think you give a damn about her life? She's safe where she is. Leave her alone until I can get the money together."

"You're sure she's safe?" I said. "But you don't even know where she is. What makes you think she's safe? And how long do you think she'll *remain* safe? And where is the goddamn wine, Spike?"

Spike smiled. "Margot has it," he said.

"What are you talking about?" Margot said.

"It's in your attic. I knew how much it creeped you out up there. So I moved it when you were hanging out at that French place across the street."

"I told you to change the locks, Margot," I said. "And it's probably too warm in that old attic. Heat's terrible for wine, even I know that."

"Who's drinking the wine?" Spike said. "It's too *valuable* to drink."

Spike's comment seemed to torpedo the discussion. Doug appeared dazed. I wanted to smack the side of his head. Instead, I dropped a business card on his lap and said, "You're a fool if you think she's safe. Those who want to find Tanya *will find her*. And here's a little secret. She has connections to organized crime. So the FBI wants to find her too. You helped fake her death to blackmail Margot. I have a feeling the FBI might want to talk to you and everyone in this room, and I can facilitate that. That's why you're going to call Tanya and set up a meeting. That's why after I walk out of here, everyone in this room is going to encourage you to do as I ask. Whether you sell the wine or use it for enemas, I don't give a damn."

47

Lying in bed, I wondered how the oddsmakers would have determined the probability of Doug following through with my request. I called Kalijero without checking how late it was. It didn't seem to matter.

"Stathmos Larissis," he said answering the phone on the first ring. "Next stop, Megalopolis, have your tickets ready." Joyous laughter.

"Jimmy?"

"Kyrios, Landau? What can I do for you?"

"What're you so happy about?"

"The *ouzo's* talking. What do you want?"

"*Ouzo* and pain killers? Is that a good idea?"

"It sure feels like a good idea."

"Is it against the law to fake your own death?"

"I've looked into this, believe it or not, and have never been able to find a federal statute that addresses faking your own death. Anything else?"

"Nope."

"Okay," Kalijero said then hung up.

Too bad. Doug's contact with the missing Tanya would've been enough to bring him in, but that's not how the Feds operated. They waited and watched. If Doug was truly obsessed, he would do what was right for Tanya, if only to stoke an idiotic fantasy, something like Tanya realizing he saved her from a crummy life in New Jersey—and into his arms Tanya would run. *She moved out a week ago to room with someone from the bar.* I thought back nine days, when Eddie first found me in Mocha Mouse. Then to the *Auvergnat Vin Bar* for a taste of Jeremy's vintage arrogance, followed by the preppy coffee shop and brokenhearted James—*someone Tanya knew from the bar.*

By 8 a.m., beautifully bobbed and tapered hairstyles hovered over laptops at Arbitrage on Armitage. The newly acquired white spot on James's bangs befitted Arbitrage's clashing decor of earthy color schemes against chrome, steel, and granite accoutrements. His reaction upon seeing me was a textbook demonstration of micro-expressions, beginning with confusion, followed by recognition, then suspicion, then fear.

"You got a few minutes?" I said.

"I still don't know where Tanya is."

"Doug said she moved in with someone from the bar."

Thud-thud-thud, the sound of ninja stars hitting James' chest. His misery washed over me as he raced through the faces of ex-coworkers. Customers started lining up behind me. I stepped away and watched him bravely dose, tamp, pull, and steam through his distress until a lull in the action afforded the opportunity to ask for a break. Sitting at a table, I waved him over.

"You're overreacting," I said. "She's just someone's roommate, nothing more."

"She could've called me. She could've moved in with me."

I wanted to grab his shoulders, shake him violently, tell him how much harder life was for sensitive guys. Instead, I lied to him. "Look, nobody's sleeping with her. Doug confessed she didn't like him *that way*. She was just a tease, to get a rich guy to spend money on her."

James's face softened just enough to suggest he believed me or wanted to believe me, and that just maybe, Tanya still thought only of him whenever she climbed into bed. I said, "So who do you think she's rooming with?"

"That's the thing," James said. "None of the girls liked her."

"So who does that leave? What about Ted, the guy who referred me to you?"

"Not a chance. She's probably four or five years older him. Way out of his league."

A bell went off in my head. I laughed. "He said the same thing about you! That Tanya was out of your league."

James didn't appreciate the humor. "I would know if Ted was hooking up with Tanya."

"Why? Are you guys close friends? He seems a lot younger than you too."

"He is younger. But we all liked him." James chuckled. "And not just because he was real generous with the sweet condo his parents bought him in Lincoln Park. Always lots of beer in the fridge. I guess because we were nice to Ted, his parents kind of adopted us, treated us like family. They would throw these huge parties at their mansion on the lake. Ted would hand-deliver fancy invitations to the whole waitstaff. I don't know. Maybe Tanya's with someone who worked in the kitchen. Ted's the only one I knew back there. But who the hell knows?"

Good question. Who the hell knew anything? I gave James another card and made him promise to call me if he thought of something.

Sitting at the counter of Buttinski's Bagels, I ate a hummus sandwich while staring out over the madness of Armitage Avenue, wondering if there had been a better way of leaving last night's gathering—besides offering an ultimatum. There were no outstanding warrants for anyone, no police reports filed. All I had was Amy's non-denial of FBI involvement to justify my cheeky exit. I had no confidence Doug would follow through or that anyone else in the room felt the least bit intimidated. Mentioning the Feds probably delighted Spike, who saw only a warped acknowledgment of his rising criminal star.

Amy answered the phone saying, "Good! I'm glad you called."

"I bet you're sitting in your car, just around the corner."

"Shut up and tell me where you are."

I obeyed. Ten minutes later, Amy pulled her silver Audi into a bus stop and waited for me to jump in. "Let me find a place to park first," she said. "Then we'll talk." She continued east on Armitage to Halsted, then north to Dickens and east again where she stopped near a small park.

"The old man was Doug in disguise," I said.

Amy's eyes widened, then she nodded, smiled. "Wow! That's interesting. I give him credit."

"He said Tanya dumped him and is now living with someone she worked with at the bar, but he doesn't know who it is or where they are. He has her phone number, but wants to leave her alone until he gets the money from the wine."

"You believe him?"

"I think he knows where she is. But he won't give her up until he can get her the money."

"Okay—"

"You're an FBI agent working in organized crime."

"No. I'm an FBI *special agent* working in art crime."

"Art crime?"

"Any high value collector's item—and that includes wine."

Considering what I had learned regarding wine as an investment and the kind of money at stake, why should I have been surprised?

"You knew Eddie was coming here?" I asked.

"Yes. I've been tracking Eddie Byrne since I got the tip he arrived. I watched him meet you in Mocha Mouse. When he gave you that wad of cash, you were officially on my radar."

"You've been tracking Margot Daley too?"

"I knew about her father's lawsuit and that she inherited the allegedly phony wine. But I'd been paying closer attention to Spike—waiting for Eddie to contact him. I'd been delayed and got to the Oriental Theatre too late to see you get jumped, but there you were, sitting in the alley."

"Using the Ghostbuster excuse."

Amy narrowed her eyes in that about-to-get-pissed-off way. "I *do* explore paranormal hotspots. I *do* feel people's energy. And, yes, I used my intuitive gift as an excuse."

"That cork you found—"

"That was real! I *did* find the cork. You would've found it too, if you had bothered looking. Clues at a crime scene, right? It just so happens it worked out perfectly with you taking the cork to the right people and learning the vintage and value.

And when you went to Margot's house, I was convinced you could be an asset."

"You used me."

"What a surprise! The FBI uses people. We wanted to follow the wine, see where it led."

"And that kiss goodbye, before I went to Irvington?"

Amy stared at me. "That was a mistake. I'm sorry."

Three teens walked off the sidewalk and started playing hacky sack in the park. "Good to know," I said.

Amy appeared tentative. "In New Jersey, they're building a big case. They want Cooper on drugs, prostitution, and other racketeering. The goal is to get RICO charges filed. My focus has always been the wine, to find out if the wine counterfeiting network has been established or is in the process of being established in Chicago."

I pinched the skin between my brows with thumb and forefinger. "So where does Tanya fit into your art crime assignment?"

"At first, she didn't really fit in. A peripheral asset, at best. But I became interested on a personal level, so I *wanted* her to fit in. I wanted to help her."

"Do you still want to help her?"

"Of course! But I was told I had to keep anything I did regarding Tanya within the framework of wine fraud—to keep my participation in an official capacity. There's only so much I'm allowed to know."

I have to cover my ass, she meant. "Did you tell anyone I was going to Irvington?"

"I told my boss." Amy closed her eyes in a pained expression. "I knew they wouldn't get involved, just watch you from afar. When I saw you all bruised and battered, it made me sick."

"Risk comes with my job, as it does yours."

"I don't investigate murder and if I did, I would have an entire agency backing me up. You have nobody. And for what?"

Please God, not another talk about my alleged depression. "I learned a lot about Eddie from that trip. I assume you already knew about that building with Cooper's bogus winery?"

"We knew," she said.

I suggested she could've lied and told me how valuable my trip to Irvington had been. She didn't laugh.

48

Amy and I parted ways with an agreement to check in with each other every day or two. Just after she dropped me off at my car, the phone rang with Brenda's name. "Something weird's going on at Margot's," she said amid the clatter of a busy kitchen. "I just stepped out for a quick smoke and saw the redheaded kid who works for Jeremy

338

walking in and out of Margot's building, carrying boxes to Jeremy's car."

"Is she home?"

"I don't know. But it didn't seem like he was trying to hide anything."

"Okay, I'm just a couple of miles away."

I raced down Armitage to Clybourn to Webster and parked in *Pâtisserie's* lot. Across the street, Jeremy's Porsche SUV was backed up to the front door with the rear hatch open. I walked to Margot's building. She buzzed me in without using the intercom. I knocked. "Unlocked," she yelled.

Margot was reading a magazine in her beloved chaise longue. A string of paper butterflies lay neatly across the coffee table. "I heard a rumor that you just gave away a fortune in wine."

Keeping her nose in the magazine, she said, "You have spies."

I took my place on the love seat. "What did you get for it?"

She dropped the magazine to the floor and looked out the bay window. "I traded it for my soul," she said.

The statement was worthy of some dead air. "I don't mean to downplay the significance of your comment, but couldn't you have dumped the wine in the sink and still recaptured your soul?"

"Spike said he had a buyer. The money will help them find Tanya."

"Suddenly you care about Tanya?"

"Sure, why not? What chance does a poor, uneducated girl have in this world? Maybe the money will free her from having to choose between working for hoodlums or finding a guy to take care of her."

"One more question. Why would you trust anything Spike said?"

Margot picked up another magazine from several stacked near her feet. "The wine is out of my life. I don't care what happens."

I watched her turn pages, stopping occasionally to read something. She hadn't once looked at me since I walked in.

"I'll see myself out," I said, then walked to the door. Margot had no comment.

"Margot told me you got a buyer for the wine," I said to Spike over the phone.

"Yeah, Ted and Jeremy just put it in the locker."

"Where are you?"

"Near the magic shop. I just got done talking to Doug."

"You wanna tell me who's buying the wine?"

"One of Jeremy's private clients. Confidential bullshit."

"Jeremy? The guy so worried about his reputation as Exalted Master of Grapes?"

"Yeah, well he wants his wet dream of a walk-in, climate-controlled vault for storing rich bastards' wine."

It took a moment to process the data. "Jeremy's getting a cut?"

"Yep. It's gonna be Tanya and Jeremy, fifty-fifty. Twenty-five hundred per bottle. I just spent the last hour trying to talk Doug into a three-way split. No way. So I'm the one getting screwed."

It took another moment to realize he wasn't joking. "What happens when Jeremy's client finds out the wine is fake?"

"Not my problem."

"You're going to tell me the plan, right?"

"Dude! You sound nervous."

"Eddie and I need to be there when Doug delivers the money to Tanya. I need to see this through with him."

"Christ, Landau! I just told you I gave my share of the money to Tanya, didn't I?"

"Damn hard to believe you're giving away 150K, but I'll go along with it for now. Tell me the plan."

"Tonight, between five and six. The buyer comes in with the cash, Doug and Jeremy split it, we help load his car, Doug calls Tanya, and we're done. Easy."

Nothing in life was easy. I told Spike I would be there, then went into Brenda's café where the remnants of her morning rush sat reading the paper or staring at laptops. Brenda walked over, carrying a cherry almond Danish. I thanked her for tipping me off about Ted.

"Did your contacts find Doug?"

"We had a powwow last night, across the street. That old man Blackstone? Doug in disguise."

I waited for Brenda to progress through various stages of disbelief before she realized I wasn't joking and screeched, "No!"

"Spike had secretly stashed Margot's wine in her own attic. Jeremy intended to sell the wine to Doug for a fraction of its value. Then Doug would resell it and give the profit to Tanya who could then flee from her past—or something like that."

"It's really Mouton Rothschild 1945?"

"Almost certainly fake. But I guess it's a damn good fake because Jeremy has a buyer coming over tonight."

"Then Doug gets his money and he takes everyone to see Tanya."

"He *calls* Tanya and sets up a meeting—or something like that."

"Jeremy? A master sommelier selling fake wine?"

"I don't get it either. Spike having a soft spot for Tanya, I can sort of understand. But Jeremy selling fake wine? One hundred and fifty thousand dollars is a lot of money, but not worth ruining your reputation."

Brenda screwed up her face. "One fifty for ten cases? You weren't kidding when you said a *fraction* of its value—for the real stuff, I mean."

"Exactly. But if you can practically give it away and pocket one fifty, who's gonna notice?"

Brenda considered my statement. "You're forgetting something. Whoever *buys* the wine is going to know how much it's worth. Does the buyer really think their sommelier seller is too stupid to know the value of his own wine?"

While I stared at Brenda, it occurred to me how fortunate I was. Apart from keeping me apprised of activities in her neighborhood, she just pointed out what should've been obvious: Jeremy's private client had to be someone involved in the world of counterfeit wine.

Brenda left me alone to assimilate the latest information while she prepared for the light-lunch crowd. The lure of easy money had been more than Jeremy could withstand. He was confident his involvement would be well concealed within a convoluted criminal structure, plus the defunct lawsuit of Margot's father helped his defense of plausible deniability. I imagined myself as Doug, secluded, cloaked in some rendition of male menopause, waiting for the money that would free his beloved. Then I tried to deconstruct Tanya. Smart, calculating, self-possessed in a poised, streetwise way. She needed a chunk of money to get away and give her time to reinvent herself in a new city. Spike could be of use, but his connection to Cooper brought risk, and she was cagey enough to know Spike couldn't be trusted. James was a friend, a diversion, but he became too attached, which made her uncomfortable. Doug served her well but the money belonged to his wife, and he too was showing signs of emotional insecurity. She needed someone to help her hide. Someone she could control, someone devoted. Someone who knew she was in a league of her own.

Eddie didn't answer his phone.

"May I speak to James?" No response, just general coffee shop chaos until James picked up.

"Yeah."

"It's Jules Landau. When's the last time you hung out with Ted?"

"What? I don't know. Why?"

"How can you be so sure Tanya isn't hiding out with him?"

"For fuck's sake! She's not with Ted. I gotta go."

49

Bruce was behind the bar, stocking glassware. I stood in front of the door and waved. He nodded, then surprised me by not immediately notifying Jeremy. Ted Goldberg was busy setting up tables for the two o'clock *Côte de Nuits* tasting. He wore a waist-high white apron over black slacks with a satin side stripe, a white dress shirt with long narrow folds in the front, and a bow tie. I watched him meticulously arranging stemmed glasses, corkscrews, baskets of French bread, and large coffee-mug spittoons. Not until he had finished with the last table and began surveying the landscape, did Ted notice me standing in the lobby.

"Uh, you want me to get Jeremy?"

"I wanted to talk to you, if that's okay."

Ted glanced at his watch and then back toward Bruce. "Well, I really should finish setting up."

"C'mon, you got at least an hour before the show starts. I need to talk to you about your pal James. I think he's in trouble."

"What kind of trouble?" Ted took a few steps toward me.

I said to Bruce, "Can I borrow Ted for a few minutes?"

Bruce shrugged. "Ask Ted."

"C'mon, let's talk outside." I moved toward the door. Ted stayed put. I satirically added, "Don't you want to know what kind of trouble James is getting you into?"

Ted untied his apron, folded it carefully, then laid it on the bar. He followed me out the door, to the side of the building that was bordered by an alley. I noticed a silver chain looping out of his pocket. The chain had that sturdy, tarnished, long-lived appearance.

"This has to do with Tanya," I said. "I think James is hiding her."

"No, he's not," Ted said.

"How do you know?"

"Because I would know. I've been to his place. He's got roommates. We all know each other. There's nowhere to hide."

I pretended to think about it. "Does he ever go to your place?"

"Yeah."

"When's the last time he was there?"

Ted shrugged. "I don't know. A few weeks ago?"

The front door opened. Jeremy appeared, then looked around. "What's up, Ted? You got all the prep done?"

Ted moved to go back inside. I grabbed his arm. "We're having a private conversation," I said. "I just need a few more minutes."

Jeremy put his hands on his hips and shook his head. "Are you ever going to disappear from my life, Landau?"

"I think soon, actually. But just as you have a *private* client coming by later—which is none of my business, of course—I need a few more minutes of private conversation with Ted."

Jeremy crossed his arms then looked at Ted. "Do you have a key to the reserve wine cabinet?" he said.

Ted pulled the silver chain out of his pocket. Numerous keys hung from a circular metal fob attached to the end. But what made the chain most interesting was that the fob also perforated the middle of a wine cork.

Jeremy looked through the keys, removed one of them, handed the chain back to Ted, then walked inside.

"I should get back," Ted said. "I don't want to piss him off."

"Is that an antique pocket-watch chain?"

"It is," Ted said. He seemed impressed. "It belonged to my great-grandfather. At least a hundred years old."

"And you have a cork on the fob. What's that about?"

Ted grinned. "It's like a good luck charm, I guess. I want to learn as much as I can about wine."

"You're smart to drill that hole in the middle of the cork. Less chance of it breaking if you snag it while pulling it out of your pocket."

Ted searched my face. "Yeah, probably."

I stared laser beams into Ted's eyes, then grabbed his arm again when he took a step to go back inside. "When you called me to ask about Tanya, you said you didn't know what Spike had been up to since Doug closed the bar. But that wasn't true, was it?"

"I wasn't sure. I mean, I saw him around, but I didn't know what he was doing—"

I grabbed Ted by the collar, pulled him into the alley, then shoved him against the wall. "You were in the alley behind the Oriental Theatre. You hit me on the head with that two-by-four."

"I—I swear, it was Spike's idea. I didn't want to do it. Then Jeremy begged me. He said he would guarantee I'd become a sommelier, you know, teach me everything about wine. He just wanted me to stun you, so we could have a head start running away. I—I'm sorry if I hit you too hard. I swear to god, I didn't want—"

"Okay, shut up." I eased up my grip but kept ahold of his collar. "Tanya's staying with you, isn't she?" Ted looked like he was going to cry. "If you care about her, you'll tell me where you live."

"I can't. I swore—"

I pushed him back against the wall. "Listen, Teddy, I know you feel real close to her, like she's your girlfriend. She's probably taught you a lot about sex. I bet all you think about is the next time you'll be climbing into bed with her. But here's the thing. She has a boyfriend and he's in town looking for her. Believe me, you don't want to fuck with this dude. And there's a big, scary gangster who's in town for one reason only: to find Tanya. So you're gonna tell me where she is, and just be happy to have memories you'll forever cherish."

I let go and stepped back. His collar and bow tie were out of whack. "She's just waiting for some money," Ted said. "She said last night that she'll be gone soon. I promised her she could trust me. Now you want me to ruin—"

"Did you notice how Jeremy backed down? He didn't really care you were out here with me on the day of a wine tasting. That's because I know about a little transaction taking place tonight. Do you know about it?"

"He's selling some wine. We carried it into the locker."

"Exactly. That's Tanya's money. Your old boss Doug is going to deliver the cash to her. And that's fine. I *want* her to get the money and get out of town. But her boyfriend Eddie wants to join her. He's paying me to help him run away with her." Not completely true, but so what?

Ted looked crushed. "She never mentioned this to me."

"Why would she?"

"She told me everything."

Ted needed a thrashing. "The gangster guy is the one I'm worried about. His name is Sergeant Blake and he wants to find Tanya *real bad*—get it? Why don't you tell me where she is so I can make sure Eddie finds her first?"

Judging from the grim look on Ted's face, I think he got it. "Look. I—I don't really know you. But I know Tanya is safe where she is. Once Doug gives her the money, she's gone. When she's settled, she'll call me."

"Don't be stupid. Doug will be followed by a Fed and probably this Sergeant Blake. Spike and Jeremy can't be trusted. You realize that, don't you?"

Ted didn't immediately respond. A bad sign. "They've always been cool to me."

Jeremy stuck his head out the door. "Ted," he shouted, "we need you inside."

"He'll be right there!" I shouted back. "What have you told Spike?" I said. "What does Spike know?"

"Nothing. I mean, he knows that I know where Tanya is. That's all."

"That's all, huh? Well, if she's at your Lincoln Park apartment, Spike and Jeremy also know."

Dazed, Ted said, "She's not there," then walked back into the wine bar.

50

Still no answer from Eddie's phone. Spike didn't answer either.

Back in Brenda's café, I called Amy. "Spike brokered a deal for Margot's wine to be sold tonight at the *Auvergnat Vin Bar*. Doug will give his share of the money to Tanya so she can flee. Doug either knows where she is, or he'll find out when he calls her."

"Okay," Amy said. "I'll follow him. I'm sure Tanya knows enough about the illegal wine biz to justify me taking her in. What time?"

"What do you mean, *take her in*?"

"In custody. To protect her."

"Then what?"

"I'm not sure, but at least she'll be safe from Cooper's reach."

"Great. And how long is it going to take to put Cooper and crew away? And what if the Feds can't prove their case? Then she's stuck in witness-limbo land."

"She's in limbo right *now* with someone trying to kill her! Wouldn't she be better off with us watching her back?"

The barefaced truth of Amy's words humbled me. "You've got to assume Sergeant Blake knows about this deal and is going to follow Doug to Tanya."

"Why would Spike tell Sergeant Blake?"

"Because he's a punk fool who wants to impress Cooper. Anything he tells Sergeant Blake gets back to Cooper. In this case, he brokered a great deal on bogus wine and made a bunch of money."

"Try to relax. What time is the deal taking place?"

"I have to talk to Tanya before anyone finds her. Maybe she hates Eddie's goddamn guts! But I can't stand by if I think Sergeant Blake is going to kill her. If Doug can get her the money, she needs to go, Eddie or no Eddie. Dumbass isn't answering his phone. If I don't find her before the others, I don't think it's gonna end well. But she could be anywhere in the city."

"Jules, you need to stay calm. *Nobody* but Doug knows where she is?"

"This little shit named Ted knows. He works in the bar. He's the last link I have to Tanya, but all he'll say is that she's not at his apartment."

"Jules, tell me when the buyer is coming."

"Tonight, between five and six. How're you going to case that whole place by yourself?"

"I didn't say I'd be by myself. Okay, one more thing to consider. Is it possible Tanya found a place to hide that's *not* in the city?"

James's deadpan look of disgust almost evoked a laugh. I stood in line as he rang up customers and shot me the evil eye as I inched closer.

When it was my turn, James seethed, "I don't fucking—"

"Where is Ted's parents' house? The mansion on the lake?"

"Highland Park. Why?"

"Do you know the address?"

"I got it written down somewhere. Why?"

"Because I think that's where Tanya is."

I stepped over to the coffee waiting area. James continued with his job, looking somewhat thoughtful, which I took as a good sign. After he finished with the next customer, I poked my face back over the counter and said, "I'm heading down there. Call me with the address."

I walked away knowing if James didn't call, I would call him or I would call Ted and, if necessary, find a way to sufficiently threaten him. One way or another, I was going to find the mansion on the lake.

Named for a Civil War general who once said, *The only good Indians I ever saw were dead,* Sheridan Road ran from the North Side of Chicago to Wisconsin, and included a twenty-two-mile stretch parallel to Lake Michigan sometimes called *Chicago's most exclusive address*. Many street names of these exclusive addresses were borrowed from General Sheridan's good Indians. One such name was Cherokee Road, where I stopped my car to stare at a house no longer resembling the one I grew up in, although the half-timbered facade was reminiscent of the English Tudor style I remembered.

It was about two o'clock. I took a photo of Tanya out of my wallet and put it in my pocket. Then I drove a few blocks east, to one of the many parks that bordered the cliffs above the beaches. The day was bright and sunny, the lake refreshingly blue, the vegetation lightly green with awakening buds. Such imagery practically compelled nostalgia. I saw myself as a kid, rummaging through the numerous ravines of the area, looking for the imaginary source of an imaginary river.

My phone vibrated Amy's name.

"I can't do anything that will influence Tanya's behavior," Amy said.

I waited for more. "But she knows about the phony wine. I thought you—"

"I can't tell you anything more. I'm sorry. I'm sure you can figure out what I'm saying. Okay?"

Amy waited for a response. "Okay," I said. She hung up.

Eddie didn't answer. Neither did Spike.

I'm sure you can figure out what I'm saying. I sat entranced on a park bench, thinking of reasons why Amy was ordered to stand down. Some kind of Fed operation was going to take place. If that was true, my presence at the mansion on the lake might be problematic for some.

James's call startled me. "What do you got?" I said. He gave me an address that dead-ended on a street above a private beach. I knew the street thanks to years of ravine exploration. All ravines led to the lake, after all.

"Let's say she's there," James said. "Then what?"

"I make sure she's okay, then report back to my employer."

"What if she's not okay?"

"You've been a big help, James. I promise to give you a full report when my job is done."

There were no cars parked on Bunnybrush Lane. Only on twisting driveways or through an open garage door was a vehicle visible. A car as old and shabby as mine clearly didn't belong on Bunnybrush Lane and there may have been an ordinance stating such.

The house itself was at the end of the street, set back and partially embedded into the side of a steep slope, maybe fifty yards from where the ravine opened up to the beach. Looking down from the edge of the property, I saw a glass wall of what must've been a stunningly verdant living space.

Since the wine transaction would not take place for a few more hours, the idea of ringing the doorbell had very little appeal compared to traversing a muddy slope to play secret agent. Slowly, I made my way, gouging the sides of my shoes into the hill, until I reached a steel column lining up with the left edge of the glass, the first of several columns supporting a balcony stretching the length of the second floor. On the wall, a huge flat-screen television played a home-and-garden show to a living room of sleek, modern furniture.

From the adjoining dining room, a young woman appeared, holding an iPad and a bottle of soda. She had caramel brown hair that reached her shoulders. A white sweatshirt fell un-tucked over tan stretch pants. She chewed gum with her mouth open.

I tried to focus on her features, but she was just beyond the range for positive identification. Tanya's photo-booth picture seemed to have the same facial structure as the woman who now sat with her legs folded underneath herself on a swayback chair facing the doorway. She wrapped her gum in a paper napkin then began reading something on the iPad.

Loose stones crunched and popped. A car door closed. I began retracing my steps along the muddy furrow I had created walking to the column, but stopped when I heard knuckles strike repeatedly on wood, followed by several muted chimes. The door opened. Male and female voices talked over each other, the female voice louder, exasperated, but gradually deferring to a more composed male voice. The door closed. On my way back to the column, the drone of a piston engine from above caught my attention. I looked up, saw a small helicopter, then slipped, smearing mud along the side of my hip and thigh. A shiver raced through me. Ravines had a cold, unforgiving nature.

I worried Tanya and guest might settle somewhere else, but she soon returned to the living room and sat in the same chair. A shadow moved across the kitchen entrance attached to the other side of the adjoining dining room. When the kitchen light switched off, a figure moved forward. His posture and gait were unfamiliar. Even when he appeared at the threshold of the living room pulling a metallic briefcase on wheels, it took me a solid ten seconds to recognize Doug Daley without the Blackstone getup.

He dragged a chair in front of Tanya, then spoke while leaning forward with his elbows resting on his knees. Tanya looked relaxed. They conversed for several minutes before Doug smiled broadly, put both hands on the briefcase handle, then struggled to lift it chest high where he held it a few seconds before dropping it back down. I had two simultaneous thoughts: the briefcase held a lot of money and Spike lied about the time of the deal. Tanya jumped up, ran behind Doug, then gave him a heartfelt hug around the neck before literally jumping back into her chair.

What the hell were they hanging around for? The sound of tires skidding on gravel. A car door slammed and then another one. I stumbled my way back across the mud, reaching the street in time to see Eddie and Spike approaching the walkway to the front door. My initial impulse was to hook my arms around their necks and smash their heads together with all my strength. Instead, I stayed behind, curious to see how they would get into the house, although I assumed I would have to rush them before the door closed. So jaded had I become with this investigation, that I felt no anxiety over reactions to my sudden appearance.

Eddie dropped to one knee. The butt of a gun poked his jacket out. He placed a black cloth on the ground then unrolled a set of lock picks. It took Eddie longer than I expected, but after several attempts, the door opened. Spike walked in first. I readied myself to charge forward, but when Eddie entered, he only nudged the door with his elbow, leaving it ajar. I followed them through the foyer into the unlit dining room, then watched the two enter the living room. I truly had no idea what would happen.

Silence happened.

Standing just outside the living room entrance, I saw Spike and Eddie, side by side, staring at Tanya. She looked more angry than surprised. Doug turned around, abruptly stood, then backed toward the window, dragging the briefcase with him.

The silence continued until Spike said, "Talk, somebody!"

"Get out!" Tanya screamed. "Goddamn you! Get out!"

"Whoa!" Spike said. "That's no way—"

"Shut the fuck up!" Eddie hissed. Watching Spike deflate and shrink away was worth the price of admission.

"Yeah, Spike," I said, entering the room. "Shut the fuck up." I circled around Eddie's right and positioned myself to face everyone.

"Who is this?" Tanya said.

"You wanna tell her, Eddie?" I said. He didn't respond and betrayed no discernible emotion. I found this unsettling. "Never mind. Eddie hired me to find you, Tanya."

Tanya looked back and forth between Eddie and me, then yelled, "I don't *wanna* be found! Don't you get it?"

"Why?" Eddie said. "What did I do?"

"Let her go," Doug said. "With this money, she's got a chance to start over somewhere."

Eddie gave Doug one of his psychopathic squint-eyed looks. It took guts for Doug to speak up, even if he didn't know Eddie had a gun tucked into the small of his back. I watched Eddie's hands closely. If he made a motion toward his gun, I was ready to draw down on him.

"Tanya," I said, "Sergeant Blake is on his way to shut your mouth for good. You and Eddie need to get out of town first, then talk about your future."

Eddie said to Tanya, "You mean you wouldn't just come with me?"

I said, "Did you hear what I just said?"

"You're crazy," Eddie said. "Sergeant Blake's not a killer."

Spike jumped in with, "That's what I told him too!"

"How do you know he's not a killer?" I said. "You've been in the can the last three years."

"Sergeant Blake was always nice to me," Tanya said. "And I don't know so much. Nothin' so important. And I haven't been talkin' to nobody anyway."

"Maybe you *should* get out of here," Doug said. "We got your money. I'll drive you to the train."

"Shut up!" Eddie said to Doug. I thought his right arm made the slightest move backward. "I got money too," Eddie said. "With what you got and I got, we can get away somewhere nice."

Shaking her head sadly, Tanya looked at Eddie and said. "You don't understand—"

"I don't care what you did with Cooper or the other guys," Eddie said. "I don't even care if you *was* wearin' a wire—"

"I never wore no goddamn wire!" Tanya said, bolting to her feet. "Did Cooper tell you that? He's a goddamn liar."

"I know, I know," Eddie said. "But that's what I mean! It don't matter either way—"

"She's telling the truth." The voice resonated over the room. Eddie turned around to face Sergeant Blake standing in the doorway, holding a semiautomatic handgun pointed down at his side. "She wasn't wearing a wire."

"Sergeant Blake!" Spike said, suddenly energized. "What're you doing here? You got your wine, now get the hell back to New Jersey and start breaking thumbs again."

Sergeant Blake bought the wine?

"Here," Doug said, rolling the briefcase forward. "Take the money back. Just leave Tanya alone."

"Come over here by my side, Tanya," Sergeant Blake said. Something about Eddie's posture bothered Sergeant Blake. "Don't be stupid!" Sergeant Blake shouted, instantly covering Eddie in a locked-arm shooting stance, both hands on his gun.

"Easy, everyone!" I said.

"What the fuck?" Spike said, walking up to Sergeant Blake, getting close enough to receive a left jab into his nose. Spike stumbled back several feet before dropping to his knees, moaning with his hands over his face.

"Stay put, Tanya," I said, then looked at Sergeant Blake. "You prepared to shoot all of us? Because you're not taking her." I pulled my jacket back to show my holstered weapon. "Either Eddie or I should get a shot off, don't you think? And you're a big fat target."

"C'mon, Tanya," Eddie said, holding out his hand. "We're gonna walk outta here." Doug rolled the briefcase closer to Tanya, then backed away slowly with his hands up, almost reaching the window. "Mr. Landau," Eddie said, "promise me you'll shoot Sergeant Blake if he shoots me. C'mon, Tanya."

"Eddie—"

"It wasn't just Cooper!" Tanya yelled, tears spilling out of her eyes. "I was tryin' to get away from you! Cooper owns your soul! You'll never get away from him. You'll always go back, just like you always have!"

Tanya's words gouged this son of Irvington's heart. For the first time, I think I truly understood when the light left someone's eyes.

"Eddie, tell Tanya why Cooper sent me here," Sergeant Blake said calmly, keeping him sighted down the barrel of his gun. Eddie looked at Sergeant Blake. Even through his leather jacket, I noticed his chest rising and falling. "Go ahead, tell Tanya," Sergeant Blake added.

Eddie turned to Tanya. "To make sure I did the job."

I slipped my hand under my jacket, removed my gun, and held it down at my side. Sergeant Blake looked at me, then back to Eddie.

Tanya stared at Eddie, stunned, trembling. "You're here to kill me? Y—you would really kill me?"

Eddie shook his head. "Cooper thinks you wore a wire—"

"I told you!" Tanya said, her voice wavering. "Cooper's a goddamn liar. I wasn't wearin' no wire."

"It wasn't a wire," Sergeant Blake said. "It was a bug. In her phone. She didn't know about it."

"You're lyin'!" Tanya shouted.

Sergeant Blake removed what looked like a small wallet from his pocket, said, "Heads up, Landau," then tossed it at my feet.

I picked it up, recognized the ID holder, then saw Sergeant Blake's photo identified by a different name. The realization was immediate, but cursory. Then came feelings of self-consciousness and abasement for missing what suddenly seemed so obvious. "Sergeant Blake's an FBI agent," I announced.

The muffled drone of the helicopter engine only added to the sense of finality permeating the silence. Eddie had known Sergeant Blake only as a cop on Cooper's payroll. Now, standing in a posh North Shore living room, Eddie digested the irrevocable meaning of the three letters associated with Sergeant Blake's name.

Sergeant Blake reached behind to take a radio off his belt. "Tanya, get out. Walk out the front door, arms raised."

"No," Tanya said, "I'm not ready."

Sergeant Blake was not pleased with Tanya's decision. Even from where I stood, I could see his jaw muscles flexing. Then he said, "Spike, get out." Spike was sitting on the floor, still holding a hand over his nose. Sergeant Blake shouted, "Spike! Walk out the front door with your hands up!" Slowly, Spike got to his feet. He left without a peep.

Sergeant Blake mumbled something into the radio. Then he looked at Doug, who stood farthest back. "You! Out the front door, arms raised."

Doug started walking. Tanya looked at him. He gave her a thumbs-up. They both smiled. Eddie swiveled his torso between the two several times. The butt of his gun was now clearly visible. When he stood square again, his mouth hung slightly open. A flush covered his neck. I shifted my index finger to the trigger. As Doug passed within several feet of Eddie, Sergeant Blake fired what turned out to be a warning shot. The blast extinguished any sense of myself as a sentient being. I had no memory of dropping to the floor and rolling to the side. When I looked up I saw Eddie's left arm around Doug's neck and his right hand holding a gun against Doug's head.

"Tanya, get back!" I shouted.

She remained standing, staring at Eddie. "Are you crazy?" she screamed. "Let him go!"

Sergeant Blake had backed up into the entryway, using the casing as partial cover. His radio crackled. He answered with some kind of code then said, "Tanya, get out of here! Go!"

"Sergeant Blake!" I shouted. "If Eddie drops the gun and lets him go, you'll control that itchy trigger finger, right?"

Sergeant Blake didn't answer. "Eddie," Tanya said, "what're you doing? Gonna shoot your way out?"

"Eddie," Sergeant Blake said. "Here's the deal. When Tanya goes out that door, she's in protective custody. You can join her. You're still a small fish. We want big fish, like Cooper. We can all walk out of here, one big happy family."

Eddie didn't have to think about it. "Yeah? And be a rat like you?"

"Goddamn it, Eddie!" Tanya said. "Drop the gun and let Doug go and then we'll walk out of here."

"You see how fast Sergeant Blake shot at me?" Eddie said. "He doesn't want me walkin' anywhere."

From my knees, I said, "There are three witnesses, Sergeant Blake. If Eddie drops that gun and you shoot—"

"Tanya!" Sergeant Blake shouted. "Go out the front door now!"

"Listen to me," Tanya said, making a move toward Eddie.

"Stay there!" Sergeant Blake shouted then stepped back into the room. "Eddie. Tanya never wore a wire, but she took notes and reported back to us. Then she decided she didn't want to help the government anymore. That's why we bugged her phone. She thought she could just run away from it all. But it's never as simple as just running away."

"You're a fucking asshole, Blake!" Tanya said.

"She performed a great service for us," Sergeant Blake said.

"Eddie!" I said. "You called Cooper a scumbag, remember? Think how much fun it will be to help send him to prison!"

"I know about the money you took, Eddie," Sergeant Blake said. "What was it? Four hundred thousand? I told Cooper about it after you left. I even know you split it up and got it in three hiding places. So if you would rather just walk out of here and hope we can put Cooper away before he finds you, go for it. Just drop the gun, let go of Doug, and beat it."

I wanted to think Eddie was rationally considering his options. Then he said, "All those years suckin' Cooper's dick? Is that what you guys call deep cover? Instead of wearin' wires, you shove bugs up your asses?"

Apart from Eddie's giggling, a grim silence settled over the room.

"Tanya, get out!" I said.

"We can try again," Tanya said, sobbing. "We'll start over—together. But we gotta go along with what Sergeant Blake says. Then Cooper can't touch us. And we'll be together. . . ."

Sergeant Blake creeped closer. "*Drop* him," Sergeant Blake said. "Just *drop* Doug, *drop* Doug."

"You shouldn't have said what you did about wanting to get away from me," Eddie said to Tanya. "You should've made somethin' up until we got out of here. Now I know you don't want me no more. So quit lyin'. I ain't that stupid. . . ."

Tanya continued sobbing, ignoring my pleas to get out. Doug stared wild-eyed at Sergeant Blake, now about ten feet away, repeating the same two words, *drop Doug, drop Doug*.

"I was never gonna hurt you, Tanya," Eddie said. "But why did you have to say you wanted to get away from me? And don't feel bad, Mr. Landau. You did your best for me and Tanya. . . ."

There was something about the fidgety movements of Eddie's left arm around Doug's neck that betrayed him as he spoke. I thought of Amy's childhood ability to gauge her father's potential for violence on a given day, and how eventually, just thinking about the man gave her a *knowingness* of what to expect. Maybe it was that same knowingness I felt, or maybe Tanya's imminent danger would've been sensed by anyone immersed in the intensity of the moment. Either way, with the first hint of Doug's descent, I was off. Three gunshots followed, two quick blasts as I tackled Tanya, then a final bang, all in the span of five seconds. I rolled off Tanya, pointing my gun at Eddie slumped over on his side, staring into the floor, blood trickling out of his mouth. He had never looked so peaceful.

"Drop your gun, Landau," Sergeant Blake said quietly, staring at Eddie's bloody corpse, his gun lowered but still gripped with both hands.

"Why don't you pump another one into him?" I said. "Just to make sure." I threw my gun across the room.

Tanya crawled to Eddie and fell over him, sobbing. I stayed on the floor, watching. Two male agents wearing navy blue Windbreakers cautiously entered the room, guns drawn in locked arm positions. Agent One approached Sergeant Blake while Agent Two circled around us, evaluating the scene.

"You okay, Darrel?" Agent One said. Sergeant Blake answered in the affirmative, placed his gun on the floor, then described Tanya as an informant and me as a witness.

Agent Two told me to stand, then led me to the window. Then he asked me if I knew the back of my neck was slightly bleeding. I didn't know. From in front of the window, I stood watching the FBI assess Eddie Byrne for signs of life and attempt to show compassion.

51

After a long conversation with Ted, I was able to piece together the events leading up to the final confrontation. Shortly after Doug's reappearance, Jeremy approached Ted with a hunch. Jeremy then suggested Ted would have a sparkling future in the wine business, if he confirmed this hunch. Ted obliged. Jeremy told Ted that revealing Tanya's location would guarantee future training in wine identification from one of only two hundred and twenty master sommeliers in the world. Ted obliged after Jeremy swore that he too only wanted what was best for Tanya.

Jeremy promptly shared this information with Spike, and the two hatched a plot in which Sergeant Blake would buy Margot's wine at a deeply discounted price, which would enable Cooper to sell it to some sucker for a huge profit. Unknown to Spike, Jeremy cut a side deal with Sergeant Blake, earning him an extra one hundred and fifty thousand dollars in exchange for Tanya's whereabouts. Unknown to Jeremy, Spike contacted Eddie, who also promised one hundred and fifty thousand dollars in exchange for Tanya's whereabouts.

Ballistics reports confirmed that Eddie's gun had fired once, grazing the back of my neck on the way to leaving a neat hole with fracture lines in the window. This finding reinforced my conclusion that Eddie had attempted a murder-suicide-by-cop maneuver. After Eddie removed his arm from around Doug's neck, the former hostage instinctively dropped to the floor. Instead of first shooting it out with Sergeant Blake, Eddie rotated left to fire at Tanya, fully aware he would be completely exposed to Sergeant Blake.

The fatal bullet struck Eddie on his right side, passing through both lungs and his heart, before lodging near his left armpit. A second bullet hit the top of his right hip, then tore into his small intestine. After an internal investigation, Sergeant Blake's shooting was deemed "faultless," since he feared for his life.

Tanya disappeared into protective custody while the Feds utilized the Racketeer Influenced and Corrupt Organizations Act (RICO) to prepare their case against Cooper. Although Sergeant Blake's years undercover provided plenty of damning evidence, it was Tanya's testimony and unwitting use of a "roving bug" that supplied the diversion the media was eager to feed a hungry public. Thanks to the Internet, crime-boss Cooper's arrogant boastings to a "mysterious young woman," detailing his mastery of bureaucratic corruption, his philosophy of crime management, and his invulnerability to prosecution, received worldwide attention.

Ultimately, Cooper was charged with thirty-one counts of racketeering, extortion, money laundering, and wire fraud. His trial lasted two months and included sixty-three witnesses. The jury deliberated less than a week and came back with guilty verdicts on all thirty-one counts. Cooper received a life term, plus five years.

I fell in love with Amy to quench the pain of Tamar's breakup. My conclusion arrived shortly after Cooper's arrest, when I first experienced a sense of closure in the case. Combined with the completion of Punim's trust and a general period of rumination on the dangerous situations I had faced, sadness dominated my spirit.

Then came Tanya's email. She was living in an undisclosed location—some place much sunnier and drier than New Jersey—and wanted to thank me for saving her life. She was very happy "wearing" her new identity, as it fit her better than anything she had worn back East. She also mentioned she had found her calling, working with cats at an animal shelter. In addition, she and her business partner were marketing flower essence remedies for cats with behavioral problems. Her email restored me.

Coincidentally, Amy called not long after Tanya's email. She asked if we could get together and properly say goodbye. I suggested we meet on the stone amphitheater steps of Diversey Harbor, a favorite daydreaming locale of mine. She agreed, and during the busy Fourth of July weekend, I waited in the humid, hazy air, cherishing the cool lake breeze.

Amy smiled and waved as she stepped over others occupying blocks of concrete. She wore denim bib overall shorts and a white T-shirt, and carried two drinks.

"Cold pomegranate yerba mate for you," she said, handing me a cup. "Iced tea with lemon for me."

"So how's the art crime business, Special Agent?"

"Booming. I already got my next assignment. Bogus Picasso, Chagall, and Degas drawings."

I decided to get provocative. "By now, you must know quite a bit about faking," I said.

Amy looked at me and burped. It was the perfect comeback. When I stopped laughing she said, "My feelings for you are real, Jules, as was the conflict those feelings produced—if that's what you're implying. But my career is important to me. I can't become romantically involved with someone I'm working on a case with."

"What if the case is finished?"

Amy took a lengthy sip. "Sure," she said. "But in our situation, there are other complications. I might be getting transferred soon—and I'm coming off a long-distance relationship. I'm not going to do that again."

Amy was probably telling the truth, but I couldn't shake the feeling she was glad to have these excuses. I said, "I'm still stuck on someone else. She's unstuck, it seems. So it's probably better that I not reattach to someone else until I feel sufficiently unglued."

Amy laughed loudly then lifted her cup. "Let's drink to freedom from adhesives," she said.

We spent the next hour talking about whatever came to our minds. When I brought up spirituality, Amy's enthusiasm lagged.

"I can only talk about it to the same person for so long," she said. "At some point you have to let go. If what I say takes root and grows, so be it. If not—doesn't matter. There is no right and wrong. There's just the truth. But truth has to be found on one's own. Nobody can do it for you."

For the first time, I really thought I understood what she meant. Sort of.

Like his character Jules Landau, Marc Krulewitch, the author of *Maxwell Street Blues, Windy City Blues, Gold Coast Blues*, and *Doubt in the 2nd Degree,* is descended from an infamous Chicagoan. He grew up in Highland Park, Illinois, and now lives with his wife in Colorado.

Thank you for reading my book. If you enjoyed it, won't you please take a moment to leave me a review at your favorite retailer?